Lizzie Fry is the pseudonym of an internationally acclaimed author and script editor. As well as working with numerous film production companies, she is a core member of the London Screenwriters' Festival board.

Also by Lizzie Fry
The Coven

KILL FOR IT

LIZZIE FRY

SPHERE

SPHERE

First published in Great Britain in 2022 by Sphere
This paperback edition published by Sphere in 2022

1 3 5 7 9 10 8 6 4 2

A CIP catalogue record for this book is available from the British Library.

ISBN 978-0-7515-7800-3

Typeset in Garamond by M Rules
Printed and bound in Great Britain by Clays Ltd, Elcograf S.p.A.

Papers used by Sphere are from well-managed forests
and other responsible sources.

MIX
Paper from
responsible sources
FSC® C104740

Sphere
An imprint of
Little, Brown Book Group
Carmelite House
50 Victoria Embankment
London
EC4Y 0DZ

An Hachette UK Company
www.hachette.co.uk

www.littlebrown.co.uk

For every woman who has been talked over, mansplained, gaslit, guilt-tripped, manipulated, whispered about, condemned or told she's 'not enough' AND 'too much' . . . this is for you.

PART ONE

Civilisation is unbearable, but it is less
unbearable at the top.

TIMOTHY LEARY

PART ONE

PROLOGUE

Nothing ever went her way.

She was used to it by now, of course; all women were. In the workplace most women soon realised they had to shrink themselves, ensure they didn't take up too much space. Their own needs, goals and ambitions were automatically suspect.

Need to leave early, to fetch your kid? You're not a team player.

You want to become head of department? But this man with less experience and talent is the more obvious choice.

You think you have what it takes, to become the boss?? HILARIOUS.

It was always thus. A man could share his vision and everyone would be starry eyed, declaring him 'one to watch'. Any woman who dared step over the line of what society deemed 'acceptable' was shot down, talked about behind her back, even called names . . . at best. Worse than humiliation, that woman could have all her accomplishments stripped away and be sent spiralling back down to the bottom.

Like she had been, now.

She limped along the Bristol streets, careful to keep to the back roads, away from prying eyes, human or CCTV. She could barely keep her eyes open; lethargy infected her bones, threatening to drag her under. She knew it was shock, that she could not afford to succumb. If she fainted in the street, some good Samaritan was bound to find her and take her to hospital.

Then it would all be over for real.

As a young girl, she had never realised her gender would stand in her way. Her heroes had been men as well as women; she'd seen no reason why she couldn't be taken as seriously as the former. She'd bought into the meritocratic idea that if she worked hard enough, she could have whatever she wanted.

It felt like common-sense advice.

She'd launched from obscurity. She'd assumed her get-up-and-go would be considered desirable. She'd figured space would be made available for her, so had done everything she was supposed to. She'd studied hard in school; got the grades; stayed away from controversy. She'd been the ultimate good girl, sacrificing partying for studying and ensuring she stayed focused on all her goals.

She concentrated on the terrible pain in her arm to keep herself awake. Had it only been yesterday she had been in that office with the Higher Ups and the lawyers? She'd finally been granted what she deserved and had worked so hard for. She

4

had left that room recognised and rewarded for her efforts, ready to begin the next chapter.

It had all been snatched out of her grasp.

She knew just who was to blame for this travesty.

And she'd make her pay.

FOUR MONTHS EARLIER

ONE

ERIN

'What are *you* doing here?'

I open one eye, fighting the urge to groan as I do so. The blind is drawn, but even the tiny sliver of morning light that pokes its way underneath and into the dim room is too much. I dare not move my head; I know extreme pain or at least greasy nausea will ensue. How much did I have to drink last night?

'Mummy!'

I blink again, my surroundings swimming into sharp focus around me. Even without my glasses I know I am not in my bedroom, though the room is familiar to me. An excited little face appears in my field of view: Joshua, my nine-year-old son. Already dressed in his school uniform, he crouches down next to my side of the bed. His face is so close to mine I can smell his breath: milk and that sugar-laden crap cereal he loves so much.

Even so, I am delighted to see him, though there's a

niggling sensation in the back of my head. I push it back down and reach out, stroking Joshua's baby-smooth cheeks and tousling his unruly curls.

'Hello, baby boy.'

Joshua grins. 'It's eight o'clock.'

We've slept in. I startle as there's a sudden explosion of noise and movement as someone sits up in the bed beside me. He hits his head on the overhanging eaves in the attic bedroom. He almost swears but manages to stop himself in time. The bed shakes like we're on a ship, making me groan as my hangover kicks in. Flashes of memory come with it: bottles of red and white; laughing, sitting on the sofa and looking through old pictures.

As I turn, I see my ex-husband David, who rubs the top of his skull with a furious gaze in those steely blue eyes of his, like it's my fault he half-brained himself. Then I remember.

I was supposed to leave before our sons got up.

'We *both* fell asleep,' I say, defensive as ever.

'We don't have time for this right now.'

David grabs the throw off the bed and wraps it around his naked body so Joshua doesn't see. He disappears into the en suite. It doesn't matter anyway; Joshua only has eyes for me. Self-conscious, I pull the duvet up to my neck. I'm naked underneath too.

'Are you taking us to school, Mum?'

I hesitate, my eye on the clock next to the bed. It kills me to see Joshua's hopeful expression and disappoint him. I have to get into work for nine. I am also loath to overstay my welcome any more than I already have with David.

I'd never meant to stay over; I'd not even meant to come over at all. If Joshua hadn't left his PE kit in the back of my car, I wouldn't have had to return it the previous evening. A flush of resentment surges through me next: I never asked to stay for that drink (or ten), David had offered. I'd tried to leave at least twice before things got out of control. It was him who'd put the moves on me, too.

Damn, I'm weak.

'I can't today. How about I take you on Thursday?'

Joshua seems to deflate. Perhaps he doesn't remember it being any different, but he knows our set up is not 'normal'. Usually it's the dad who leaves the homestead after divorce, but not in our case. It had seemed the sensible thing at the time – I earned more than David – but I'd completely under-estimated how much I would miss my boys. Though I see them several times a week, it's not the same as living with them every day.

Ten minutes later, I've gathered my clothes, changed in the bathroom and kissed Joshua goodbye. Sniffing my blouse's armpit, I decide to take a detour back to my basement flat to shower and change. Our eldest, Dylan, had rolled his eyes when he'd seen me creeping back downstairs in the same outfit I'd worn the night before. If a self-involved fourteen-year-old can spot 'The Walk of Shame' a mile off, I can't risk the rest of the office noticing too. It's a new job; I'm still trying to make a good impression.

I make it back to my basement flat as fast as I dare for a Tuesday rush hour in Bristol; it feels like time is collapsing around me like a house of cards. I race down the steps, run through to the skanky box that calls itself a bathroom and jump in the shower. The water is cold which makes me swear and gnash my teeth but helps me keep up my rocket-like pace.

Casting an anxious eye at the clock, I dress and brush my teeth at the speed of light. Stumbling out of the bathroom, I pull a boot on. I hop around, finding the other abandoned underneath the breakfast bar.

Behind the scenes of my life, rushing around like a headless chicken is typical. My personal life might be a disaster, but I always think of my professional life as being the ultimate stage play: on the actual boards, everything's perfect and going according to plan. There's great lighting above me, fantastic scenery behind me. I look fabulous. I say my lines and do whatever I need to do to earn respect, money and to get ahead.

People fall for the charade, every time.

Grabbing my keys and my bag, I run for the door. Almost falling to one knee up the concrete stairs, I career upwards, nearly colliding with someone sitting at the top.

'Shit!'

It's one of the young lads from the student house on top of my basement. They're not much older than Dylan: maybe nineteen or twenty. With hooded, sleepy eyes, this one's dark hair is in disarray, his clothes crumpled; it's obvious he's been out all night. I know his name is Asif, but only because I get all his post downstairs. He's laconic and laid-back; he's also an A1 wind-up merchant.

'All right, Karen,' he says in a London accent so low it sounds like it belongs to someone else, 'keep your knickers on.'

My nostrils flare; he always calls me this. 'My name is *Erin*. I'm late for work!'

He puts a hand-rolled cigarette in his mouth and lights it, expelling a puff of smoke that seems to envelop both of us. Jealousy pierces through me. I haven't smoked in twenty years, but I would kill for one right now.

'Aren't you a good little worker bee,' Asif drawls, 'or should I say drone?'

This again. I know Asif's type: supposedly anti-capitalist to the bone, he wears a Che Guevara T-shirt and thinks he's invented socialism. The fact the T-shirts are mass-produced in sweat shops seems to escape him.

'Some of us have to work for a living.'

Asif's chuckle falls on my back as I scurry towards my car, parked further down the road. As I get in, my heart is thumping erratically.

The clock reads nine. I'm going to be late now, whatever I do. I sit at the wheel for a moment so I can compose myself. I take a deep breath in through my nose and out of my mouth. My calm lasts for all of thirty seconds.

I jump as my mobile rings; DAVID is emblazoned on the display. I stare at it for a second, my heart buoyant, before punching the button on my phone for loudspeaker as I reverse out.

'Hello, lover.' The smile is evident in my voice.

'Seriously, Erin? I can't believe you let the boys see you.'

My calm evaporates and injustice sticks in my throat. Before I can reply, he continues his barrage.

'I can't believe you sometimes. Have you any idea what it

13

was like, trying to answer all Joshua's questions after you left? Now Dylan is in a foul mood too. We agreed we mustn't get the boys' hopes up.'

I interrupt him. 'I didn't force you to sleep with me. In fact, *you* came on to *me*.'

David tuts. 'It doesn't matter, anyway. Last night was a mistake.'

'You don't mean that.'

'Don't I?' David declares, the bitterness in his voice as clear as the January sunlight caressing the Bristol skyline. 'Maybe I think a night of sex is not enough recompense for having to deal with your mess.'

'*My* mess?' I can hardly believe my ears. 'We both slept in. Not just me!'

I don't have time for a full-blown row, so tell David I have to go. I cut him off before he can say anything more, savouring the win, even though it's petty. I need one after this morning and I haven't even got to the office yet.

I count to ten as I take the roundabout. I travel past the concrete monstrosities and the modern, shiny chrome and glass buildings on the way to the university. I take the next left and park up in the underground car park at Queens Mead Tower, where my new job is.

None of the morning's strains show on my face or in my body language as I stride into the glass atrium of Carmine Media. The interior is a stark contrast to the building's ornate façade: bar our offices on the top floor the whole place is a building site. I greet people pleasantly as I go, even the security men or interns. It's an old habit, but I am struck by the way people at Carmine regard me like I am some kind of visiting angel just for remembering them. That figures. They're used to being ignored at best.

Media people can be such elitist arseholes sometimes. I'd begun way down the industry pecking order at the Bristol Journal Group in sales and subscriptions. One particularly delightful line manager used to flick spitwads at all of us with his ruler. Another had a 'no coffee' rule until you closed a sale. When she noticed several of us didn't care about this or brought our own Thermos flasks, she upped the ante and said no loo breaks.

With this hell still fresh in my mind years later, I take an interest in workers below me, no matter who they are. I enquire after people's children or cats or plants.

It's the little things.

The Bristol Journal Group is no more, officially: it's been absorbed into the Carmine Media collective like the Borg from *Star Trek*. Once upon a time, the *Bristol Journal* had been the paper everyone read in the city and its surrounding towns and villages. The internet started killing off the group's circulation years ago, with social media sounding its death knell late last year. I'd been limbering up for redundancy and what that would mean for me and my (estranged) family when Hugh Carmine had appeared with an offer we couldn't refuse.

I weave my way through the cubicles, grateful that no one appears to realise I'm late; one of the few benefits of working in an office with hundreds of people, instead of fewer than fifty. Various faces pop up over the walls to greet me. I smile and wave, remembering the countless hours I'd spent behind similar cubicles, grafting my way out like a miner in the dark. Those were *not* the days.

I make it to my office on the far side and close the door, breathing a sigh of relief. The office is small, but mine. Unlike my flat, which permanently looks like a Sharknado has swirled through it, this space is immaculate. Airy and light, the lack of furniture, books and papers makes it seem bigger. I can see right across Bristol: streets and car parks, rows of multi-coloured houses and murals, construction sites, shopping malls and multistorey apartment buildings.

On the desk, a little wooden block with my name carved on it: *Erin Goodman*. It's one of the last things David bought for me, before our marriage went tits up. I run my fingertip across the grooves of the carved letters.

There's a bold knock at the door. I don't call 'come in' because the knock's owner appears over the threshold straight away, as ever: John.

'All right, maid.'

A dyed-in-the-wool Bristolian, John stands in my office, hands on his narrow hips, chewing gum. His fly is unzipped. I don't tell him. I'm not tall, but everything about John is tiny, like he's been shrunk by a miniaturising gun. He is bursting with energy, positively crackling with it. If life was a cartoon, he would have wavy lines all around him constantly.

'Hello, John, sorry I was late.'

'Were you?'

John flicks a hand at me; he couldn't care less now. Once upon a time he'd roasted latecomers but now, on the brink of retirement, he's mellowed out.

'What can I do for you?'

He grins. 'I got a favour to ask.'

Uh oh.

I've been working for John for so long I know that phrase from his lips can mean literally anything. Forty hours of extra unpaid work on a project, perhaps; or maybe he'll ask you to phone his wife Bobbi with some bogus excuse about why he has to stay at the office. I brace myself for whatever it is.

'There's a girl crying in the toilets. Can you deal with that?'

I blink. 'A little girl? However did she get past security?'

John laughs and clicks two finger guns at me. 'You're right. I mean "woman", of course. One of ours, apparently. Y'see, this is why you're good for me, Erin. Keep me on my toes. Anyway, can you sort it? Thanks, you're a star!'

With that, he breezes back out of my office. Irritated at being stuck with an obvious babysitting job, I sit and stare into nothing for a moment, trying to channel out the noise in my head. Not for the first time, I wonder if I'd been right to follow John to Carmine Media. Though I made rapid progress up the career ladder at the *Bristol Journal*, in recent years I've stalled. Maybe I keep bumping my head on the glass ceiling because I've gone as far as I can go? It's not like I don't have transferable skills. I could start my own business, be self-employed like David. Set my own hours. See more of the boys. Except . . .

. . . No steady pay cheque.

. . . Not enough money for the mortgage AND rent.

. . . Most new businesses lose money in their first few years.

. . . My maintenance payments for the boys would have to go down.

Sighing, I pull myself to my feet, grabbing my handbag. Time to sort out whoever is crying in the toilets.

I know just how she feels.

TWO

CAT

Once she heard the last of the other employees get bored of calling to her and shuffle back out, Cat emerged from the toilet stall. She regarded her image in the mirror. She couldn't have let any of them see her like this. She looked a right state. Tear tracks down her face; the mascara she'd taken pains to apply this morning was ruined; her cheeks were red and puffy. She looked like she'd been punched in the face.

'*She* who dares wins.'

Cat conjured the words into being for her reflection and felt the weight fall from her shoulders. Those words were a promise to herself, but also a reminder of what she was fighting for. She'd had dreams of being an investigative reporter, holding politicians, corporations and institutions to account. She would be an avenging angel, known for being tough-talking, but fair. Men would flock to her, bewitched by her charm and mystique; women would want to *be* her. Because, obviously.

It hadn't worked out that way. Cat slumped against the toilet wall, her optimism fading as quickly as it had appeared. Working in the cubical farm at Carmine Media was not her dream job. When she accepted the position, she thought she would be Lois Lane, filing scoops and falling in love with a dashing investigative reporter. In reality, she had no friends and was rewriting press releases when she wasn't making tea. She hadn't even left the office on an assignment in weeks and even that had just been to cover a bloody school fete because no one else wanted to do it.

Worse than that, though, Cat was out of her depth. She'd completely underestimated the classism that was shot through British professional society like words through a stick of rock. She could never hope to compete with Oxbridge graduates and old-school luvvies. She lacked polish, which in turned affected her self-esteem.

No one said anything, but it was obvious: the sudden lulls in conversation, the glances between other workers. Cat didn't understand their in-jokes, nods or winks; nor could she bond with colleagues by talking about expensive holidays or going drinking and buying huge rounds. She was working class to the bone. Everyone in the office could see it even without an X ray.

As this thought occurred, steely resolve bloomed in Cat's chest. Okay, journalism wasn't like she imagined. But she could still do this, make her parents proud. Hell, she might even make Lawrence proud.

'One of those days, isn't it?' a soft voice said behind her.

Cat turned, ready to bawl out whoever had slipped so

noiselessly into the ladies. Her eyes grew wide when she took in who it was. Wearing a cashmere sweater, a mid-length A-line skirt, high heel boots and a concerned expression, she was immaculate. More than that, her reputation preceded her.

Erin frikkin' Goodman!

Cat already knew everything there was to know about Erin. When she had joined, barely six weeks earlier, Cat had been excited to see a woman in a senior position; Carmine was notoriously male-centric in most of its leadership roles. Cat worshipped Erin from afar across the office, bringing her coffee with stars in her eyes. Erin always thanked her with a beaming smile.

'Cat, isn't it?' Erin smiled, pulling a wad of tissue from a dispenser on the wall and proffering it to her.

'That's right.' Cat couldn't believe she'd remembered her name.

Erin raised a single eyebrow. 'Man trouble?'

Cat fought the urge to stab herself in the eye with the mascara wand. If only her problems were as simple as Lawrence being a dick. She couldn't get into it now, no harm going with it.

'That easy to tell, huh?'

To be fair to Erin, the day *had* started with Lawrence ripping the duvet off her and telling her to fuck off because they were finished again. He'd shouted in her face that she was a user, a gold-digger and a whore. He'd reminded her yet again that he owned the flat (a graduation present from Mummy and Daddy) and could chuck her out any time he wanted.

Cat had been stung, especially since she paid for all the

utilities, food and pretty much anything else Lawrence wanted, including weed. She was tired of walking on egg-shells around him for fear of being homeless, but she knew she could not afford such a nice building on her own. She'd end up in some backstreet dive if she went it alone, or worse: a house share like an overgrown student. She'd worked so hard to get where she was and she *couldn't* take a step backwards.

That morning wasn't the first time Lawrence had finished with her in the eight years they'd been together, or even the last few months. Cat missed the mild-mannered, self-assured young man she'd met at university. Now Lawrence's self-pity and general misanthropy were getting out of control. He spent most of his time hanging round the flat, making con-spiracy theory-based TikToks, watching television with the cat and gaming. Still, that was an improvement on last year when he wrote and self-published a mildly racist book that failed spectacularly to get the negative attention he craved. It sold four copies, one of which was returned to Amazon. It currently languished on the site with a single one-star rating.

Erin tilted her head at Cat. 'You have "that" look. You know the one.'

Cat did.

Erin sniffed and grimaced. Cat noticed the smell of urine and old pine air freshener in the toilets for the first time.

'How about a drink?'

Habit made Cat check her watch. Lawrence always got extra-antsy if she wasn't in before six without calling first. Despite it feeling like the day must be almost over, she'd been in work for less than three hours.

'It's not even eleven.'

Erin copped Cat a conspiratorial wink. 'Let's call it a work brunch?'

Her make-up repaired, Cat slunk back to her desk to grab her handbag. She enjoyed her cubicle competitors' curious looks as they clocked Erin waiting for her. A particularly gossipy young woman called Helena caught Cat's eye. Unlike Cat's natural look, Helena's foundation was schoolgirl bright orange, a horrible contrast against her deep red lipstick as she smirked over her keyboard. Her deduction was obvious: she thought Cat was in trouble, or even about to be fired.

Well, screw that.

'Just off for a work brunch,' Cat declared.

That wiped the smirk off Helena's neon face.

There was a Bill's a block away from Carmine Media. Even though Cat knew it was just a chain restaurant, it felt fancy to her with its wooden floors, glass bottles lined along the wall and large cacti and floral arrangements. Her parents had never been able to afford dinner out. The most Cat had ever got was a Happy Meal from the McDonald's Drive Thru as a treat on the way home from school on the last day of term.

A serious-looking man in his early twenties seated them, drawing their attention to the various specials on the board behind him. Erin thanked him, engaging him in conversation. Cat was agog as she watched Erin put him at his ease, asking him about his university course. Was there anyone this woman couldn't break open with a smile and a friendly enquiry?

Cat wondered how and where Erin had learned to do this. The world seemed relentlessly hostile to Cat. Sometimes it felt

23

like someone had changed the rules especially for her. There was an invisible line in the sand drawn between her and other people. Every time Cat attempted to cross it, she got her head bitten off or worse.

Erin ordered black coffee, poached eggs on toast, with a side of crispy bacon and mushrooms. Unused to being able to eat out because she always had no money, Cat felt flustered by the size of the menu. Rather than keep Erin waiting, Cat smiled and said that she'd have the same.

'When did you come to Bristol?'

Erin was not looking at Cat, but at her food. This, plus her kindness in bringing her to brunch, gave Cat the bravery to answer honestly for once. She normally hid anything pertaining to her past close to her chest. Her mother had instilled in Cat the need to be discreet.

If people don't know anything about you, then they can't use it against you.

'When I was eighteen.' Cat speared a mushroom on the end of her fork. 'For university . . . then I stayed.'

Erin grinned at her. 'So, you've been here a while. You must like it in the big city?'

'Yes. It's great.'

Cat could feel the lie radiating off her like a heatwave. Erin seemed like she detected it too.

'Took some getting used to,' Cat conceded. 'I grew up on a farm. Out in the middle of Exmoor.'

It was the right thing to say. This nugget of information seemed to unlock something in Erin. She sat back in her chair as she grabbed her coffee cup.

'Wow, big change then. You didn't move up here with friends from school, share a house?'

Cat had been a bit of a loner at school, but Erin didn't need to know that. She didn't want the older woman feeling sorry for her. She wanted Erin to continue thinking she was a go-getter, willing to change her entire life for the sake of her career.

'No. They . . . went to different unis.'

'Must have been tough, growing up on a farm in the nineties and early noughties?' Erin let her cutlery clatter on her plate. 'CJD . . . milk quotas . . . foot-and-mouth disease. Hard times.'

Cat nodded, astonished a townie like Erin would know anything about rural struggles. She mentally kicked herself: *of course* she would remember. Erin was much older and working in journalism during that time.

'It was hard for me too, growing up.' Erin leaned forward, like Cat was her confidante. 'My mother tried as hard as she could and worked two jobs, both "zero hours" contracts. Her employers acted like they were doing her a favour giving her any shifts at all.'

Cat tutted like she sensed she was supposed to. Erin was on a roll.

'My school uniform was second hand, including my shoes. My home clothes had come from charity shops and jumble sales. The flat was always cold; the fridge was nearly always empty. I never got to go on school trips or go on family outings with her to the cinema or anywhere that wasn't free. Friends didn't come over because Mum couldn't

25

afford to feed two kids instead of one, or the meter for the extra electric.'

Erin caught the eye of the waiter and signalled for the bill.

'Even so ... we're lucky, you and I.'

Cat tamped down the urge to laugh in Erin's face. She felt many things, but 'lucky' had never been one of them.

'How so?'

'There's a predictable road meant for people like me and you – school, maybe marriage, maybe a kid; part-time work at *whatever* to make ends meet; on a good week a single drink at the pub on a Friday. We've dodged all that. Guess your mum must have been like mine, working all hours to make sure you can have more than she did. Right?'

'Yes,' Cat replied, meaning it this time.

The brunch over, the waiter appeared with the card machine. Cat offered to pay, for fear Erin might think she was a freeloader like Lawrence always said she was. But Erin smiled and waved her card away, saying Carmine Media would take care of it.

As Erin tapped her company credit card against the young waiter's handheld reader and took the receipt, Cat noted they'd scoffed and drunk forty quid's worth of hospitality ... for no real reason. They hadn't discussed work, just Cat. But someone like Erin would justify the expense as investing in her employees, a kind of pastoral care. This realisation added to the euphoria.

Cat was sorry when they had to part ways back at Carmine Media. Erin left her at the lift, smiling and squeezing her arm again as she did so.

'It'll get better, you know.'

Cat grinned back, feeling truly enthusiastic for the first time in weeks. Rather than slaloming at speed through the maze of cubicles, she took her time, head held high so all her competitors could see her. She relished the high. She could feel their jealous gazes like cartoon arrows pointing straight at her.

As soon as Cat sat down at her desk, Helena's bright orange face popped up over the cubicle wall like whack-a-mole.

'Nice brunch?'

The other woman's tone was sour. Cat decided she could afford to be charitable, so kept her reply breezy rather than smug.

'Great, thanks.'

Helena's brows knitted together. She looked like she wanted to say something else but thought better of it. She disappeared again behind the cubicle wall.

Cat clicked her mouse and her inbox swam up on the computer screen. In the short time she'd been away from her desk, she'd received no fewer than fifty-six emails. Normally this Sisyphean practice depressed and overwhelmed her, but not today.

She'd gone for brunch with Erin Goodman.

Despite its rough start, today was a good day. Erin was right: things would get better, especially as it had prompted Cat on her new goal to get ahead at work. It was so obvious, she wasn't sure why it hadn't occurred to her before. Erin's arrival at Carmine Media presented an opportunity for Cat. The media was about creating relationships, after all.

Cat would become Erin's new best friend.

THREE

ERIN

As I leave Cat back at the cubical farm, I check my phone for the umpteenth time for notifications. Nothing from David, of course. Irritation and disappointment niggle at me: I'm just like a heartbroken teen girl, waiting for her crush to text her back. Despite the hangover, I'd felt so hopeful when I'd woken up in my old bedroom, my little boy next to me. I should have known David would slam the shutters down, just like he always does.

I make my way back to my office and slip my phone from my bag. I scroll down the screen and tap out a quick text.

> You're right, last night was a big mistake. It won't happen again.

I'm gratified to see bubbles pop up right away in answer as David types a reply. But he must change his mind because nothing comes through. After five minutes of waiting, I give up. I am not sure what I want him to say anyway. It's not like my contrary declaration is going to make him do an about-turn and beg me to come back to him. David is not wired for reverse psychology. The best I can hope from him is an agreement that getting drunk and having sex was a big mistake. Exactly what I *don't* want. I enjoyed our night together and I want more.

Just as I am about to abandon my phone on the desk in favour of some copyediting, a text appears on screen. It's not David this time, but Dylan.

You should stay away from the house.

A ball of pain forms in my throat and hot tears prick the backs of my eyelids as I read and reread my eldest son's missive. He doesn't mean 'the house', of course; he means his father. Him. His brother. He doesn't want me in his life, he's made that clear for a good while. He'd been just ten when David and I had split and taken it very hard. I'd expected tantrums and ultimatums; instead I'd got the silent treatment and other passive-aggressive ways of making me feel like abject shit.

Like father, like son.

Dylan hasn't spoken to me properly in weeks. Angry with my absence in the home, he's been punishing me. He's not wanted to come out with me on Saturdays with Joshua, either, pleading coursework. I know my own son well enough to realise he's dodging me. The polar ice caps are more likely to melt in the next week than Dylan do his homework. I tap out a quick reply.

If that's what you think best.

I grab a pen and start my copyedit. I can't keep my mind on the job in hand and find myself staring through the internal window, out into the cubical farm, the home of the 'word monkeys'. I watch as a variety of university graduates and bored old-timers sit cheek by jowl, staring vacantly at their computer screens, separated only by partitions. No music plays and conversation is limited to queries about toner for the photocopier and who was the last person to use the kitchenette.

I gravitate back to my phone. Another text. This time it is David. Still eager for his change of heart, I open it to find my hopes dashed again.

Don't forget you promised Joshua you would take him to school on Thursday. You know what you're like.

This really smarts. Whilst I've never been what you might call a perfect mother or domestic goddess, I've always provided for our sons and I've never broken any promises to them. Being a journalist, it's not easy for me to get away; unexpected things happen all the time which can mean staying late to do new reports or reorganise copy. David is a self-employed graphic designer, so can pick his own hours; another reason why we'd agreed it made more sense I would be the one to move out.

David and I had been in our early twenties when we'd met. I was working in Rough Trade's bookstore, a stop gap I'd had all the way through university to help fund my way. I'd loved that job, hanging out with fellow book nerds and writers, sometimes helping out in the vinyl section too. The café was always full of young, bearded musicians promoting their latest gig, asking shyly if they could leave their flyers on the cashier's desk.

When David walked into Rough Trade there had been a ring through his nose and one in each of his ears, like a pirate. Back then he had long, flowing black curly hair and was the most beautiful man I'd ever seen. The fact I'd only ever had one boyfriend – a laconic, self-involved vampire literally called Edward – all the way through university might have had something to do with it.

When David asked me out on a date, I'd promptly broken up with Edward via text. His only reply: *OK*. (Despite spending most evenings and weekends with the vampire for four years, I never heard from him again.) Our courtship was rapid, but it didn't matter to me and David or everyone around us, who declared we were soulmates. We left our respective shared houses and moved in together.

Married life started out well. It was just us for the first seven or eight years, content as we built up our careers and saved up a deposit for our own place. Back then, David worked in a graphic design firm in the city centre; I was a junior at the *Bristol Journal*. I made it up the ladder rapidly, making assistant editor before I was thirty-five.

Looking back, that's where the rot started. Like many men,

David talked the talk about not feeling emasculated if his wife earned more than him. The reality was far different. He never said anything, but I saw the steel glint in his eye and the tightness around his mouth when I got promotions or had to stay late at the office.

Sometimes I think back to that Rough Trade job and wish I could travel back in time and tell my younger self to stay there. I'd have less money, but I'd have a predictable nine to five job. Maybe I wouldn't feel like I was missing out on so much of my boys' lives?

Maybe I wouldn't have even got divorced.

Through the internal window, I spot Cat in the corner. She has headphones on, zoned out to all her colleagues around her. I watch as another woman, Helena, approaches her, empty coffee mugs in hand. Even through glass I can understand what she's doing: attempting to get Cat's attention, ask if she wants a drink. Cat remains oblivious. Eventually Helena gives up, making a rude gesture behind her back. *Ouch.*

So much of Cat reminds me of myself. I'd been single-minded just like her when I first came up, keen to get ahead. I'd had to learn my colleagues were not my competitors; that it was better to work *with* people. It looks as if Cat will have to do the same.

'You still with us, Erin?'

I return from my dreamworld and discover my office door is wide open again. John stands over me for a second time, a grin etched on his amiable face as usual.

'Of course!' I return his wide smile, on autopilot as ever: 'How can I help?'

John sniffs and sits down, rearranging his crotch. 'Well, as you know, my role here was only ever in a transition capacity.'

'Right.'

A flurry of butterflies dances in my solar plexus. Could this be the moment I've been dreaming of? I've wanted to go all the way and be editor since I joined the Bristol Journal Group. John's sixty-nine, way past retirement in real terms. I've known him for the best part of two decades and despite his benevolent sexism, he has been a mostly good boss. More importantly, he'd argued for my inclusion in the transfer of the *Bristol Journal* to Carmine Media. He's always said I'm the natural choice to be his successor as editor.

I cross my fingers under the desk, hopeful my crappy day might be about to get better. Perhaps if I was editor of the *Bristol Journal*, David and I could work out our differences and be a proper family again? I push this ridiculous thought back down; things between us are too fraught and tangled right now.

'Anyway, Hugh decided me leaving was a good opportunity for a knees-up.' John yawns. 'And I figured you gals like organising parties – am I right?'

My smile freezes on my face. I'm unsure I've heard correctly. I am assistant editor of the newspaper and yet I am expected to set up a bloody leaving party? John grins across the desk. For a second I think he's going to guffaw and say 'Gotcha!'

He doesn't. Instead he pushes a memo from Hugh across the desk towards me, detailing the types of things he wants or might want, plus the funds available and possible dates. John rises from his seat and claps two hands together.

'So, I'll leave that with you, shall I?'

I watch him meander back out of my office.

FOUR

CAT

As Cat crept in that evening, Lawrence greeted her with enthusiasm, swooping on her as soon as she made it through the door.

'You're home!'

Suspicious and used to his hot/cold treatment, Cat flashed Lawrence a wary smile. He was neither drunk nor high and seemed more together than usual; so did the flat. The usually fetid air in the small space was gone; Lawrence had opened the windows and given the place the once-over. Cat's nostrils flared as she took in the smell of furniture polish and something with gravy coming from the slow cooker on the narrow counter.

'What's brought all this on?'

Cat deposited her bag and keys on the rickety old sofa, wondering if it might all be a trick. Not missing a beat, Lawrence pulled her to him and enveloped her in his bony arms.

'I've missed you.'

Cat was much shorter than him, only up to his armpit. Normally this was an unpleasant place to be, given his aversion to washing every day. Today he smelled clean: he'd dressed in a fresh T-shirt and jeans, a welcome change from the manky old sweats he slept it. His skin smelled clean too: her expensive papaya shampoo and body wash wafted off him, but Cat didn't mind. Despite her initial reticence, she felt herself relax against him.

'I'm so sorry about this morning.' Lawrence rested his chin on top of her head. 'I'm a total wasteman.'

'No, you're not.'

Cat's mumbled reply was automatic against his scrawny chest. There was something quite ridiculous about a public school-educated white boy using Jamaican slang, but she let it go. Lawrence was trying. For once.

'Yes, I am.' Lawrence's tone was firm. 'And I'm going to make it up to you.'

Cat was agog as he took her by the hand and led her to the sofa as if she were a delicate Victorian lady who'd just had an attack of the vapours. He presented her with both remotes for the television and, seconds later, a large glass of white wine.

'Dinner started off as beef Wellington.' Lawrence fretted with a tea towel, pulling it through his spindly fingers. 'I got the recipe on Pinterest, only it turns out I am totally shit at making pastry. So now it's a stew. Hope that's okay.'

'It will be lovely,' Cat assured him.

Lawrence beamed at her. He looked like the young man she'd fallen for back in university, when they both had that

36

optional novel-writing module together. They'd been paired as study buddies by their mentor but neither of them had done quite enough studying. They had managed to scrape through delivering that final project at the last minute. The difference between them was Cat knew her 2:2 for that half-arsed novel was well deserved, whereas Lawrence still believed his was a masterpiece.

Cat marvelled at the turnaround as Lawrence chatted away, peeling potatoes for mash to go with the stew. Just under twelve hours ago she'd left him cussing and throwing himself around the flat, spittle on his lips. She'd said nothing for fear of enraging him further. She'd just skulked out like she usually did, hot tears stinging her eyes. She hadn't sent him any pleading texts or ultimatums during the day. In truth, she'd forgotten all about him in the high of having brunch with Erin Goodman.

'So, how was work?'

She chose her words carefully, for fear of bringing back the morning's rage. From bitter experience she knew Lawrence could turn on a sixpence, from reasonable and lucid to full of venom. If she waxed lyrical about how she'd managed to score a lunch with one of her personal sheroes, there was no telling how Lawrence might react.

'Oh, you know . . . dull.'

It was the right answer. Lawrence turned from the pan of salted, boiling water as he dropped the potatoes in. He smiled, his gaze sympathetic.

'Well, you'll find a way to make 'em see.'

Cat shrugged, non-committal. She'd been at Carmine

Media for nearly two years now and felt like she had made no headway whatsoever: hardly anyone even knew her name. They still called her 'new girl' because she was the last hired. To still be at such a junior level at twenty-eight felt excruciating. But Erin knew her name, and that counted for something.

Cat took her place at their tiny trestle table. Lawrence had laid it like their flat was a fine dining establishment: cutlery lined up just so, vase with a single rose in it, white tablecloth. She didn't even know they had a tablecloth. Perhaps Lawrence had bought that too, along with the food? Their cupboards had been bare that morning.

'Here we go.'

Lawrence brought two plates over and placed one in front of her with reverent care.

'Looks delicious.' She meant it.

As they raised their glasses, it dawned on Cat that she had been waiting to get picked. For someone to really see who she was, her potential, and pluck her out of the cubicle farm like a rare wildflower.

Erin hadn't done this. Cat knew it for a fact. Listening to her at brunch that morning had been a revelation. Erin had talked about 'making things happen'. She'd nodded in sympathy when Cat had expressed disbelief at this, saying that doors kept slamming in her face. Then Erin had dropped the greatest pearl of wisdom Cat had ever heard.

If you can't get in through the front door, try the window.

It was obvious now Cat really thought about it. *Of course* she would be overlooked, trying to get in through the same old ways in, along with everyone else. That's what gatekeepers were for: they created bottlenecks, making the whole system back up. It was inefficient, but it worked. As various frustrated people gave up and fell away, only the most dogged and determined would make it through. Survival of the fittest.

But what if she didn't go through the door at all, like Erin said?

Cat felt certain she wouldn't be the only one trying this metaphorical route; she wasn't even sure exactly what it would entail. But it had to be worth a go. Cat felt like she was standing still where she was. She'd wanted to clamber up to the next level for so long, but had been clueless how. Then Erin had arrived, with the answer. It was like fate.

Cat had nothing to lose and everything to gain.

'To the future,' Cat said, clinking glasses with Lawrence.

'To the future,' he echoed. 'Now eat up.'

FIVE

ERIN

By the time I drag myself into my poky little flat and eat a Pot Noodle that evening, my eyelids start to droop. I brush my teeth, dress for bed in a clean pair of pyjamas and settle down for a late night looking through Hugh's memo.

There had been so much copyediting and website maintenance to do for my actual job that day that I'd had no time for planning John's retirement party. I'm shocked by the amount of money that's been put aside for such a shindig, so I call Hugh Carmine from my bed as I scroll through my computer looking for ideas.

Hugh's a typical playboy, modelling himself on internet entrepreneurs like Mark Zuckerberg and Steve Jobs. In love with nostalgia, Hugh acts and looks like a forty-five-year-old teenager: jeans, trainers and T-shirts with slogans for movies from three decades ago. None of Hugh's laissez-faire attitude does not make a dent in the fact that Carmine Media is one of the top media conglomerates in the country. Owning numerous companies involved in mass media enterprises, it has its fingers in all kinds of digital or real brick-and-mortar pies: television, radio, blogs and YouTube channels, motion pictures, even a theme park.

'Yeah.'

Hugh always answers the phone with a bored timbre to his voice, like he's a kid minding his parents' mansion, rather than the one with the keys to the kingdom. I greet him as social norms insist for the rest of us plebs, then enquire whether he *really* wants to spend six grand on cupcakes and booze in paper cups?

'Why not.'

There's no question mark, but I make a stab at answering Hugh anyway.

'Because the tower is a wreck! Wouldn't it be better spent on the renovations?'

I wince as I say this, worried Hugh might slap me down as having ideas above my station. We've only been working together a short while. Hugh sniffs, like he's thinking my point over. We both know he's not really.

'It's all in hand.'

He hangs up before I can argue the toss with him any further. I stare at my mobile handset, unable to believe how the other half lives. Six thousand pounds is an absolute fortune to me, but for someone like Hugh it is pocket money. *WTAF.*

Hugh's indifference almost makes me wish I had criminal

tendencies. I could take ninety per cent of the cash and still deliver John a night to remember. Hugh probably wouldn't even notice any shortfall. I could take the boys on holiday somewhere abroad and still have money left over to buy them anything they wanted. But of course, I can't and won't do either of those things. Damn having a conscience!

I blink and slide into sleep, my laptop still on the bed with me. What feels like moments later I startle awake, unsure for a moment what's slammed me back into the waking world. My mobile vibrates on the nightstand. I snatch it up and press the green button when I catch sight of the word DYLAN on the screen.

'. . . You okay?' A flutter of emotions surge through me: irritation that he's woken me; pleasure that he's called me at last; concern that something bad might have happened to him.

'Mrs Goodman?'

Momentary disappointment comes next: the youth's voice on the end of the line is not Dylan's. Next, the worry floods through me with a vengeance.

'Who is this?'

'It's Tom.'

'Who—?' I interrupt myself. That doesn't matter, I have more pressing worries right now. 'Why have you got Dylan's phone?'

The boy sighs and I hear a discordant whistle down the phone, along with sirens. My heart makes a sick lurch. Tom is outside. This means Dylan is probably with him, in the middle of downtown Bristol somewhere. Presuming his friend is the same age, that means two fourteen-year-old boys are walking the streets late at night. Shit!

'I don't grass, okay?' Tom's voice is shrill. 'I just didn't know what else to do!'

'It's all right, Tom. In your own time. I'm right here.'

I don't press him even though my heart is hammering around my ribcage. I might not live with my teenager, but I've read enough parenting articles online to know squeezing teens for information is an exercise in futility. They either shut down or freak out, or both. Even if Tom doesn't, he could cut me off. Then I'd have no clue where Dylan is.

'We're on Turbo Island.'

I know it. It's a small triangle of land at the junction of Stokes Croft and Jamaica Street. It's become synonymous with late-night drinking and general antisocial behaviour. It's maybe a ten-minute drive from my flat. At this time of night, I might even make it across the city in less.

'Okay, I'll be there very soon. Stay where you are!'

I leap out of bed, grabbing a cardigan and pulling it on. I fit my bare feet into a pair of trainers and pluck my car keys off the hook, racing up the basement stairs towards my car.

Asif stands at the top, smoking a joint and chatting with a Deliveroo driver on a bicycle. Does that boy ever go inside?

'Whoa! Where's the fire, Karen?' He cracks up laughing again.

'Fuck off!'

I dodge round him and make it to my car. As I slide behind the wheel, my focus on getting to Dylan is interrupted. Knuckles on the passenger side window.

Asif again.

He gestures for me to roll the window down. I shake my head and raise a finger, like I would at a pet who'd done wrong. He chuckles again, barely audible behind the glass. He grabs the car door handle and opens it before I can snap the central locking down.

Damn my shitty reactions.

Agog, I watch him pull a belt across his chest, make himself comfortable. He looks over the gearstick at me and gives me that devil-may-care grin. It's not often I am rendered speechless, but this boy is something else.

'So where are we going?' Asif enquires, like we're friends and this is a perfectly normal, everyday outing.

'*I'm* going to fetch my son,' I hiss, '*you're* getting out!'

'Nah.'

'No?' Red mist descends; I don't have time for this. 'Fine!'

I slam my foot on the accelerator. I savour the momentary delight of Asif's grin disappearing as the sudden forward momentum makes us lurch back in our chairs. He grabs the dashboard to steady himself before releasing an impressed titter.

The backstreets of Bristol on the way to Stokes Croft are all but empty. As we make it onto the bigger roads, I start to see people milling about from pubs and clubs; others joining queues for takeaways, the occasional police officer overseeing them. Next to me Asif chatters away, rolling himself another cigarette. I ignore him, focused only on making it to Turbo Island. I can feel the anxiety roiling in the pit of my belly.

What if Dylan isn't there after all?

What if he's hurt?

What if . . . what if . . . WHAT IF?

We park up outside a neon-shuttered off-licence, just off Turbo Island. I am out of the vehicle the moment we're at a standstill, barely remembering to turn off the engine.

'Mrs Goodman?'

A youth's form appears from the shadows by the traffic lights to my right, making me jump.

'You must be Tom.'

The lad in front of me is much more developed than Dylan. Unlike my son's smooth cheeks, stubble dots Tom's jaw. He's substantially taller, with broad shoulders and wiry chest hair peeking out of the top of his shirt. Even so, it's not difficult for me to see he is roughly the same age as my son, fourteen or fifteen. The panic in Tom's eyes and his apologetic gait marks him out as more child than man.

'I'm so sorry, Mrs Goodman, I—'

'It doesn't matter right now.' I am careful to keep my tone friendly. 'Where is he?'

Tom folds in on himself, like he might faint from relief. We step under the dim glow of the streetlights as he takes me and Asif onto the vacant lot.

Two sofas sit opposite each other under the big advertising billboard. I hadn't noticed them against the riot of colour on the wall behind, which is papered by hundreds of activists' flyers. On one of the sofas lies my errant eldest child, eyes closed but mouth open, catching flies. Even before I take in his greenish hue, I realise he's drunk and passed out. Brilliant.

'I told him to take it easy,' Tom mutters, 'he was knocking it back like Fanta!'

45

'How many units has he had?' When that doesn't seem to land with Tom, I reframe it: 'Think of it like pints.'

Tom blows out his cheeks. 'I suppose . . . three? Maybe four.'

I groan. No wonder Dylan is sparko: he's skinny and not used to that kind of volume. When Dylan had become a teenager, David and I had agreed he could have small measures of alcohol at home to hopefully avoid scenarios such as this. So much for that idea. We should have known teens always find a way to rebel.

Before I can say or do anything else, Asif sniffs and steps forward, peering over Dylan like he's a museum exhibit.

'Mate . . . what was he drinking?'

I hadn't thought to ask that. I award Asif a few extra brownie points in my mind, not that I will be telling him, of course. It will go straight to his head.

'White cider.'

Tom pushes an empty plastic bottle into my hand. I note the label says it's over seven per cent proof. No wonder my boy is hammered. I sigh, recalling all the times I drank this crap as a teenager. Some things never change. Blurred vision, stomach cramps, dry mouth, banging head. Dylan will pay for this tomorrow.

'Has he thrown up?'

'Yeah.' Tom motions vaguely at the street behind him. 'Back there somewhere. Like a fountain. It was even coming out of his nose! Rank.'

I shudder but concede it's good news. Much of the poison will have left his system. I pay attention to Dylan's lips: they're not blue, as far as I can tell under the muted streetlights. I press a hand to his pale forehead: he's cold, but no more than I am. I sit down next to Dylan, who promptly attempts to sit up. Not comatose, then.

'Hi, Mum.'

Dylan's gaze meets mine and he gives me a sloppy Cheshire cat grin. I grimace at his sour breath as it wafts over me.

'I'm sorry,' Dylan slurs. 'I don't want you to stay away. I love you really.'

I don't trust myself to reply; I might start crying grateful tears. I can't remember the last time he's been pleased to see me. It's been all scowls and avoidance, either literally or whilst he hides in his phone, doom scrolling rather than deigning to look at me.

Asif helps me get Dylan to his feet. We guide him and Tom to my car. I drop the other boy off at his parents' two or three blocks away. I ring the doorbell to ensure Tom makes it back inside. Moments later his mother answers the door in her nightie, blinking furiously against the hallway light and horrified to see her son on the doorstep. I assure her I will take Dylan back to mine and fetch his things another time. At the sight of her mortification and seething anger at Tom, I'm glad I won't be sticking around.

I try and leave Asif on his own doorstep, but he's adamant on helping me get Tom down the steep steps into my basement flat. As I fuss around Dylan in my room, encouraging him to take off his vomit-stained T-shirt, Asif pours my son a large glass of water. He also presents him with two paracetamol from my medicine cupboard in the postage stamp-sized bathroom.

'Take these before you go to sleep, works a treat.'

Dylan just accepts them and pops them in his mouth, eyes wide. He takes the glass, then turns to me as if he's forgotten Asif is even there. 'Is he your boyfriend?'

'Oh God, no.'

I wave Asif out of the bedroom, back to the front door. He laughs and tips me an imaginary hat.

'Hey, you're welcome.'

His facetious smile makes me spit out a retort as he goes.

'I didn't even ask for your help!'

'Night, Karen!'

The front door closes behind him. I go back through to the bedroom and discover Dylan has fallen asleep on my bed sitting up, shirtless, the empty glass still in his hand. I take it from him and gently move him, rearranging his limbs in the recovery position, just in case.

I retrieve my phone from my pocket and see it's getting on for two in the morning. I sigh, knowing I won't be going to sleep in a hurry after all the adrenaline and worry. While I have the phone in my hand, I drop David a quick text so he can pick it up in the morning.

Dylan at mine. Don't freak. Come by in the morning when you've dropped Joshua off. We can talk. E x

I add the kiss at the end without thinking. Not wanting to antagonise David further, I press the back key and delete it, then send. Still wired, I crawl into my bed next to Dylan and wait for morning to come.

*

48

I wake late again the next morning, calling in to work to say I have a family issue to attend to. I'm thankful it's John, not Hugh, who answers. Dealing with the playboy would be just too much.

'I remember our Maya at the same age, she was a right terror.' John chuckles on the end of the phone. 'Come in when you've got it sorted with your ex.'

'Thanks, John.'

Sure enough, David descends like Samael, the 'venom of God' and angel of rage. The piercings and long hair might be gone now, but David has not let himself go like so many men in their mid-forties. His salt-and-pepper hair is cropped short; there's no hint of a paunch or moobs. Vanity means he only wears his glasses for reading or driving, which also means he no longer dresses like a tramp like he did at university. Today he's wearing designer jeans, a well-pressed shirt.

Even so, he is a formidable sight at my front door so early. He appears after dropping Joshua at school like I'd suggested, hollering and banging on my front door with both fists. I rush to let him in, hoping Asif and the other boys upstairs won't notice.

Too late: Asif is on the top step of the basement steps as usual, watchful and smoking. How he's always awake during my family dramas is anyone's guess. Maybe he's an insomniac – or a very annoying guardian angel?

'It's fine, don't worry,' I find myself saying over David's shoulder to Asif.

'Who the hell is that?' David spits.

Asif narrows his eyes at David. 'Okay, boomer, I'll leave you to it.'

'I'm forty-five!' David hollers after Asif.

'For crying out loud, David, you're making a scene.'

I pull him into my flat, closing the door.

'Where is he?'

I shush him, try and ensure he keeps his voice down. 'He's in my room. Believe me, he needs the sleep.'

'Don't tell me what my son needs,' David hisses.

I don't trust myself to reply. I might slap his face. I'd forgotten my ex-husband can be a sanctimonious twat who loves to score points.

'Why the hell have *you* got Dylan, anyway? What's happened? Is he okay?'

The subtext is obvious: I shouldn't have our firstborn son with me. I can't be trusted to keep him safe. I am a selfish woman who thinks only of herself. A bad mother.

'Of course he's okay!' I retort. 'But he nearly wasn't, thanks to you!'

David takes a step backwards, as if I've struck him.

'What are you talking about?'

I sigh and count to ten. I need to keep my head, or this could all go downhill fast.

'Where did he tell you he was?'

'At Tom's.'

'Doing what?'

'Studying, of course. What else would they be doing on a Tuesday night?' David bristles, his blue eyes flashing. 'I met the mother. Nice woman. Nice family. Tom's on the school newspaper with Dylan.'

'Then explain to me why I had to go and rescue both

of them, drunk, from Turbo Island in the early hours of this morning?'

David freezes in horror as his overprotective mind rattles through a litany of what *could* have happened to Dylan. I wait for him to catch up with me.

'Jesus Christ.'

He looks absolutely gutted and grateful, all at once. I can't deny the satisfaction of seeing the self-righteous anger wiped off my ex-husband's handsome face.

'Don't you remember telling your parents you were studying, then sneaking out to get drunk with your friends?' I sigh. 'David, you fell for the biggest teenage play in the book.'

'Don't talk to me like that.'

'Like what?'

'Like I'm an idiot!' David stakes a step forward and for a moment he almost looks threatening. 'I've sacrificed everything for those boys.'

'Oh and don't we all frigging know it.' I shake my head. 'David the martyr.'

Before he can utter his riposte, Dylan skulks into the main area of my basement flat in just his jeans, bare chest and feet. He hangs his head, hugging himself. He's so skinny he could probably wrap both bony arms around himself at least once, bless him. His face is gaunt, the hangover making it look grey.

My gaze meets David's and the situation flips on its head: we smile as if we were just laughing together, rather than wanting to rip each other's guts out and then bathe in the mess.

'Dylan, buddy,' David says, raising an arm to our son for

a hug. 'What's been going on? I thought you were at the Gaskills'. Got anything you want to tell me?'

Dylan ignores his father. He just stands there, a dark expression on his pale, narrow face. His eyes meet mine.

'Thanks, Mum. For taking care of me last night.'

I'm taken aback. My eldest born is not known for even understated displays of gratitude like this.

'Erm . . . you're welcome.'

A beep behind me alerts me the tumble drier is finished.

'Oh, your shirt.'

I pull his clean, dry T-shirt from the machine. Moments later Dylan has it and his shoes on, ready to go. David threatens to take him back home to change into his uniform before going into school. Hoping this is a bad joke and his anger has passed, I make an attempt to chivvy him out of it as they leave. David seems to accept this, but once he's sent Dylan on with the keys to the car, he turns back on the basement steps, a feral snarl on his lips.

'You think you're there *one time* and you can undermine me?'

I blink, shocked at the sudden about-face in his demeanour.

'No, of course not.'

'Let's get one thing straight, Erin. You might be anxious to embrace this "cool mum" thing, but it isn't you who's been there every day of that boy's life. You were given a choice: career or family. You chose career. You don't get to swap back when it suits you.'

There's a hard lump of pain in my throat. It's never been that simple; David knows it too. I've made sacrifices, too, not least living in a shitty basement flat so he and the boys can have the house. For all David's talk of how I'd left the boys and never looked back, he's conveniently forgotten how I'm there every Saturday to take them out. He's ignored all my phone and FaceTime calls with them, not to mention the school plays and sports days I've booked holiday to see. Also yes, how I dropped everything last night to rescue our child in the middle of the night.

Because, obviously.

Whatever David thinks, I love my kids and want what's best for them. I'm not just a cash machine. I am a good provider *and* a good mum. Screw him.

I'll show him.

SIX

CAT

'Going already?'

What a difference a day made. Twenty-four hours earlier he'd thrown two scatter cushions and a vase of dead flowers at Cat and told her to get out and never come back. Today, Lawrence sounded disappointed she was leaving.

He rolled over, reaching for her, but Cat smiled and stepped out of his range, buttoning up her jeans as she did so. Last night they'd polished off the stew, the rest of the wine and then fallen into bed together. It had been a lovely night.

Now she had work to do.

''Fraid so.' She kissed his lips. 'See you tonight.'

Cat left her flat building and stepped out onto her street, raising one palm to check for rain. Dark clouds gathered overhead. She was glad she'd thought to bring her umbrella. As she power-walked down the road, her senses were assaulted by the city: traffic fumes, a cacophony of human voices, the odd car backfiring.

None of it bothered her today.

She was never usually in a hurry to get to work, but that Wednesday was different. She was anxious to get to the office and see Erin again.

Cat already had her plan of attack all worked out: she would take Erin a coffee around half nine, along with a small gift. She had lain awake most of the night trying to figure out what she could give her. She didn't have much time to go shopping on the way to work, plus she also didn't want to embarrass Erin. She was all too aware of the fact some people who came from nothing often found unexpected gifts stressful, as it plunged them into the spotlight without warning. Some even thought of spontaneous gift-givers as attention seekers, or as having sinister agendas. Cat didn't want to put her foot in it and ruin any chance of becoming friends with Erin before she'd even begun.

That's when her brainwave had struck. Cat had access to Erin's office. She needed to come and go freely, not only to bring Erin coffee and the odd message, but so Cat could empty the wastepaper basket. Litter patrol was supposed to be the duty of *every* low-rung employee at Carmine Media, doled out weekly via rota so everyone received a turn. Needless to say, that wasn't how it worked in the cubicle farm. Long before Cat had even left school, some bright spark had proposed the *newest* low-rung employee do *every single wastepaper basket every night*, not only in the cubicles but every single solo office as well. Since Cat was *still* the last in, she'd been stuck with the dubious honour for the past two years.

Cat had never shirked litter patrol but had resented it hugely up until that point. Now, she recognised it as a boon. Having access to Erin's rubbish could give Cat an insight into her line manager's psyche.

Result.

Half-walking, half-running down the street with a dozen other office workers in raincoats with briefcases, Cat caught sight of her reflection in a newsagent's window. She stopped, as if halted by the sight of herself.

That was it!

One thing Cat could be certain about Erin: she had a sweet tooth. Every single day there was at least one wrapper in her wastepaper basket. Through the internal window that backed onto the cubicle farm, Cat had seen Erin devour enough sugar to rival Homer Simpson. She could get her something sweet as a small gift.

Congratulating herself, Cat slipped inside the dark little shop. It was one of those lone traders that couldn't quite decide what their USP was, full of newspapers, confectionery, buckets of soft toys, tourist paraphernalia, gift boxes and bottles of craft ale. Towards the back were commemorative china plates, a chiller cabinet of essentials, plus what Cat had come in for.

Sweets in big glass jars.

Cat ran her eyes across them all, trying to decide what she could give Erin. Lemon sherbets, cola cubes, humbugs and Americandy seemed to be right up there in Erin's estimation. All of them were dust when compared to Erin's real favourite:

toffees. Cat directed the little old lady towards the chewing nuts, right in the middle of the shelf two rows down from the top. Ultra-hard caramels wrapped in silky milk chocolate.

Perfect.

The old lady measured out one hundred grams onto the shiny, silver scales, deposited the chewing nuts into a pink and white striped paper bag and twisted the corners closed. Cat handed over her coins, excitement fizzing in her veins at the thought of handing the sweets to Erin later that morning.

She would love them, Cat was sure of it.

Reaching Carmine Media at last, Cat floated into the building. Turning on her computer and firing up the coffee machine, she kept a watchful eye on the strip of carpet that led from the lift towards Erin's office.

When Erin hadn't made an appearance by breaktime at eleven, Cat pretended she needed something from the kitchen at the back of the cubicle farm. She might have missed Erin making her entrance, but this route took Cat past Erin's internal window. When she spotted Erin's office was empty, the lights off, Cat stopped and stared through the glass, willing her to pop up in her chair like the genie from the lamp.

'Erin not in today?'

Cat attempted to keep her tone light and nonchalant as she rinsed mugs out in the cubicle farm kitchen. A colleague was seated at the Formica table in the corner next to the water dispenser; his name was Michael, though Cat couldn't ever recall being introduced to him. A bubble appeared, taking an age to travel up to the top of the tank. Christ, even oxygen was depressed in this place.

'Dunno.'

Michael was staring at the newspaper in front of him. He was in his late forties, balding, with red ink dotted on his top lip. He looked like a vampire. As she watched, he filled in the crossword.

Cat knew he had never made it out of the cubicles and was now stuck there. He was destined to rewrite press releases for ever as more ambitious, younger and prettier things overtook him on the corporate ladder. She also knew Michael had a bunch of ungrateful kids and a wife who liked to keep up with the Joneses. When Cat looked at him she heard a bitter recital of endless credit card bills, swapping of cars and booking of holidays they could not afford. Cat wasn't certain how she knew any of those details, but she figured his complaints must have made their way across the cubicle farm and into her ears.

'Hey there, Catrin isn't it?'

Dustin from marketing appeared, all swagger. Marketing had their own kitchen, but Dustin preferred the hunting grounds of the cubicles. Bored female drones swarmed to him like insects to the blue light of electric fly killers.

'*Cat.*'

She corrected Dustin automatically, fighting the urge to shrink away from him in distaste. With his sandy blond hair, clean-shaven face and trim body he was classically good-looking, but nevertheless a sleaze. He grinned as he moved 'accidentally' too close to her while he reached across to the fridge to retrieve a carton of milk for his coffee.

Her eyes met with Michael's across the kitchen; he rolled

them in solidarity with Cat. The fact he didn't like Dustin either gave Cat the strength to be a little more strident with her riposte.

'Will you get out of my space?' she hissed.

Dustin stared at her, like he had no clue what she was going on about. He probably didn't. Why did every single office worldwide have one of these jerks!

'Sorry.'

Dustin lifted the milk carton to his lips. He took a long swig, even though it was communal. Cat got the feeling Dustin was the protagonist of his own mind movie; he probably thought he was a young Brad Pitt.

Muscling past him, something occurred to Cat. Dustin was one of the Higher Ups at Carmine Media; he should know where Erin was. If she'd called in sick, then their shared calendar would have been updated. At last, a way he could be useful to her.

'Erin in today?'

'Should be. Not heard anything. Maybe she's coming in late.'

'Okay, thanks.'

Anxiety coursed through Cat's chest as she left the kitchen. She thought back to the previous day and her brunch with Erin. She'd thought they'd got on well, even possibly 'clicked'. But what if she was wrong? Maybe Erin was working from home today, avoiding her. Perhaps she'd put a call in to get Cat disciplined or even fired for being overfamiliar or inappropriate.

Cat arrested these thoughts, breathing in through her nose and expelling them through her mouth. She was being ridiculous. She had done nothing wrong. Accepting an invite to brunch was not a deal-breaker in the working environment. Despite his recent change of behaviour, Lawrence's face returned to her again, that sardonic smile he'd affect when Cat expressed such insecurities at home.

Why do you always think everything is about you? Lawrence would chide. *Most people don't even notice stuff right in front of their faces.*

Though Lawrence had been sneering at her like he so often did, Cat had nevertheless discovered his words were correct. People would see and forget people, places, world events, appointments, even their own family. It wouldn't even matter how important those things were to them, either. In the struggle to put one foot in front of the other and battle on through the daily grind, only the 'now' mattered.

This realisation was not only eye-opening, but potentially profit-making. She'd spent a long time watching Lawrence online, doing his TikToks and Insta reels filled with pop psychology and conspiracy theories. He was full of shit, but he was right about one thing.

If people only noticed stuff that mattered to them in the moment, then Cat could use this to her advantage.

She could blag her way into the most exclusive of old boys' networks.

She could climb the ladder of any institution she wanted.

Once at the top, everyone else would be at her mercy. She could choose to help others up the rungs or pull the ladder up after her. All Cat had to do was hold her head up high and act as if it was all hers for the taking – because it was.

Fake it till you make it.

At school and university Cat hadn't found it too difficult to make out she was doing great, but the working environment was a whole different ball game. Cat discovered the problem with faking it was you're on constant red alert, in case you're unmasked as a fraud. You have to plan ahead, rethink your strategy and position, halt potential problems in their tracks before they begin. It was exhausting.

It's also impossible to keep juggling everything, 24/7. Certain things tended to fall by the wayside. Cat's love life was the obvious one. She knew, deep down, she wasn't meant to be with Lawrence. Whether he treated her like a princess or like dirt, the end result was the same: she didn't love him. She never had.

Lawrence had been company at university, the relationship equivalent of a security blanket. That had been fine as she started out alone on her adult adventures, but she'd outgrown him now. She wanted to live by herself, decide how to spend her own wages, enjoy a few years of selfishness and solitude. But Cat knew Lawrence wouldn't go quietly and she dreaded causing such a tsunami of bad feeling.

Just as she was trapped at work between the expectations of two classes, Cat was trapped at home with Lawrence in a cycle of abuse and insecurity. She couldn't afford a flat on her own and she couldn't bear to leave him, no matter how much of an arsehole he could be.

As Cat filled her coffee cup, peacock blue streaked past the internal window in her peripheral vision. Looking up, she spotted a harassed-looking Erin stalk through the cubicle farm. Erin looked as immaculate as ever: blue cardigan and black mid-line skirt, blue low-heel boots. She didn't smile or wave to any of the cubicle drones as she usually did.

Intriguing.

Moments later Cat abandoned her own coffee and was knocking on Erin's door, a cup in hand for her boss. Inside, Erin barked 'come in'. Cat walked as confidently as she could over the threshold, the bag of sweets in her left hand and her mother's face imprinted on the back of her mind's eye like a cinema projector screen.

Act like you own the place, Judith Crawford would always say. *The men think they do, but show them all who's boss. She who dares wins.*

Erin proffered her a tight smile as Cat placed the coffee on the desk for her. She was pale and had large dark circles under her eyes. She seemed upset or angry about something. Was it her fault? No, she had to pull herself together. Whatever had ruffled Erin's feathers couldn't be work-related, she'd only just got there. Cat's gift would make her feel better.

'I got you these, as a little thank you for brunch yesterday.'

Cat put the pink and white-striped paper bag next to the coffee. Erin didn't react. Embarrassment and awkwardness flooded through Cat, but sheer bloody-mindedness forced her to stay where she was. Following Erin's gaze, Cat realised she was staring out of the window, at the city below. She narrowed her own gaze, trying to work out what Erin could be looking for out there.

'Oh! Thank you.' Erin's attention flitted away from the

window to the coffee and sweets, then back to Cat as if seeing her for the first time. 'That's very kind.'

'Don't mention it.'

Cat turned on her heel to leave. As her hand grabbed the door handle, Erin called after her.

'Cat?'

She turned back towards Erin.

Erin was standing up, an appreciative smile on her cherry-red lips. She had the striped paper bag in her hand.

'How did you know these were my favourite?'

Cat licked her lips. She wanted credit for being thoughtful, but she didn't want to appear like a needy fangirl or a stalker either. Damn it, office politics were draining.

'I noticed you liked toffees,' she said, 'and those are my favourite, too.'

Erin beamed at her and Cat found herself beaming back. Cat dithered; she could tell Erin wanted to say something else. She didn't want to miss anything, but she also didn't want to out-stay her welcome and make it weird. Just as Cat was about to leave the office, Erin sat back down, kicking back in her chair.

'I was wondering – would you do me a favour?'

'Anything.'

Cat cursed herself inwardly; she sounded too eager. Erin didn't appear to notice, though. She was staring out at the Bristol skyline again.

'I've been tasked with organising John's retirement party.'

Confusion struck Cat. Erin was far too senior to be doing such grunt work. Perhaps she'd been chosen because she had worked with John for so long?

'I see.'

Erin raised an eyebrow.

'Apparently women *like* organising parties.'

'Men are such arseholes.'

Cat clamped a hand over her mouth as the words escaped before she could stop them.

'You see, that's what I like about you, Cat. You say what you mean and mean what you say.' Erin laughed. 'Anyway, if it's not too much trouble – and please, feel free to say no – would you mind giving me a hand with it?'

Pleasure bloomed in Cat's chest. She could not believe the turnaround in the past twenty-four hours. Just yesterday she'd been crying in the toilets, sure she would never level up. Now she was helping Erin Goodman! Okay, it was just a retirement party, but it beat rewriting press releases and it was bound to lead to other opportunities, too.

'I'd be delighted.'

'Fantastic. How about another drink tonight, after work? We can get started then.'

Cat forced herself to stay nonchalant. 'That would be great.'

Once Erin's office door closed behind her, Cat skipped all the way back to her desk.

SEVEN

ERIN

Despite promising myself I'd never drink again after over-indulging with David on Tuesday night, I'm now in need of a drink or ten.

Cat and I don't go far, just a cellar bar two streets away from Queens Mead Tower. I'm too tired to think about traversing Bristol's winding streets into the city centre. Cat wants to get the first drinks in, but I sweep her aside and wave some cash at a bored-looking barman with a tea towel in his back pocket and a sour expression. Seconds later we have a bottle of rosé and are chinking glasses.

'To you,' I say.

She titters like a schoolgirl. 'Oh, I'm nothing much.'

I've only had a few sips, but my tongue feels loose like I am already drunk.

'Oh no you don't, missy. Society will tell you you're

"nothing much". It tells all women that. We have to make ourselves smaller, not take up space. Well, fuck that!'

My loud tone and swearing make a small group of other office workers look over. Cat gives me an embarrassed smile, like she's not used to the spotlight being on her. Maybe she isn't. I know she's been in the cubicle farm a good while, but I've heard no buzz around her work since I joined Carmine. Not that there's any shame in that. For every star in the making, there needs to be at least ten cogs, keeping the machine running.

'That man of yours behaving himself now?'

Cat looks puzzled for a moment, like she's not sure what I'm talking about. Then she grins and nods.

'Oh . . . he's fine.'

'Just fine?' I pour myself more wine. Some slips over the rim of the glass onto the tablecloth. 'What does "fine" even mean?'

Opposite me, Cat takes another tentative sip. Her eyes shift sideways, like she's not sure she should answer. Oh my, the poor girl. This is waaaay worse than I thought.

'Let me guess,' I muse. 'You're still with your university boyfriend? All spark is gone. It's a hassle being with him, but it's even more of a hassle to split. You outgrew him years ago, but you can't face breaking it off with him. Am I close?'

Cat averts her eyes. Poor thing is probably embarrassed. Bless her.

'This is the thing.' I shift in the booth, cradling my wine glass in one hand; I like how it makes me feel like an old-style mentor from the movies. 'Some people say passion is the key, but that's bullshit. Others say security is everything, but that's bullshit too.'

'So, what's it all about?'

'Balance.'

'Is that why you're divorced?'

Cat gives me an apologetic smile as she sees my eyes bug out. A smirk tugs on my lip; there she is again, saying what she means and getting straight to the heart of the matter. She's also not too wide of the mark: perhaps if I had been less of a workaholic, David and I might have been able to deal with our problems instead of always being at each other's throats.

'That's right.' I drain my glass. 'I was dealing with the fall-out only this morning, so that's how I know.'

'I won't ask,' Cat says.

'Probably for the best.' I smile. 'So, about this party – any ideas?'

'Honestly, I haven't been to many retirement parties.'

'Nor me.'

My nostrils flare as I consider this fact is going to change. As I get older, more and more of my colleagues will start to retire. Hell, it won't be long before I retire. I might only be forty-three, but the last twenty years have disappeared in a blink. The next twenty-five are bound to vanish as quickly. Ugh.

'I googled "retirement party" ideas.'

Cat consults a reporter's notebook from her bag. I notice it's embossed with her initials. Cute. She flicks through the pages.

I'm a little embarrassed I hadn't thought to do something

as simple and sensible as this. I'd waded through Pinterest, looking at décor and party favours so detailed and complicated it would be easier for me to build an Eiffel Tower model entirely out of toothpicks. I'd only served to freak out and depress myself in equal measure.

'I made a list. We need a cake, a playlist of the retiree's favourite songs, party games and things to do. One article suggested a piñata of an alarm clock, since everyone hates getting up in the morning.'

'That's kinda genius.'

'Right?' Cat grins. 'Another article suggested a travelling petting zoo or reptile roadshow.'

I'm less enthused by this idea. If nothing else, the renovation of Queens Mead Tower is still ongoing. The thought of any of the animals – or God forbid, a snake – escaping and making it under the floors and into the wall cavities of Carmine Media sends a shudder up my spine.

'Yes, I didn't really like that idea, either.' Cat strikes a pencil through that one. 'How about an "oldy but a goody": a photo booth, with props?'

'I love it.'

I can feel the anxious weight of John's retirement party falling from my shoulders. Cat has a real knack for this. I pick up my glass and discover it's empty; so is the bottle.

'I'll get us another.'

I order at the bar feeling better than I have in days: I can't believe how easy it all is with Cat on board; all my previous worries and resentments vanish. I would never admit it to John, but I am enjoying organising the party.

'You're an absolute star, Cat. Thanks so much.'

'Oh, it's nothi—' Cat catches herself before I can jump in and tell her to stop denigrating herself. 'I mean, you're very welcome.'

We pick up our glasses again.

'To John's retirement party,' I say, 'and to you.'

EIGHT

CAT

Cat excused herself to Erin around half eight. She did not have a long commute. It was just a twenty-five-minute walk home, but it was dark and her carefully calculated budget couldn't stretch to an Uber. She was also anxious about Lawrence's reaction if she was out too late. After his turnaround in mood the day before, she didn't want him to plunge back into dark suspicions and accusations.

As she emerged from the cellar bar, Cat reached inside her pocket to retrieve her phone to let Lawrence know she was on her way. Her fingers grasped at nothing; her phone was not there. Sighing, she unzipped her bag and peered inside. Notebook. Pencil case. Make-up bag. Tampons. Gum. No phone.

Shit!

Burgeoning panic began to surge through her veins. Cat was less worried about the cheap handset itself than the fact

Lawrence might have been texting or calling her. He hated it when he couldn't get through to her. This was why she usually checked her screen for notifications every ten to fifteen minutes. Once, she'd not checked for just over an hour and returned to find six missed calls and no fewer than thirteen messages on a variety of social media platforms. He'd hit the roof when she got home that day.

Cat had worked hard to ensure that hadn't happened again. It just made sense not to provoke him, like it had with her mother too. Judith Crawford had been a mercurial woman; you never quite knew what you were going to get with her.

When had Cat had her phone last?

Of course. She'd texted Lawrence back at the office to say she was going for a drink 'with a colleague' after work. She'd been careful to ensure he knew said colleague was female. She'd known he would have laughed or sneered if she'd mentioned helping Erin organise John's retirement party, so she'd invented something about 'reviewing targets' and other bullshit office-style phrases she knew would impress him, or make him back off.

Cat normally would have slipped the phone back in her pocket or bag, but she recalled the landline had rung. A crazy old dear had told Cat she had a story, but really it was yet another conspiracy theory about 5G towers. Apparently the one near her home was making her cat jump up in the air like a jack-in-the-box and had caused her granddaughter's Non-Hodgkin lymphoma. Cat had sympathised and got off the phone quickly, returning to her work. She could now wager real money where her mobile was.

On her desk, next to the bloody landline.

Cat entertained momentary indecision about returning for it. She was over a quarter of the way back home. Perhaps she should just push on through? She had no real friends, so it was not as if anyone apart from Lawrence ever texted or called her anyway.

On the other hand, the phone would provide her with clues as to Lawrence's state of mind. If there were a gazillion texts and voicemails waiting, she could prepare herself for the onslaught when she returned to the flat.

Cat turned back.

Her calves were stinging with exertion as she hurried back to Carmine Media. Re-entering the building was easy. A single, aged security guard patrolled the large atrium at the bottom of the building. He opened the double doors for Cat without a second glance, without even asking to see her ID. Cat had never been in the office by herself. A couple of lights on her floor had been left on as a security measure, but this somehow made it more eerie. As she slipped inside Carmine Media and slalomed her way through the cubicle farm, she discovered to her surprise she missed the sound of fingers hitting keys, or laughter behind grey walls. The air, normally alive with various clashing aromas like coffee and cologne, now felt heavy and stale.

Just as she suspected, her mobile was next to the landline in the cubicle farm. Relief, then perverse disappointment shimmered through her as she saw there were no notifications from Lawrence – or anyone else – on the screen. She fired off a quick text to say she was leaving the bar and would be home in half an hour. Lawrence's reply popped up a nano-second later:

XXXX.

Just kisses. *Phew.*

As Cat slipped her phone back in her backpack and over her shoulders, a sixth sense skittered down her spine. She turned sharply, expecting to see someone behind her.

No one was there.

This did little to comfort her; somebody could lurk behind any of the cubicle walls. The farm was a maze. The security guard downstairs had let her in so readily. Could he have let an intruder in, too? It wasn't so much of a stretch.

Cat scurried towards the Carmine Media front doors to let herself back out again so she could go downstairs and get the hell out of this ghost office.

'Catrin.'

She screamed as a reflection in the glass of the doors appeared behind her. She registered a dark shape in the periphery of her vision, making her whirl around, arms up in a defensive pose.

A self-conscious chuckle from the other person made the shadowed man reconfigure in front of her. The threat evaporated as she took in the details of him: slumped shoulders, bald head, yet more pen ink – this time leaking through the pocket of his tan trousers.

'Jesus, Michael.' Cat felt herself deflate in relief. 'You nearly gave me a heart attack!'

Awkwardness bloomed in the space between them. Cat had expected him to laugh, to say sorry and exchange pleasantries before they both went their respective ways.

Michael stood where he was.

'Did I, now?'

His expression was curiously impassive. He bobbed his head, a bit like a bird. His voice was higher than she remembered, but there was something intangible beneath it that sent a flurry of alarm through Cat. The awkwardness morphed into disquiet. There was something she was missing. It was definitely there, like she was grasping for pennies in murky water.

Trust your instincts, her mother had always counselled her, *they're rarely wrong*.

'Out drinking?'

'Not really.' Cat felt the urge to over-explain, fill the space between them. 'Just a work thing.'

'Well, aren't you a good girl.'

Good girl. Lawrence had said this to her on more than one occasion. Usually when she capitulated to whatever it was he wanted. It might be a sex act; giving him money; or something as simple as making him a sandwich. It was a phrase that sent uncertainty, self-loathing and rage coursing concurrently through Cat's veins. As ever, she tamped it down.

'Well, night then.' Cat injected a breeziness into her voice she didn't feel.

'How about a drink?' Michael took a step forwards, almost in her space. 'I've got a bottle of whisky in my desk. One for the road?'

Cat took a careful step back.

'I have to get home, my boyfriend's waiting.'

Boyfriend. Husband. Partner. Magic words, designed to tell other men to stay in their place, to back off: this woman is taken. The vast majority will take the hint. They'll smile, maybe even raise their hands in mock surrender. *Hey, I tried.*

Not Michael. He didn't move. Worse, there was a steely glint in his eye. It was one Cat felt a curious familiarity with, yet she was not sure how.

Then it clicked.

She remembered seeing foxes and rabbits on the farm do this dance. Rabbits would stay stock still, sometimes as many as six or seven of them, right out in the open. The fox would transfix them, double-daring them to run. The rabbits knew that as soon as they moved, the fox would move too. But the rabbits had numbers on their side, the fox could not chase all of them.

Here and now, Cat was the predator's only prey. She fought the urge to ask Michael what he thought he was doing, what he wanted.

She knew what he wanted.

'Going so soon?'

She did not back up hard against the office doors of Carmine Media or say anything more. She knew Michael would count on that.

She lunged forwards at him.

Caught by surprise, Michael took an involuntary step backwards, allowing Cat enough room to turn on her heel and grab the door handle again.

Cat felt his meaty hands grab her backpack and pull. She had expected him to do this. She let her arms and shoulders go slack, shrugging it off. Cat was through the door and out into the corridor before Michael realised he had captured only her bag.

Lungs and legs burning, Cat careered down the stairs to the next level, then the next. The lift was out of the question. She didn't dare box herself in there. The doors may not close quickly enough and she could end up trapped in the steel compartment with him.

She heard footsteps above, Michael's calls after her. She couldn't make out the words, just the tone of his wheedling pleas. No doubt he was telling her it was all a big misunderstanding.

Cat knew she had understood only too well.

She had to make it back downstairs, to the atrium. The security guard would surely give Michael pause for thought, plus he had a radio. Cat wondered how many times Michael had attempted this before, or even got away with it with other women.

Cat made it onto a wide landing with two staircases off it, one leading right, the other left. Indecisiveness flitted through her for a second before she looked up and saw Michael through the banisters. The look of unbridled fury on his face sent stabbing pains surging through her chest.

She'd read somewhere that crowds most often veered towards the right, because most people were right-handed. She hoped that applied to individuals too and raced down the stairs on the left-hand side.

It was darker down there. She took a corner, then another. Where the hell was the atrium? She was completely disorientated.

As Cat glanced up, she saw the strip lights overhead were missing. Almost tripping over some debris, her eyes picked out sights in the gloom: a dustpan and brush. Bags of unmixed plaster. Piles of broken ceiling tiles. Sheets of plastic wrap. One of those large industrial vacuum cleaners.

Blood crashing in her ears and adrenaline coursing through her veins, Cat had missed the carpet stopping and the concrete beginning under her rubber-soled shoes. Now she heard them squeak as she had to halt in her tracks, windmilling her arms to arrest the momentum. For one hairy second she thought she was still going to pitch into the gloom. At the last moment she rocked back on her heels, avoiding falling straight into the open chasm where the stairs used to be.

There was no time for relief. Cat could hear her pursuer thundering up behind her, about to turn the corner into the corridor and join her. Terrified, she looked side to side for another door, a way out to the next floor below.

There was none.

Cat did not dare to jump into the gloom of the missing stairs and hope for the best. She was fairly sure she was too high up for that to work. She also knew in her heart she'd reached the end of the line, just like the rabbit facing down the fox.

She was trapped.

'Cat.'

The arrogance in Michael's voice was as abrasive and obvious as a car alarm. He was not breathless, despite pursuing her down so many storeys. Shaking, Cat rose to her feet, picking up a piece of crumbling breeze block as she did so. Michael clocked her aggressive stance and whistled, as if impressed. With nowhere left to run, she stood her ground, determined not to let her fear show.

'Didn't think you had it in you.'

Cat pursed her lips. People always underestimated her. 'Well, you thought wrong.'

With a scream, she ran straight at Michael.

He was ready for her this time. He didn't take that involuntary step backwards but matched her, racing towards her with his own guttural yell. He raised one of his forearms to protect his head, anticipating a blow from Cat's piece of breeze block as she neared him.

Cat did not strike him. She knew she didn't have the strength necessary to halt his attack. Instead, she lunged from her right foot to her left like a boxer feigning in the ring, leaving a gap where he expected her to be.

Michael dodged, Cat kept running towards the end of the corridor, intent on grasping as much of the advantage as she could. She felt the breeze against her cheek as they passed each other, with Michael surging right towards the chasm where the stairs had been.

'Shit!'

Cat's head turned back as she reached the corner. Agog, she watched Michael teeter on the edge of the chasm. She expected to see him recover like she had. He would push himself back, then turn on his heel and give chase again. He did none of these things.

He pitched headfirst into the hole.

His howl accompanied him all the way to the bottom, then it was cut off abruptly as he hit the concrete below.

Shock immobilised Cat, for what felt like hours. Adrenaline making her woozy, she eventually managed to put one foot in front of the other like a newly born calf. She peered into the darkness of the hole, giving it a wide berth just in case.

There was no mistake. She could just about make out a dark shape at the bottom, the head a growing black mass as blood seeped around it like a macabre halo.

Michael was dead.

PART TWO

Victory comes from finding opportunity in problems.

SUN TZU

NINE

ERIN

'This is a nightmare. A nightmare!'

John stands in my office, pacing. His remaining hair stands up at all angles where he's pulled it through his hands. He has a pyjama shirt tucked into his jeans and odd shoes on: one a brown brogue, the other a black Doc Marten.

I can't judge him. I have no make-up on and my coat covers my own nightclothes. I feel hot but daren't take it off in case John sees my braless nipples straining through my PJ top's thin material. Why am I even thinking about that at a time like this, for God's sake? But I am. I grow irritated by John's relentless pacing and chuntering to himself.

'John . . . *John!*'

He freezes where he is. His mouth drops open in an 'o' of surprise like he'd not even realised I was present. Maybe he hadn't. I can see the endless cycle of questions, *what ifs* and *WTFs* swirling in his eyes.

'Erin, how could this have happened?'

I'm at a loss too. Nothing like this has ever happened to either of us, or in the entire history of Carmine Media before. Michael Froud, one of Hugh's most loyal and longest-serving word monkeys in the cubicle farm, stayed back late to run some updates on the computer system. Apparently he's done this many times before, without overtime, which now makes me suspect he'd been avoiding something at home. As if eavesdropping on my thoughts, John lowers his voice to a conspiratorial whisper.

'Do you think . . . do you think he *meant* to do it?'

I know John means suicide, but neither of us can summon the word. I understand why he thinks Michael might have taken his own life, but I know better.

I'd received a call from Cat about an hour earlier, just as I was getting into bed for an early night. It was the second night in a row I'd had my sleep interrupted by the phone. Any uncharitable, weary thoughts vanished as soon as I heard her hysteria. She'd been babbling about holes and chasing.

Still not knowing what had happened, I'd told her to sit tight at the office, then thrown on my coat. I'd suffered approximately five seconds of guilt as I contemplated the fact I must be over the limit, but according to my app there were no Ubers in the vicinity. I slid behind the wheel, telling myself it was an emergency.

I'd called the police and John on the way via speakerphone. When I'd made it to the office, Cat's hysteria from the phone had been downgraded to an eerie, monotonous telling. The timbre of her voice sounded like a robot's. I was reminded of

Joshua's reading when he was six or seven. Something about her demeanour felt staged, but then I'd had a word with myself. How the hell would I know what was the 'appropriate' way to act after you just saw a man fall to his death? I needed to listen and not judge.

Cat told me that Michael had 'accosted' her. When I asked her what she meant, she'd eyeballed me, her manner both defiant and defensive.

'What do you *think* I mean?'

Like most of the female population, my own life path is littered with near-misses from men who hadn't known how to behave and wouldn't take 'no' for an answer. I've also been told it 'can't' be what I'd thought; that I was overreacting, or even an outright liar.

I chose my next words with care.

'Tell me what happened. Every detail.'

Cat nodded and told me.

'He must have got confused in the dark. That's why he fell.' Tears well up and spill down her cheeks. 'Is this my fault?'

'No!' I am mortified she could even entertain such a self-destructive thought; the poor girl. 'He came after *you*. This is on *him*.'

Now there's a small contingent of officers downstairs, at the hole, recording all the necessary details with a stern-looking pathologist. Another young female officer stands nearby babysitting us. Her eyes are all over the place, taking everything in. I'm not sure what she's looking for, or whether she's just anxious to avoid my gaze and any potential questions she can't answer. I can't blame her.

There are a million unanswered queries squalling through my mind, just waiting to be breathed into being.

Still dazed, Cat sits in my office wheelie chair, one of those foil blankets around her that I've only ever seen on television, wrapping marathon runners like roast turkeys. She stares at her shoes, which she clacks together like Dorothy trying to leave Oz. A middle-aged, tattooed paramedic talks to her in a soothing voice, trying to get her attention. He doesn't seem very successful. Cat's jaw has snapped shut with the force of a steel trap. Shock, I suppose.

None of us can know how we would react in devastating situations. I remember my mother saying this when she was first diagnosed. Before that, she'd always been incredulous that people would hear terrible medical news like cancer and other conditions yet refuse to face them. Wouldn't you *want* to get started right away on treatment?

Then Mum had received such heartbreaking news herself. In contrast to what she'd believed she would do, her first action was to get in the car and drive away, to the coast. She'd lain low in a B&B up the road near Nailsea. She'd dodged my calls and attempts to find her for three whole days. When Mum had finally answered and told me where she was, she'd confirmed she had motor neurone disease like I'd merely asked what her Christmas plans were.

At Queens Mead Tower, I blink and Hugh Carmine's arrived. His eyes are wild but he otherwise looks the same as always: like he'd just got out of bed. He's shouting, gesticulating, his tone accusing. John mutters something about keeping his voice down so as not to spook Cat, but Hugh ignores him.

He crouches next to the poor girl, barking questions at her. The paramedic tells him to take his leave, but Hugh ignores him too. The young police officer seems to switch on at this point, putting one hand on Hugh's shoulder. He jerks it off, rounding on her when she does it again. The young woman shoots him a grim smile and manages to extricate him from the room, promising to hear him out in his statement.

The police will want my own statement soon, so I work through what I've learned from Cat tonight. I try and focus on what she'd first said on the phone.

'Michael . . . he's gone!'

'Gone where?'

'In the hole.'

'What hole?'

'The one where the stairs used to be – on the left side of the building. You know, where the lifts are going in. Oh God, Erin, what am I going to do?'

What am I going to do.

What else was there to do? We have to pick up the pieces and trudge onwards. I suppose Cat had lived a sheltered life up until this point. Most of us have. Death is stage managed in our lives in the Western world. It is kept away under the cloak of hushed reverence, limited to nursing homes and hospital side rooms, like my poor mum.

Most of us will not see someone die at work. Unless employed in the police, medical, construction or transport institutions, you have to be very unlucky to see the results of terrible accidents or suicides. Even all the golden agers and gammon, harking back to eras where health and safety standards had not 'gone mad', did not really want to return to a time when people had zero rights and took their lives in their hands every time they went to work.

Health and safety. Shit.

How liable is Carmine Media for Michael's death? My beleaguered brain tries to sort through the details. If one colleague attacks or tries to attack another at work, where does the employer stand? What's more, though Carmine Media only takes up the very top floor of Queens Mead Tower, the whole building belongs to Hugh Carmine. He'd started the refit last March to make the old high rise more attractive to businesses looking to rent. He'd had a vision of making it a whole media hub, even kicking off his own Bristolian version of Canary Wharf. As ever, up until this point Hugh's had only one eye on the project. Longer-serving word monkeys tell me he's cut corners, employing cowboy builders in the first instance. This had meant having to employ better ones to put right what the first lot screwed up, which is why the refit is so behind.

Have I been much better than Hugh? I've been preoccupied with relaunching the *Bristol Journal* with John. I've ignored the daily deluge of dust and seemingly never-ending piles of rubble. I've promised others I would 'look into' their concerns about the noise and mess. Whilst I'm not a head honcho by any stretch of the imagination, I am still one of the Higher Ups. I might have only just started my career at Carmine Media, but it could be hanging in the balance already. My lack of action would have been recorded on meeting minutes somewhere if the police do enough digging.

Does that mean my head is on the block too, now?

Shame floods through me as these self-interested thoughts register. A man is dead. Whoever is liable will get what is coming to them. A huge fine for the company, probably. This in turn will no doubt mean several redundancies to make up the shortfall. I will argue for the cutbacks not to fall on the cubicle farm, but on the Higher Ups. If necessary, I can nominate myself. Since I am one of the last in, few people if any would oppose this. It would be a bit of a disaster in my personal life, especially regarding my maintenance for the boys, but I will figure that out if and when I have to.

It's the least I can do.

After what seems like an age, the paramedic announces his initial checks are done and that he's taking Cat into the hospital for observation. She says nothing, just stands like a good robot and follows him.

Eager to help and assuage some of my guilt, I pick up her rucksack and move after them, the bag banging against my leg in tandem with my heartbeat. On my way past, John tells Cat to keep her pecker up, which is ridiculous *and* inappropriate, but I let it go. We are all in uncharted territory here.

Downstairs, we're bathed in the ambulance's blue light which turns idly, the siren off. I see a coroner's van arrive. I imagine them picking up poor Michael's broken body, zipping it into a body bag. I turn my face away, but I am not fast enough. My stare draws Cat's, who looks across the car park and sees the dark vehicle. Seeing her face crumple, I push some words out, any words, in an urge to stop her feeling quite so bad.

'It's not your fault,' I remind her.

Cat's lower lip quivers, but I'm surprised to see her eyes are now free of tears. Her gaze is hard and sharp as she clambers inside the ambulance. Her tone and body language match her demeanour.

'No. It's not.'

The paramedic slams the ambulance doors after her, leaving me perturbed again.

TEN

MAN DIES AFTER PLUNGING FIVE STOREYS INSIDE BRISTOL TOWER

THE TRAGEDY HAPPENED AT THE QUEENS MEAD Tower around 9 p.m. on 20 January, police said. The 47-year-old man was pronounced dead at the scene.

Cat Crawford reports.

HORROR FALL

MICHAEL FROUD, 47, HAS BEEN FOUND DEAD AT THE bottom of a large hole in the Queens Mead Tower, near the city centre. Home to conglomerate Carmine Media, the old building has been undergoing an extensive refit after being bought by media tycoon Hugh Carmine two years ago.

Police and ambulance crews descended on the scene, but Mr

Froud had already passed away. Police are investigating but say there are no signs of suspicious circumstances.

A police spokesperson said: 'Police were called around 9 p.m. on Wednesday, 20 January, following a report a man had fallen approximately five storeys through a large hole in the floor.

'It is our understanding Mr Froud was working late and that the hole was for an elevator shaft.'

THE TOWER

STARTING IN MARCH LAST YEAR, THE MULTI-million-pound refit was supposed to take just twenty weeks. It was to include a suite of luxurious offices and conference rooms, as well as a gym, coffee bar and crèche.

The refit was also supposed to update the old building to more modern, inclusive standards such as a new set of lifts to accommodate disabled workers and visitors.

Some ten months on, the refit's end is not in sight, and it provides the backdrop not only for Michael's untimely death, but his alleged attack on me, Cat Crawford.

LAST DAY

AN INDISPENSABLE PART OF THE CARMINE MEDIA team, Michael had been working for the company since its inception. He'd spent two decades working for Charles Carmine at its previous home near Brandon Hill. When Charles left his empire to his son Hugh, it seemed only right that Michael and other such loyal workers would be moved with the company to the Queens Mead Tower.

I've known Michael, a married father of two, since my first day at Carmine Media two years ago. He congratulated me on getting the job and made me a coffee, delivering it to my cubicle with a wink and a smile.

With such a cheery disposition, Michael was popular in the office. He could frequently be found in the office kitchens doing the crossword or chatting with others by the water cooler. He'd told me he was always happy to help if I had any questions or worries. At least, that was the persona he liked to project.

I never imagined I would be present on his own last day on this earth.

HOW IT HAPPENED

I'D RETURNED TO THE OFFICE FOR MY PHONE, WHICH I'd accidentally left behind. I didn't see anyone else in the empty office. A little spooked by the deserted workstations, I found my phone and attempted to leave.

That's when Michael made his appearance, startling me.

'They' say there are moments that are written in time, unavoidable; that everything leads to that event and there is no going back. That night my first impulse was to laugh, saying he'd made me jump. Yet Michael didn't find it funny, or even interesting. His face was as impassive as a death mask.

Instinct told me I was in trouble. Despite his vacant

93

expression, Michael seemed spring-loaded, like he might pounce on me. Something rippled between us: dark and threatening. I knew that I couldn't just turn my back on him and leave. His demeanour put me on edge. I froze, my anxiety spiking.

Though Michael had never behaved inappropriately around me before when the office was busy, he seemed like a different person now no one else was there. Knowing I had no other way out, I feigned advancing on him and when he retreated, I ran for the office door.

Sure enough, as I attempted to escape, he grabbed my backpack to yank me back into the office with him. I shrugged it off without missing a beat, racing for the door and leaving him holding my bag.

Michael chased me down flight after flight of stairs. Disbelief, horror and anger powered me to run faster than ever before. Like so many women, I'd imagined predators to be obvious; that I'd somehow 'just know' who the bad men were. Yet I'd had no clue about Michael's dark intentions towards me.

Considerably younger than Michael, I managed to outrun him. We got separated in the labyrinthine corridors of Queens Mead Tower. When I found myself nearing the atrium, I heard a man's harsh scream from the left side of the tower where the renovations were undergoing.

When he did not make a reappearance, I retraced my steps back. I discovered a huge hole in the floor where stairs had been on the fourth floor. My brain incongruously reminded me a disabled lift was meant to have been in their place. Instead the hole ran straight through the heart of the tower to the underground car park, five storeys down.

At the bottom, splayed on the concrete, Michael's body.

He must have stumbled in the dark and fallen straight in. Relief flooded through me, followed swiftly by guilt. A man was dead. Had he really been chasing me with ill intentions? Could I have been mistaken? Could he have been pursuing me only to tell me I'd got it wrong? Perhaps if I had never run, he would never have fallen.

Then I remembered. Michael had attempted to manhandle me in the office; I'd left him holding only my bag. Also, men don't chase women they don't know to tell them they've made a 'mistake'.

What I also know: I am willing to wager there are more women like me, some perhaps not as lucky as me.

I can't be Michael's only victim.

ELEVEN

ERIN

'What the hell is this?'

I let my iPad clatter on John's desk. Through the internal window, I see a couple of investigators bagging up Michael's belongings from his workstation and unplugging his computer. The Friday after Michael's death, Carmine Media is still super-quiet. Hugh had sent most of the cubicle farm home, as well as the podcast and internet television studio. All of these employees are still working from home, of course. Our boss loves money and there's no way he's going to let a prime bit of news escape the organisation just because the police have a job to do.

John picks up my iPad in one hand and his glasses in the other, peering at the screen like Grandma at the wolf. 'Ah, yes. Poetic, don't you think?'

I arrest the automatic retort in my mouth, counting to

five as I do so. John really is a test to anyone's patience, but especially mine right now. I collapse in the chair opposite his desk, my feet and lower back almost screaming in relief.

'Yes, it's a nice piece of writing. Heartfelt, but still tells us the facts without resorting to sensationalism. That's not my point, though.'

John just looks askance at me. I roll my eyes. All he sees are the multiple likes and shares of Cat's article. It's been trending on Twitter and created an uptick in follows for the paper on a variety of platforms. I will have to spell it out for him.

'Did you have Cat write this? A man tried to attack her, then bloody died. She's still in shock!'

John's wide forehead furrows. 'Of course I didn't. I told her to take the next couple of weeks off, paid leave. She pleaded to come in, so I said yes.'

My mouth drops open in shock. It hadn't even occurred to me to look for Cat at her cubicle. I'd assumed she would be at home, hopefully waited on hand and foot by that otherwise useless boyfriend of hers.

'She's *here*, in the building?'

John kicks back in his chair. 'Some people need time alone to process trauma. Others need to work straight on through it. It's not unusual, Erin. You of all people should know that.'

He has me there and knows it. When my mother died five years ago, I was back at work the very next day. She went slow, hanging on for days and days. Despite being up all hours that last night, I plastered on make-up over the tracks of my tears and reapplied a bright red lipstick. I deflected others' concerns and sympathies like light off a reflector board in an Instagrammer's photography set up.

Determined to push on through, I buried myself in work and didn't come up for air for the best part of a year. Shortly after that, I inexplicably started crying in the bath and couldn't stop for approximately four days. *Delayed onset grief*, my therapist called it.

I don't want that for Cat.

I am unsure why I am so invested in the younger woman. I suppose part of it is vanity; Cat reminds me of me at the same age. I was isolated and alone back then, albeit for different reasons. Though I climbed the corporate ladder relatively quickly, I was a new wife and mother and totally out of my depth at home. David was – *is* – the love of my life, but my workaholism came between us. I was always focused on the newspaper at the expense of our marriage. I can see that now.

My time as a mother at home was hardly a roaring success, either. I'd believed having children would come to me as naturally as it had my own mother. Yet Dylan was a colicky baby, crying for hours and sleeping in fitful starts of ten to twenty minutes at the most for his first six months. He didn't take to the breast, was late crawling and prone to chest infections. I became trapped between the walls of our home with him. I dreaded David going out to work and started counting the days until I could return to the office myself.

I told myself it would be different with Joshua, that he was my second chance at getting motherhood right. I would forget about my job and take my full complement of maternity leave. I would be a domestic goddess, making home-cooked meals and trawling Pinterest for salt dough recipes. Then David lost his job and I had to return to the office before I wanted to, whilst David was stuck at home looking after another squawking infant.

David called me that morning after Michael's death, waking me after a broken night full of dreams in which I chased a wailing Cat through debris-filled corridors. I felt around on the nightstand, grabbing my mobile and putting it on speakerphone without opening my eyes. I told myself I couldn't go on a third mercy mission in as many days. I just couldn't. I had nothing left.

'Erin?' David's voice had that shouty quality somewhere between fear and anger. 'That you?'

'Yeah, it's me.'

'Jesus . . . I just saw the news. It just says someone died in your building. I just wanted to check . . . '

He trailed off altogether. A warm feeling blossomed in my chest. He *did* care about me after all.

'Y'know, for the boys.'

His words were a blow. 'Oh, cheers. Disappointed?'

'Of course not!' David was full-on rage now. 'How can you say that?'

Maybe we'd just always been doomed.

I leave John's office and make my way through the maze of cubicles. It feels odd to see them all empty in the middle of the day. They are all identical, but different at the same time. Tidy ones next to ones hosting tsunamis of clutter; ones with posters of celebrities, motivational quotes or movies next to ones with ornaments, mascots and family photographs. The mark of humans: all the same, yet also diverse.

Sure enough, Cat is at her desk, cradling an empty mug and staring into space. Even so, she looks very different to Wednesday night when I'd last seen her, after Michael's fall. There is colour in her cheeks and she doesn't seem as vacant or robot-like. As I approach, she looks up, her face breaking into a broad smile as she clocks me.

'Erin.'

She stands, abandoning her mug on her desk. She steps forward and hugs me, enveloping me in her floral perfume. I accept her embrace. She smells clean, her body is not wary under my touch. Though no one can ever know exactly what's going through someone's mind, she seems all right. My expression is grave as I release her.

'How are you?'

'Oh, fine.' Cat averts her gaze, stares at the natty cord of the office carpet.

I don't let her brush me off. 'Cat, a terrible thing happened to you. Are you sure you should be here?'

'I had to come.' Cat lifts her chin; it juts out in defiance. 'Got to get back on the horse.'

I can understand why she feels like this. Staying away from the scene of such an awful event could make it grow like mould spores, take over her mind. Maybe if she didn't come back right away, she'd never be able to walk back through the doors of Queens Mead Tower ever again. Perhaps I'd even say the same to myself if I was in a similar position. Scratch that. I know I would.

I look at my iPad screen. On the LED it reads past two o'clock. An idea occurs to me.

'How about another drink?'

Cat blinks, surprised I am no longer trying to persuade her to go home. She looks back to her work, in two minds about abandoning it. It's not a difficult decision for her.

'You're on,' she says.

TWELVE

CAT

'Your piece about Michael . . . it was very brave.'

Cat sat across from Erin again. This time they were in some overpriced Mexican chain restaurant with sombreros on the counter, a huge, badly painted mural of a desert scene and salt and pepper shakers in the shape of cartoon cactuses, replete with comical expressions.

'Thank you.'

Erin had declared a need for nachos with their wine. She'd ordered a large platter of them, smothered in bright orange plasticky cheese sauce, chemical-tasting red salsa and fiery green jalapeños. Cat had never been one for spicy fare; her mother considered lasagne to be foreign food. Even so, she nibbled at the tortillas for the sake of politeness. Erin didn't appear to notice she was eating the lion's share.

'Thank you as well for . . . you know, believing me.'

'Why wouldn't I believe you?' Erin seemed shocked by Cat's gratitude. 'Those types look normal, they could be anyone. We have to be on our guard, always. It's exhausting.'

Uncomfortable, Cat proffered a wan smile. *Schrodinger's Rapist*, Cat's mother had called it. Like the cat was dead and alive simultaneously, the male species was both benign and malevolent, Judith Crawford believed, often at the same time, even to the same women. She'd insisted no man could be one hundred per cent trusted, not even Cat's own father Ernest. Maybe *especially* the men women invite into their lives: too many were wolves in sheep's clothing.

This thought sent her accompanying images of Lawrence. She'd written the piece to get her thoughts in order and process what had happened that evening. Cat tapped the article out on her phone while Lawrence lumbered about in A&E, making various demands of harassed nurses and busy doctors. Cat needed water. An extra pillow. To be discharged. She'd asked for none of these things but let him get on with it. Like many men, Lawrence felt the need to take charge when his woman had a problem.

When they made it home he showed his true colours. As soon as they were back in the flat, all pretence of being the caring boyfriend was gone. Lawrence grabbed Cat's arm and twisted it behind her back, a feral snarl on his lips as he hissed in her ear.

'What *really* happened with that guy tonight?'

'Exactly what I told you and everyone else,' Cat insisted, squealing as he twisted harder. 'Lawrence, please – don't!'

'He just tried to attack you out of nowhere?'

'Yes!'

Lawrence let go of Cat and pushed her away. Cat held her arm, snivelling and rubbing the pain from it. Nostrils flared, he looked her up and down like she disgusted him.

'Who'd want to rape *you*?'

He shook his head and ambled to the bedroom in search of cigarettes. Tears still in her eyes and on her cheeks, Cat regarded herself in the smeared mirror by the bookcase. She was not much to look at, that much was true: fine, mousy-brown hair; moon-like face; greasy skin across her cheeks and chin she had to exfoliate every night or risk breakouts. Her body was no better, with her too-wide bottom that was matched by small breasts and rounded shoulders. She knew that for a man like Michael none of that would have been a deal-breaker. It was about power and opportunity.

It hadn't occurred to Cat that her article could go viral. She'd still been in two minds about telling the truth about what had happened with Michael. There was a part of her that hated the idea of casting herself as the would-be victim of a creep like him. Cat didn't want to be known as the girl a dead man had tried to assault. The notoriety would not only be hard to deal with, it would follow her throughout her career.

The thought of being vulnerable like that in front of her colleagues made Cat feel sick. But Cat hadn't invited Michael's interest, nor had she been 'asking for it'. She'd returned to the office only to fetch her phone. Everything that had happened – including Michael's death – was on him, even if she didn't tell the story exactly as it happened.

Feeling steely and resolute, wanting to stick it to Lawrence and his cruel disbelief, Cat attached the article to an email and sent it to the night subeditor. She hadn't expected them to accept it, let alone run with it on the front banner of the website. She'd thrown up when she'd seen it that morning.

'John is very pleased with the piece; it's doing extremely well online.'

Cat suppressed a yawn, not wanting to appear rude. She had only been able to nap since the accident. Every time she closed her eyes she saw Michael overbalance and topple headfirst into the chasm.

'Anyway, don't take my word for it. Look at this.'

Erin turned her phone screen around so Cat could see. At the bottom of her article were the visible shares, which had hit almost one hundred thousand. Underneath were scores of comments, all expressing various emotions and emojis, from anger and hearts through to crying faces.

Cat swiped a finger across the screen and another platform opened. #MeToo was trending, with women coming forward and sharing their own stories of sexual assault at work. Several Bristol women were even claiming Michael had been their assailant too. As Twitter, Instagram and Snapchat demanded, these women were providing 'receipts', which included dates, times, text message chains and even photographs of them with Michael. Bristol police were promising to investigate all allegations.

In addition, #HealthAndSafetyGoneMad was trending too, an ironic hashtag asking why the hell there was such a large hole leading down five storeys right in the middle of Queens Mead Tower. There were gifs and memes, some referencing horror and thriller movies set in tower blocks where bad things happened, such as *Attack the Block*, *High-Rise* and *Die Hard*. That self-appointed guardian of the people Piers Morgan had retweeted Cat's article, with demands that the Powers That Be take the matter seriously. In response, several prominent MPs were asking for their party leaders to look into it, plus the mayor of Bristol was saying it was his 'number-one priority'.

'Wow.'

Cat didn't know what to say. Erin gave her a sympathetic smile.

'I know this is hard, but you mustn't feel guilty. Michael was the one in the wrong, not you.' Erin shoved yet another tortilla smothered in sour cream into her mouth. 'I think you know that, really. That's why you've been brave enough to turn your traumatic experience into a story like this and show it to the world. Never doubt the healing power of telling your story, Cat. You will have changed other women's lives.'

Cat blinked, unsure she'd heard Erin correctly. Whilst her viral article on Michael's death had been a welcome distraction, it didn't mean anything. It couldn't . . . could it? Cat's main job was dealing with press releases and 'N.I.Bs' aka 'news in brief', just like all the other juniors at Carmine Media. She wasn't supposed to leave the office to do any investigating without permission from the Higher Ups. Any phone calls she made were to double-check tiny details like names or locations. If she was lucky, she got to help out in the podcast department or the TV studio. Whilst that got her away from her cubicle, it wasn't much of a break in routine: she was still making coffee or writing boring announcements for them to record.

'But I'm not supposed to write anything other than what they tell me?'

Erin wiped her hands on a napkin and picked up her phone. She showed Cat the viral article again.

'Did they tell you to write this?'

Heat crept up Cat's neck. 'Well, no. But—'

'No buts,' Erin interrupted. 'Look, I get it. A man has died. It feels horrible and opportunistic. But you have to remember this story could have ended much worse for you, plus he would never have fallen into that hole had he not been after you. You need to make sure you build on this. It could be the start of something really big for you.'

She signalled for the waiter, who approached with a card machine in hand. Waving Cat's card away, she tapped her own. Checking the time, she gathered her things and rose from the table, all smiles. Cat mirrored her, sliding out of the booth and escorting her to the big glass double doors of the restaurant. She was surprised to see it was dark. They'd been talking for hours. Out of habit she checked her phone for notifications from Lawrence. None.

'Gotta leave you here,' Erin said. 'You take care, okay?'

Cat nodded and accepted an awkward hug from Erin. She watched as the older woman stalked off in the direction of the multistorey car park, before turning and shouting something back to her. Something Cat had heard before in her mother's parlour.

'Remember, she who dares wins!'

It was a sign.

THIRTEEN

ERIN

Finally, the weekend rolls around. It's been a hell of a week, but today is my day to see the boys. Determined to enjoy my allotted time with my sons, I don't even let the likelihood of Dylan dodging me yet again crash my mood. If he does, he does. Teenagers are a law unto themselves. I know at least Joshua will be pleased to see me.

David answers the front door in a black T-shirt and chequered pyjama trousers, bare feet and white whiskers on his chin. He seems surprised to see me, like this hasn't been our weekly arrangement for the last three years. This gets my back up, but I plaster on a smile and make no attempt to come into the home I pay for. David has made sure I know better than that. Even so, he leans on the doorframe, his body a barrier just in case I charge at the hallway. For God's sake.

'Hi, David.' I keep my voice and tone measured. 'The boys ready?'

David nods and yells into the house. I hear the clatter of feet overhead on the stairs in the large hallway, but not which boy they belong to. My ex-husband turns back towards me on the doorstep, his face grave.

'I thought you might want to give this week a miss' – David chooses his words carefully – 'after what happened at your work.'

'What happened at work?'

Joshua pops up under David's armpit. I bite my tongue as I see David has had my youngest son's hair cut. His beautiful curls are all shorn off, grade number two. This dismay is eclipsed as he grins at me: he's lost another tooth since last week. It's brought home to me in even the smallest things how much of my sons' lives I am missing by not seeing them every day.

'Oh, nothing much, just boring grown-up stuff.' I force breeziness into my tone, running my hand over the fuzziness of Joshua's head. I glance up and see David's challenging stare, so add: 'Your hair looks great.'

My heart sinks as I hear more feet on the stairs. David couldn't have someone staying over – could he? Children are not known for their discretion, so I'd already heard that David had been working his way through a selection of the single mums at school. Dylan had told me to hurt me, but it wasn't as if I'd been living like a nun. Though I'd sworn off long-term relationships, I'd enjoyed a few brief dalliances of my own since the divorce. That cute young actor-slash-barista

110

from Starbucks had made me feel good about myself again, then Carlos from finance had been my fuck buddy for two or three months until he'd been let go by the *Bristol Journal* when Carmine Media had bought the asset. Carlos had decided to use his redundancy money to take a trip around the world. Good for him. After he'd gone, I'd joined a few dating apps and swiped right on a couple that had taken my fancy. Because, why the hell not?

As far as I knew, David didn't have a girlfriend right now, plus we'd spent the night together only that week. I still harboured feelings for David, not just as the father of my kids but as a lover. The thrill of the chase aside, it's boring to have to train new partners. The pull of history is hard to resist, plus David is a good-looking guy who knows what I like. There's still something about him that sends the tingle to my you-know-what. I hope I make him feel the same way, but the truth is I just don't know. David is infuriatingly secretive.

'Here he is,' David says.

I'm flabbergasted as my eldest son appears on the stairs. Dylan nods at both me and his father and jumps the last few steps.

'Hello, Mother,' he says, a touch of irony to his voice.

'Hello, son,' I reply, determined not to make a big deal of it. I don't want to make him change his mind and scurry back to his pit.

Dylan grunts at me and sweeps straight past to the car. Brandishing a plastic sword, Joshua skips after him. I look to David, eyebrows raised.

'We had a little word.' David shrugs.

'Thanks.' I mean it.

Before I can turn on my heel, the *bonhomie* is broken. David fixes me with a stern glare.

'Remember, back by six.'

Caught on the back foot, I nod.

'I won't forget.'

'You were late with Joshua last week.'

I grit my teeth. 'Just twenty minutes.'

'It's the principle of the matter, Erin.'

For a split second, I see myself in my mind's eye flying across the threshold and throttling the life out of my ex-husband. Who does he think he is? Dylan and Joshua are my children every bit as much as his. I provide for them and look out for them and love them as a mother should. I can almost feel the tendons of David's neck under my hands. I can see his eyes bug out and feel the flush of heat as his face turns red and mottled as the life starts to leave him.

I blink and the image pops like a soap bubble.

'Of course. Six it is.'

In the car I quiz the boys about what they want to do. Joshua has a million and one ideas, nearly all of them revolving around ice cream. That's the beauty of smaller kids: they find joy in the smallest of things. In stark contrast, nothing is good enough for teenagers. I am met with utter contempt or indifference from Dylan.

Not for the first time, I find myself frustrated in trying to keep two age-gap children occupied. I'd planned on taking Joshua to the farm park again that day, but Dylan's appearance puts paid to that. Every other suggestion is either inappropriate or met with apathy from my sons: the cinema, shopping, coffee and cake, the museum, a gallery or even leaving Bristol altogether for the countryside. I can't win when I'm with both boys.

Stumped, I take them back to my flat where I make them some lunch. Shoving a ham sandwich and half a dozen crisps in his mouth at once, Dylan proposes a video game marathon. Joshua's eyes light up. I'm delighted they are agreeing at last and no more of our precious time together will be wasted when I suddenly remember one huge problem: I don't have a games console. But as this issue occurs, so does the solution.

I know where I can get one.

Upstairs, Asif opens his front door bare-chested in just his undies, utterly oblivious to my discomfort.

'All right,' he says.

I avert my eyes in case I end up looking where I shouldn't. I am old enough to be the boy's mother, for God's sake.

'Weird request, any chance I can borrow your games console?'

Asif's eyes narrow. 'Didn't have you down as a gamer.'

'Oh, I'm not. My sons are visiting.'

'They're not both drunk this time?'

Despite myself, I laugh. 'No. Also, the other one is only nine.'

Asif nods. 'Okay, gimme five and I'll be right down with it.'

Before I can object and say it was just the console I wanted, Asif's front door slams in my face.

An hour later and Asif has installed the console and himself in my front room. Dressed now, he is a big hit with the boys, giving them high fives and chatting with them about school. He shows them his vast array of games which he's dragged downstairs in an old milk crate.

'Your mum's gotta pick, though.'

I shoot Asif a grateful look. Knowing David won't want Joshua – and maybe even Dylan – to play the military ones, I end up picking a heist game set in a Wild West storyworld. David is a big fan of westerns, so I don't see the harm. It's only when Dylan feeds one of the female non-player characters to an alligator that I begin to think it might be a little too violent after all. I decide not to worry or claim any responsibility. David will think the boys will have played it at a friend's house. He knows I don't have a console, so he can't pin this on me.

Screw him.

The rest of the afternoon passes in a good-humoured blur. The boys get on well with Asif – Joshua especially, who looks at him like he's one of those YouTube celebs. I have a go on the game but die almost immediately, so I keep the boys supplied in snacks and pop out to the corner shop to fetch them a ten pack of Coke.

I blink and it's quarter to six. I'm gratified when the boys don't want to tear themselves away, even though I figure it's probably Asif they want to stay with. Wary of antagonising David further, I shepherd my sons into the car and drop them off outside my old home with two minutes to spare.

I watch them go inside and notice David comes to the door. He looks around, surprised (disappointed?) I haven't tried to follow the boys in. When he spots me still in the car, he waves and smiles at me. I'm peeved by the absurd skip in my heartbeat when he does this, reminding myself it means nothing. He said Tuesday was a mistake and I agreed. That's all there is to it.

When I let myself back into my flat, I discover Asif still on my sofa playing video games instead of letting himself out like I'd told him to. I'm momentarily annoyed *and* grateful he is still here. I had not been relishing having the place to myself after having my beloved boys all afternoon. There is something especially sad and lonely about my poky basement flat after it's had children in it.

'Want some dinner?' I keep my tone nonchalant, like I don't care either way.

'Don't want to put you out.'

Asif's eyes are still on the screen. I can hear the duty in his voice. I feel a rush of maternal affection for him. He's not much older than Dylan, but I do like his company. He probably has a few dried goods and cans upstairs, maybe half a box of cereal. I open the fridge and cast an eye over the shelves. There are some carrot batons; bean sprouts; five or six mangetout, a couple of sprouts of purple broccoli, a jar of half-finished sweet chilli sauce and a defrosting pack of prawns. It's not much, but I can do something with it.

'Stir fry okay?'

'Lovely. Thanks.'

Fifteen minutes later, I place two plates of food and cutlery on the breakfast bar. He abandons the games console and lopes over, his mouth and eyes wide with hunger. He tucks in and slurps the noodles up, nodding his head.

'It's probably not very authentic,' I fret.

'If it tastes all right, who cares, I say.'

'So where are you from?' I realise my gaff immediately as his eyes narrow, so hurriedly add: 'I mean, you're from London, right? I meant whereabouts *there*.'

Asif appears to relax. 'Oh. Slough.'

'Ah, I know it,' I say. '*Come friendly bombs and fall on Slough, it isn't fit for humans now, there isn't grass to graze a cow, swarm over, Death!*'

'Bit harsh.' Asif's face is impassive, chilli sauce on his chin.

I chuckle. 'John Betjeman. He was pretty harsh. How come you're here in Bristol?'

'It's a cool city. Lots going on, but smaller than London, so my mum doesn't worry.' His eyes sparkle as he does air quotes: 'We "compromised".'

'Mummy's boy, huh?'

'No.'

Asif's tone is defensive, meaning he is. No wonder he's drawn to me, my boys and my crappy attempts at cooking. That's okay; it's what both of us need at this moment in our lives.

'So, you're not doing English literature then? That's what I did.'

'Yeah, I guessed.' Asif polishes off the last of his cola. 'No, I'm not. I'm doing education studies. I want to be a primary school teacher.'

This information makes everything fall into place. I don't know him that well, but instinctively realise it is the perfect career for him. Asif is good with Joshua, chatting with him

116

like an equal. He was also able to coax Dylan out of his shell and away from his phone today. I can see why he was able to deal with Dylan when he was drunk, too. Asif is a natural.

'I can see that.'

Asif's face splits in two with a wide smile. He looks like a little boy presented with a gift from Santa.

'Really?' He sighs, his expression changing. 'My mum – she wanted me to be a lawyer. Like my sister.'

'Is your sister good at being a lawyer?'

'Yes. Too good, to be honest. She is scary as fu—' Asif's words trail off, suddenly worried about swearing in front of me. 'She's very ambitious. Let's just say that.'

'Good for her.' I arch an eyebrow at him. 'If she was your brother, you wouldn't say she's scary AF. You'd say she was a great leader.'

'Well, if she was my brother, that would depend on how many purple nurples and atomic wedgies she gave me,' Asif declares, 'which, by the way, is a *lot* . . . and Mum says I can't retaliate 'cause she's a girl. Even though she's four years older and should know better. How is that fair?'

'You make a valid point.'

I try to keep a straight face and fail. I start laughing. Asif joins me even though it's clear he's not sure why we're both in stitches.

'To you, Asif. You are a tonic.'

I raise my glass and clink it against Asif's empty one. He looks at his plate, now almost clean but for a couple of stray noodles and a streak of chilli sauce.

'Got any more?'

'You bet.'

I take his plate to the cooker to refill it. I place it back in front of him and watch him shovel more food into his gob. Even though I always claimed to hate the daily chores and drudgery, I've missed cooking for others, just like I've missed being part of a home. The divorce and working all the time means I have fallen out of touch with most of my friends; some of them even stuck with David over me. I should have expected it: he was the one who stayed, after all. The path of least resistance.

As unlikely as mine and Asif's burgeoning friendship is, it's a comfort after Michael's death in what had been a shocking and terrible week. I might not know what will happen next with company liability, health and safety and the police's ensuing investigation, but I feel able to deal with it.

Life is looking up. At last.

FOURTEEN

CAT

Never doubt the healing power of telling your story, Cat.

Erin's words returned to Cat again and again on an endless loop as she walked home from the Mexican restaurant, prompting her to ponder her next move. Michael's death had provided Cat with an unexpected opportunity. She'd risen to the occasion and told the story of his demise and the internet had responded. She knew John would be open to seeing more pieces from her. He'd told her as much.

Cat also knew she couldn't expect a promotion on the basis of one piece. She knew for a fact there were other people still trapped in there with her who'd done what she had, then faded back into obscurity. Last year her colleague Scotty, a big guy with hamster cheeks and braces, had a random meeting with *The Avengers*' Loki, aka British actor Tom Hiddleston, in the freezer section of Bristol Co-Op. He'd even taken a selfie with him. The picture had got 56,000 retweets and ended up reposted on Buzzfeed.

Despite this brush with internet fame, Scotty had received the dubious honour of coming up with content for the Carmine Media Twitter feed ever since. If anything, his star turn had delivered him more work for less reward.

Cat didn't want to end up like Scotty.

What could she write about next?

Cat's assigned work at Carmine Media would not present her with many exciting, intriguing or heartfelt human-interest stories. She was not supposed to leave the office without permission, which meant she had to do it all in her own time. She had to go out there and find something – and keep finding things.

Lawrence was unaware of her preoccupation. Cat discovered he was out again when she let herself into the flat that evening. Only a terse note pinned under a SpongeBob SquarePants magnet on the fridge reading *I can go out too* gave any indication of his state of mind. Cat was pleased to dodge him after his vile behaviour when they'd come back from the hospital. She crumpled it into a ball, letting it fall into the wastepaper basket, and took herself to bed. She had bigger things on her mind than Lawrence and his never-ending pre-gammon tantrums.

The flat was still empty on Saturday morning when Cat awoke late. She padded through from the tiny bedroom into the living area to find the cat had returned. He was a huge black and white grumpy feline called Chairman Meow that Lawrence had adopted a couple of years before. Lawrence cradled the animal like a large, furry baby in his arms while he watched television and would kiss the animal on top of its head with such reverent care it creeped Cat out. Cat hated Chairman Meow. The feeling was mutual: he matched her hiss for hiss.

'*You.*'

Turning her sights away from the pesky animal, Cat took in the state of the flat. Somehow in just a couple of days, Lawrence had managed to wreck the place again. Their flat was light and up-to-the-minute, but like so many modern buildings, small. Developers really liked to stack 'em and pack 'em. Anything out of place made it look like a whirlwind had squalled through. Now there were dirty dishes piled high; books and papers scattered all over the coffee table; used bowls and mugs took up every surface.

Cat set to work cleaning it all up.

After a couple of hours, she heard Lawrence's heavy tread on the stairs. Marching over to the flat's front door, she wrenched it open, intent on giving Lawrence a piece of her mind.

'Where the hell have you . . . '

Her words trailed off when she saw Lawrence was not alone. He was carrying two shopping bags in his arms, both made of brown paper like groceries from US sitcoms of old. Next to him, her head thrown back in a throaty laugh, was Leila, who lived opposite them across the landing. Leila was one of those string-bean-esque ultra-thin women.

'And here she is, *my beloved.*'

On the landing, Lawrence caught Cat's eye. She could sense the hostility in his demeanour. She did not miss the steely glint of sarcasm in his eye as he said the words. She knew already Lawrence did not like Leila. He'd complained endlessly about their neighbour: she set the smoke alarms off with her incense and cooking disasters; she drummed on bongos until the early hours.

Behind closed doors, Lawrence also called Leila 'mutton dressed as lamb'. Like most misogynists, he presented this as fact, pointing out to Cat Leila's heavily lined face, especially around her eyes and forehead. Her veins and sinews stuck out in her neck and arms, her hair bleached so bottle blonde it was white, piled on top of her head in a topknot like one of those Yorkie dogs.

Today, even though it was January and had to be five degrees outside, Leila was wearing a light jacket, short skirt and her tanned legs were bare. She completed the look with strappy sandals, brightly painted nails and a toe ring.

'Thank you ever so much for your help.'

Leila gave them both an indulgent smile as if to say 'young love'. She had one of those quiet, husky voices like female actors who narrate ice cream and topical ointment commercials. She gestured to Lawrence for her grocery bags, who dutifully handed them over, having done his (one) good deed for the day.

'You're welcome.'

Lawrence stood and watched the oblivious woman as she turned her back on him, letting herself into her flat. He cocked his head, leering obviously at her skinny arse for Cat's benefit. Even though she knew Lawrence despised Leila, he'd told Cat many times how fat and frumpy she was.

Humiliation and self-loathing surged through Cat's veins, pinioning her to the spot in their own doorway. When the door closed on their neighbour, Lawrence turned towards Cat, the smug triumph etched on his features.

'You wanker,' said Cat.

Lawrence raised a hand to his scrawny chest. 'I don't know what you mean, Catrin.'

'It's *Cat*!'

She tried to slam their front door in his face but was too late. In two or three steps, Lawrence had his foot over the threshold, meeting the wood with his shoulder so it bounced off him. He was thin, but still much stronger than Cat. His hands met her shoulders and pushed her backwards into the apartment.

Cat windmilled her arms but couldn't stop herself falling. She landed on her decidedly *un*skinny arse with a bump on the natty cord carpet. Hot tears of fury sprang up in her eyes as Lawrence shut the door, letting the lock snap and pulling the chain across. He made no move to help her up.

'That was your own fault.' Lawrence regarded her on the floor, hands in his pockets. 'You shouldn't have stood in my way.'

Cat scrabbled onto her hands and knees. Keen to get control back, or at least not let Lawrence get one over on her any more, she hauled herself to her feet.

'Are you going to tell me where the hell you were last night?'

'Out and about. I'm sick of being left here alone.'

She rolled her eyes. Cat could still feel the jolt in her spine where Lawrence had pushed her down. It was more difficult to get back up than she liked. Though she was still young, her joints were screaming in protest. Her lower back hurt from sitting in that damn office chair in the cubicle farm all day.

'I told you, I just went for a drink last night with a work colleague.'

If Cat hoped her clarification would make Lawrence realise his suspicion and subsequent vitriol towards her was misplaced, she was wrong.

'I know,' Lawrence declared, 'I came and saw you through the window.'

'What?'

Cat's mind whirled as she rose to her feet, perching on the sofa arm. She'd texted Lawrence as always, but she hadn't known where she was going until Erin led her into the Mexican place. It was on an out-of-the-way side street, too.

How could Lawrence have found her?

'Oh, Cat, you're so naïve.' Lawrence pulled his mobile from his pocket and showed it to her. 'I used "Find My Friends".'

'I didn't consent to that!'

'No, you didn't have to. I set it up on your phone.' Lawrence's face was incredulous, as if this kind of stalkery behaviour was normal, a no-brainer. 'Why would it matter to you? We live together. Got something to hide?'

'That's not the point.'

'It very much is the point. You're my girlfriend. I have every right to know you are where you say you are.' Lawrence's expression softened. 'Anyway, you of all people should know it's more about safety than anything, Cat. C'mon.'

He meant Michael, of course, but Cat wasn't having that.

'Safety?' A cynical bark of laughter escaped Cat. 'You were out all night last night without a word! So you need to know where I am at all times, but I'm not allowed to know where *you* are?'

Lawrence shrugged. 'I'm a man. You don't need to worry about me. But I'm talking about *protecting* you, Cat, and you're making it some kind of feminist conspiracy?'

'You and your conspiracy theories!' Cat shrieked. 'You're ridiculous!'

She braced herself for another onslaught. Though Lawrence was averse to punching, kicking or hitting (that would mean owning up to being a woman-beater), other tactics were on the table. He'd shake her, pull her hair, wrestle her to the ground. Anything to prove he was stronger than her.

To Cat's surprise, Lawrence just stood there.

'Wow. It's because I love you, Cat. What don't you get about that?'

Self-doubt pierced the bubble of Cat's anger at last. Maybe she was being too harsh on Lawrence. Negotiating the world *was* a nightmare for women; she'd found that to her cost with Michael. A predator had been right under her nose the whole time, yet nobody had noticed. Trying to work out which men posed a threat and which didn't was exhausting, just like Erin had said. Perhaps she should just accept Lawrence could help with this.

'Thanks,' she muttered, her gaze downcast.

Lawrence grinned and opened his arms to her. She moved towards him and rested her head against his pigeon chest. He folded his thin arms around her.

'No one will ever love you like me,' he said.

A high-pitched miaow drew Lawrence's attention. The cat came running towards him, tail up and perky. Lawrence let go of Cat as his pet weaved itself around his legs.

'Here he is!'

Lawrence picked up the hefty animal in his arms. Chairman Meow headbutted him, overjoyed to see him too. At the sickening sight of this genuine affection, Cat felt her resentment return with silent, seething fury. Lawrence disappeared into the bedroom with Chairman Meow.

Bastards of a feather flock together.

Cat rolled her head around her shoulders, feeling the satisfying *crick* in her neck. She was annoyed with herself for letting Lawrence humiliate her like that, pushing her to the floor like a playground bully. She might have been childish too trying to shut the door in his face, but there was only one person who'd put their hands on the other.

No one will ever love you like me.

FIFTEEN

ERIN

The next few weeks rocket onwards in a buzz of activity. Once the police complete their investigation, the cubicle farm appears back at work. It no longer feels like a ghost office.

Hugh puts a bomb under the latest set of contractors, offering generous bonuses in exchange for covering the hole and making the lifts operational before March. The left side of the building erupts in banging, clanging and swearing as a swarm of builders attend to the refit. I see more progress in just ten days than I did in the two previous months, making me wonder why Hugh had not offered this incentive before. Probably because no one had died. Nothing like a little human misery to make capitalism grow a conscience, always far too late.

Another bit of good news is the police eventually cleared Carmine Media of any wrongdoing. They accepted Cat's version of events, as well as the other women's who accused Michael of past wrongdoings. They told us the coroner is likely to record 'death by misadventure'.

This is not good enough for his wife, who insists Michael was a stand-up guy. I schedule a meeting with her and John, where she regales us with her belief it's all a massive cover-up. I manage to bite my tongue and don't tell her that she has it the wrong way around: that it's women like *her* who cover up for men like Michael. I stop myself from sticking my fingers down my throat as she tells us of a gentle husband who couldn't do enough for her; how their children miss him terribly and that we are an evil conglomerate who don't put the safety of their workers first. We nod in fake sympathy and offer the usual platitudes because there is nothing else we can do.

Downstairs, in the midst of the construction site, the dust settles metaphorically, even if it doesn't literally. Annoyed it ever came to this, I'm nonetheless grateful no one has to put their head on the block to appease the authorities or the Powers That Be. It's a curious anticlimax.

Events muddle on in my personal life, too. David is needlessly spiky with me as always, but since the video games marathon with Asif at my place, Dylan has accompanied me and Joshua on an outing every single week. I'm delighted at this development.

I take the boys on a variety of outings, determined never to take them to fast-food joints. 'McDonald's Dads' were such a thing when I was growing up in the nineties. Every Monday so many of my school mates would come in, complaining about making small talk over burgers and fries with their estranged fathers. I might not be a dad, but I don't want that legacy with my sons.

It's weird how quickly your perspective changes. Back when I'd still been married to David, I'd felt harassed and put-upon by the demands of small children and earning money at the same time. I felt trapped within the concrete walls of our house, flattened by smaller and smaller windows of time to get it all done. I'd seen only my home's flaws: what a mess the front room was because Dylan had taken all his Lego out while I was busy typing; or how David had wrecked the kitchen cooking dinner, or the bath was full of old scum and Joshua's rubber ducks.

The calm, quiet and safety of my old home was a huge contrast to the environment I'd grown up in. I'd lived on the top floor with my mother in a leaking, cold flat in a converted Victorian semi. Wind whistled ominously around our little studio in the eaves, making the rotting windowpanes rattle. Breaking glass and hollering was the background noise of my childhood. Our downstairs neighbours were mostly single men, from whom we'd hear brays of laughter and the furore of arguments and threats, a.m. or p.m. From my bedroom I could see the motorway which lit up like an arterial system at night. Mesmerised, I watched the white and red lights zoom on through like fireflies on speed.

One day, I'd think, *one day I'll get out of here.*

I got out. I created the life I'd always wanted: a career, a family. Yet it hadn't been enough for me. I'd felt I was wasting my time kicking my heels at home; I'd not seen I was raising a child, creating a home, building a marriage. I'd placed everything on proving myself at work. I'd told myself I was doing it for women everywhere – yet ended up a woman alone when my family realised they could live without me, since I was never there anyway.

I pull the latest copy from my tray as John enters my office, not waiting for my response to his knock. He sits down in front of me with a wide smile.

'I've had an idea.'

My heart sinks as I wonder whether I'm going to be roped into more party planning. 'Shoot.'

'Recently I've been thinking about a new, relaunched *Bristol Journal*.' I can see his excitement and I lean in, putting my elbows on the desk. 'We could plug into Bristol's vibrant music scene and start a *What's On*-type publication that would be offered as a free pull-out from the newspaper. I want it to include TV listings, interviews with bands and musicians and a gig guide for young people. It could be a new start, with the backing of Carmine Media this time.'

He's practically beaming, and I know it's my job to bring him back down to earth.

'I love the idea,' I lie, 'but young people don't watch television in real time and they get their information on gigs from Instagram and Snapchat.'

I catch John's eye and he looks on the verge of apoplexy. I seize my chance to pitch my idea whilst his brain has too many tabs open.

'How about something for women? And let's keep it online. Remember, Hugh wanted to pull back from hard copies, thanks to those falling sales figures.'

Which is why we're here at Carmine Media in the first place, I avoid saying, keeping my tone light and breezy.

John makes a face. He wants to do something funkier, something cooler. His benevolent sexism means that, as far as he's concerned, 'cool' has a penis. I go in for the kill.

'I'm thinking something about the ins and outs of female life and problems.'

My deliberate, targeted word choice has the effect I desired. The euphemistic phrase *female problems* always makes men like John uncomfortable as hell. It's as if the temperature in the room has gone up five degrees. He loosens his tie, his cheeks bright scarlet. Stifling a chuckle, I continue.

'I'm thinking mainstream, about stuff the *everywoman* cares about. Equal pay, career progression, contraception, birth and fertility, beauty and fashion, how to find reliable childcare, awareness campaigns for breast cancer—'

'Yes, yes that sounds fine,' he cuts in.

John dumps the entire relaunch of the asset on me with a sigh of relief, but it's still a win, one which I'm relieved to have. I'll have to pitch my idea to Hugh as well, but he rarely has much interest in editorial. Since I am the natural choice for John's job when he retires, I figure I can do what I like for once and prove my worth with a project that's completely my responsibility, not just organise a leaving do.

I'd also not been entirely honest with John. I might have sold the *Journal* relaunch as mainstream, but it's not going to be as fluffy as he assumes. I've spent many an hour the past few weeks combing through issues of magazines and sites like *Marie Claire*, *Teen Vogue* and *Vanity Fair*. Though they all contain articles about the things I told John about, they also have hard-hitting opinion pieces and investigative journalism too.

I envisage the perfect combination of popular culture meets social justice through the prism of local Bristol politics, maybe even opening it out to the world. I close my eyes and see myself accepting awards and adulation for me and my team of groundbreaking journalists.

John's approval in the bag, next I call a meeting with the Cogs. They shuffle into the boardroom like corporate zombies, looking at phone screens or around them with suspicion. When they see it's just me they relax as it means they aren't about to be fired en masse. As the newest member of the Higher Ups, I don't have that power. Yet.

I do a short PowerPoint presentation on my vision for the relaunch and explain that every one of them has first refusal in pitching me articles, dangling the carrot of a permanent place on my team.

In response, a good percentage of the cubicle farm old-timers sit back in their chairs, arms folded in a defensive pose, their feelings on the matter clear. They don't want any extra work; they're happy where they are. That's fine by me: I don't want anyone on my team I would have to carry.

I am gratified to see many of the newer and younger workers' eyes light up at the possibilities. One such worker, as I'd privately expected and hoped, is Cat. I'd spotted her in the corner of my eye taking copious notes and nodding to herself.

As the meeting draws to a close, Cat makes a beeline straight for me, eyes glittering. I smile, expecting her to have various questions about the relaunch, but she blindsides me with a question I was not expecting.

'So, the whole local news angle is going?' she queries.

'Not completely,' I reply. 'We'll still cover major events. But I'm thinking more opinion-led, rather than facts and events.'

Cat's eyes narrow. 'Sounds a bit . . . y'know, Fox News.'

My face freezes in a rictus grin. 'Absolutely not. Don't worry about that.'

Cat just nods and mutters something about sending me copy. Then she ambles off with the rest of the Cogs.

Within forty-eight hours I am sent her first submission. Excited to find out what pushes Cat's buttons and makes her want to write, I'm disappointed to discover she has not followed the submission guidelines. In the Cogs meeting I'd asked for an overall short pitch about the topic, followed by four or five bullet points for rounding out the body of the article.

She has done neither of these things.

Instead, Cat's submission seems to be a stream of consciousness. It's every thought in her head while she composed the document. Sighing, I call her into my office.

Cat appears seconds after I buzz her. From her mannerisms and body language, it's clear she expects good news. I take a deep breath, my brain spasming under the weight of having to burst her bubble.

'Thank you for your submission, Cat. Can you talk me through your main ideas?'

'It's . . . it's in the submission,' Cat mumbles.

'I know.' I fix her with a friendly smile. 'Indulge me?'

'Sure.' Cat casts her eyes at a spot over my head in an

attempt to look like she's not quaking in her boots. 'How about "Women Can't Have It All"?'

I can't really argue with that. I've tried and failed to combine work and family in the most spectacular manner. Even so, I can't commission yet another article about women getting the short straw in society. I'd googled the phrase that morning when I reviewed Cat's document and discovered it had over twelve million hits already. The whole point of the relaunch is that we stand out.

'It's a bit generic, I'm afraid.' I keep my voice soft and my gaze sympathetic. 'Do you have anything else?'

Cat stands stock still for a second too long; it's like she is a wind-up toy, run down. Then she snaps back to life and retrieves her reporter's notebook from her pocket. She rifles through the pages. Something tells me she's playing for time, rather than looking for something in particular. I let her get on with it.

'How about something on books you should read before you die?'

I wrinkle my nose before I can stop myself. 'Bit safe.'

'An article about the drug cartels in Mexico?'

'It's the *Bristol Journal*,' I remind her.

She flips through more pages.

'Okay,' she says, her voice too bright, 'how about productivity tips for people who find it difficult to get organised?'

I fight the urge to stick a pen in my eye. The search term 'productivity tips' is even more generic than 'women can't have it all'. Rejecting so many ideas makes me feel uncomfortable, so I decide to give her a chance to improve on it.

'I see. What USP would you bring to this topic?'

Cat's lower lip trembles. 'U . . . SP?'

Oh, Jesus.

'Unique selling point. What would you bring to the topic that no one else has thought of yet?'

Cat just blinks. When it dawns on me she's not going to answer, I indicate for her to sit down. I can see it written all over her face that she realises she's fucked up. Her lip quivers. She strode into my office full of confidence, but now I can see the meek girl I took under my wing. Pity and empathy swell inside me.

'It's okay,' I reassure her. 'Think of it like your driving test. None of us gets it first time.'

Silence follows that seems to stretch on for ever, even though it can't be more than a minute or so. I watch her face, bracing myself: is she going to start crying? The first time we'd met she'd been in tears in the bathroom, but that hadn't been my fault. She's clearly a fragile girl. I hate the idea of upsetting her.

Finally Cat nods, her gaze directed at the floor. Relief surges through me. I feel grateful I can direct her at this critical point of her journey. She doesn't want to go from rewriting press releases to writing filler content for the internet about stereotypical female problems or getting organised. Cat has a much bigger future in store for her than that. She may not thank me for it right now, but she will look back and see it as a dodged bullet.

'That's not how we're going to do things here.' I smile again, so she knows I am not mad with her. 'But thank you for your submission. I appreciate your hard work and know you can come up with another that will nail it.'

Cat scurries from my office. She's so sensitive, bless her. It must be difficult to have such a strong rejection on the back of the success of her piece about Michael. She probably feels like she's blown it.

Before I plunge into the rest of the pile of pitches from cubicle farm workers, I resolve to do something with Cat so she can see she hasn't reset to zero. I could invite her for another drink, or perhaps over for dinner at my place. It would be nice to have another woman over, for once. I write a note to self on a Post-it and attach it to my computer, reminding myself to ask her.

Tomorrow.

SIXTEEN

CAT

Who the hell did Erin Goodman think she was?

As soon as work was over, Cat power-walked all the way back from Carmine Media to her apartment building. She absorbed the ache in her calves, the chafing of her shoes on the backs of her heels. Sticky blood made her socks fuse to her flesh, causing stinging pain to set her teeth on edge. She didn't stop. She crashed through the double doors at the bottom of the flat block, taking the stairs two at a time.

The vision of Erin and her patronising smile was tattooed on the back of Cat's eyeballs. She saw nothing of the flat block's magnolia walls or the muted graffiti that had been painted over. All she could hear was Erin's rejection, over and over, an endless loop of humiliation.

That's not how we're going to do things here.

Yet again Cat was the outsider who didn't understand the

rules. What Erin called 'generic' or 'safe' were popular topics. Cat had taken the time to check Google and viral sites, that's how she knew. As for 'USP' – that was just jargon, a way for Erin to lord it over her, pretending she knew more just by virtue of being older. Cat let a bark of frustrated anger escape her as she grabbed the handrail to stop herself falling back as she climbed higher upstairs.

Erin was jealous.

Cat's mother had warned her about this. Every time a woman had even a smidgen of success, the harpies came out in force to bring her down a peg or two. Erin had pretended to be interested in Cat's career, but really she'd been protecting her own position. She'd seen an opportunity to grind Cat's face into the dirt and crow over her while she was doing it.

Duplicitous bitch!

If Cat closed her eyes, she could see her mother's ruddy cheeks and worn hands feeding meat through the grinder; her father carrying hay bales over his shoulders like they weighed nothing at all. She'd loved life on the farm when she was a child, but her mother had been adamant Cat get out.

Judith Crawford never wanted Cat to be trapped like she was, not expecting that Cat would find herself in another kind of trap: stuck somewhere between the working and professional classes. Cat was too worldly now to go back to her roots, yet too naïve to make it to the next rung. Ironic.

It had been Judith Crawford who'd been instrumental in opening Cat's eyes to the ludicrous hypocrisy of feminism. In her parlour Cat had learned all about the games women played, screaming out against supposed oppression and then collecting the spoils for their own benefit. It had been brought into sharp focus for her today.

Erin was doing it to Cat, right now.

Gasping for air by the time she reached the top-floor landing, Cat was grateful she lived in a low-rise building. When she'd originally left university, she'd spent six stressful and horrible months in one of Bristol's tallest high rises. A hotbed of petty crime and drug dealing, Cat had felt she was taking her life in her hands every time she ventured into the stairwell. When she'd been on the farm, she'd envisaged living in a building like the one in *Friends*. Instead, she'd ended up in a concrete prison that exuded despair and was known for being used as the exterior of Nelson Mandela House where Del and Rodney lived in *Only Fools And Horses*.

Cat stopped and leaned on the banister, her door just a few steps away. Everything hurt: her head, chest, throat, feet. Lights twinkled in the corner of her peripheral vision like a threatening migraine. She inhaled through her nose like her mother had shown her, breathing out in a steady flow.

Cat listened carefully at her own door. She couldn't hear Lawrence in there. Maybe he had gone out? Whatever the case, she had to get a handle on her anger and her ensuing anxiety before she went home. She didn't want to create any more angst with Lawrence, even inadvertently. Things had been slowly improving since he'd pushed her to the floor after taunting her with that gristly stick of beef jerky across the landing.

The memory of this encounter refuelled the embers of her dying fury, making Cat look towards Leila's door.

It was ajar.

Like a bug mesmerised by light, Cat drifted across the landing and pushed the door. She let it swing inwards, staying on the threshold in case her neighbour was in. It was quiet in the living and kitchen area, the television off. The smell of incense hung in the air.

The room itself was clean, but organised chaos: there were books and trinkets everywhere, with multiple sun catchers and even bunting hanging from the ceiling. A large batik wall hanging claimed the back wall. There were large overgrown plants, like a mini jungle; their neighbour must have spent an inordinate amount of time tending to them. Cat could see a large potted palm tree on the balcony.

Cat felt another surge of displeasure as she noted the flat was larger than theirs. She'd mentioned to Lawrence before that they could afford one of the bigger flats if he got a job.

Lawrence had been furious, telling her he already had a job. He'd cited various facts and stats, claiming it took time to build an online platform. Cat had backed down immediately, suggesting he just get a part-time position at something like Costa or McDonald's so he could work on his sites at the same time.

If she had hoped this would assuage some of his anger, she'd been sorely mistaken. Lawrence had become incandescent, telling Cat she had no idea what pressure creatives and entrepreneurs like him had to go through. He'd advanced on her, making her shrink against the wall, afraid he was about to strike her. But he'd just laughed and grabbed his coat, which was hanging on a hook behind her. Then he'd strode out of the flat, leaving Cat wishing he'd just get on with it and beat her up. The endless intimidation and fear of violence had to be worse than the actual act ... didn't it?

That's what her mother always said. Cat saw no reason why Judith would lie. Her father Ernest had been a quiet man, barely saying a word most days when he was back at the farmhouse. He would sit in his favourite threadbare arm-chair, poring through the local paper or guarding the remote control under his gnarled hand. There would be no warning before he erupted; Ernest's fury rode a wave neither Judith nor Cat could predict. It could happen frequently for several weeks, then nothing for years.

This sporadic violence forced Cat and Judith to tread on tiptoes around him, just in case. Though Ernest would shout at Cat, the bulk of vitriol – and his violence – would centre on his wife. His sudden rages did not seem connected to everyday events going badly in the home, nor even the farm. When foot-and-mouth disease arrived in the West Country with dev-astating ferocity, both Judith and the six-year-old Cat braced themselves for Ernest's wrath, yet nothing was forthcoming.

Then the night sixteen-year-old Cat brought home a cluster of A* grades for her GCSEs, Ernest descended onto one of the worst warpaths she'd ever witnessed. She couldn't remember how it began, but she could still envisage him grabbing her mother by her ponytail and bashing her face against the big oak table in the parlour. Cat had frozen in shock and horror. She watched him do it once, twice, three times before letting Judith slump to the floor, holding her broken nose with both hands, bright red blood pouring between her fingers.

141

Later Cat had tended to her dazed mother's mangled face, mopping up the blood and listening to Judith's rambling through the pain.

Promise me, her mother said, *promise me you will get out of here and never come back. Not for me, not for any reason. Say it.*

I promise, Cat replied, ever the dutiful daughter.

Her anger in check, Cat suddenly remembered she was standing in her neighbour's open doorway and surveying an apartment that was not her own. Advance mortification flooded through her at the thought of her neighbour arriving behind and finding her there. Cat grabbed the Yale lock and snapped it, so she could shut the door properly after herself.

'Hello?'

Leila was home after all. Shit!

Cat froze where she was as her brain and body rebelled against her. Her limbs wanted to take flight, race out the door and across the landing to the safety of her own apartment. Her mind wouldn't let her do it, reminding her that hers was the only flat opposite her neighbour's. Cat was exposed regardless, and racing off could only make her look worse. She didn't want to have to stake out the landing every time she came and went for fear of embarrassment at seeing this woman again.

Cat composed herself with a ready smile. Leila appeared from the bedroom, looking sleepy in sweatpants and an oversized man's T-shirt hanging off one shoulder. Cat decided the truth was her best option.

'Hi, so sorry to intrude, but did you know your door was ajar?'

It was the right call. Leila wasn't suspicious or even sur-prised to see Cat there. Her gaze went to the door and the Yale lock. She rolled her own eyes, indicating several big bags of shopping abandoned on the nearby counter. Cat could see coat hangers and clothes bulging inside. Retail therapy.

'Right. I had to get these inside. I must have forgotten to take the door off the latch. Thank you so much for looking out for me! Cat, isn't it?'

A warm feeling spread through Cat's abdomen.

'That's right. And you're welcome.'

Before Cat could make her excuses and leave again, Leila opened a drawer underneath the counter. For one mortifying second Cat thought she was going to offer her money, like she was a bellboy or concierge. She was relieved when the other woman drew out a small plastic bag.

'Want some?'

Leila said the words as if she was offering a cup of tea, or a bar of chocolate. Cat's stomach lurched as she took in the contents of the small cellophane bag: white powder. Though she'd seen multiple drug deals in Bristol since leaving the farm, even out in the open, Cat had never done drugs herself. She wasn't even sure what the powder was. She guessed cocaine.

The words *no thank you* came automatically to her lips, but Cat sensed Leila was not the type to take a refusal as an answer. Lawrence was the same: he loved to have a buddy on all his trips and bliss-outs. He was always smoking weed or popping pills. She'd played along with him many times.

'I don't know how to do it.'

'I'll show you,' Leila said.

Retrieving some more cocaine from an ornate box on the mantelpiece, then more from behind the television, Leila showed Cat how to do it over and over again by demonstrating on herself. When it was Cat's turn, she simply hovered her nose over the straw and sniffed loudly, knocking the powder from the mirror into her cupped hand.

'How do you feel?' Leila demanded.

'Great!' Cat lied.

Within half an hour the older woman's pupils were dilated to twice their usual size. She did not appear to notice Cat was much more together than she should be. The older woman chatted at Cat with incessant ease, revealing endless personal details like a shopping list. Leila told Cat her entire life story: from her girlhood attending Bristol Grammar through to her three failed businesses and that she'd broken up with her boyfriend several weeks earlier.

'Still in love with his ex, I reckon.' Leila collapsed back on the sofa. 'Won't admit it, of course. Aren't men the worst?'

Cat agreed men were indeed the worst. 'At least you got rid, though. If it wasn't working, what's the point?'

More thoughts of Lawrence crowded through her brain as she said this. Cat chanced a surreptitious look at her watch: he was bound to be back soon from wherever he'd jaunted off to. Leila was off her head. Would she even notice if Cat snuck off now?

'Uh oh, trouble in paradise,' Leila cackled. 'I thought you and him were loved up over there?'

Cat's eyes bugged out at the thought. She and Lawrence

had never been love's young dream; they'd liked each other well enough, then tolerated each other. Now it had all irretrievably broken down. They would never be able to make it work. Right now, there was part of Cat that wished she never had to set eyes on him again. If she could walk out of the flat without looking back and find somewhere to live just as nice without him, she would. The last thing she wanted was to end up back in a dive like Nelson Mandela House, though.

'It's complicated.'

Leila was no longer listening. Complaining of feeling hot, she stripped off her oversized T-shirt, thankfully revealing a bra top underneath, her nipples sticking through like acorns.

'I need a smoke,' Leila mumbled, crashing against the coffee table as she rose to her feet. 'Come with me?'

'Oh no, I have to get back.'

Leila was having none of Cat's protestations. She grabbed her hand and pulled her towards the balcony door, leading them out into the fresh night air.

Below them the city lights stretched out into the distance like stars fallen to earth. Growing up in the middle of nowhere with zero light pollution, Cat always found herself transfixed by such scenes: they were strangely beautiful, even if the sounds of buses and other traffic spoiled the ambience somewhat.

'If you're not happy, you should get rid of him.'

Cat's attention snapped back to Leila, who was attempting to roll a cigarette rather laboriously. Sighing, she took the tobacco pouch from her new friend's bony hands.

Though Cat had never smoked herself, she'd rolled her father's when his hands were covered in cow shit or he couldn't be bothered.

'It's not as simple as that.'

'Yeah it is. You a doormat or something?'

Cat thought back to Erin that afternoon, patronising her over her copy. She had just stood there, mute while Erin trashed her writing ability and called her suitability to journalism into question. Why had she let her do that to her? Cat was a great writer. She shouldn't let poisonous old women like Erin make her doubt herself. Cat was destined for greater things than the *Bristol Journal*, anyway. Maybe she *was* being a doormat? She ran a hand over the balustrade of the balcony, peering over the side.

'I don't have any money.'

'So?' Smoke streamed from Leila's nostrils like she was a dragon. 'You going to put up with him just for the sake of living in a nice flat? There's a word for women like that.'

A flush of anger surged through Cat, making her clench her teeth.

'You're calling me a whore?'

Leila grinned. 'Oooh, touched a nerve, did I?'

Weariness crashed through Cat next. It all seemed too much. Michael, Lawrence, Erin, now Leila. Everyone was against her. She should just go back to the flat and climb into bed, pull the covers over her head.

'I have to go.'

Leila let out a sympathetic croon, grabbing Cat by the elbow.

'I was just trying to provoke you, help you release the negativity. You look like you need it. Let's try something else.'

Leila let out a scream, making Cat jump. The older woman laughed.

'Sorry, sorry! But gotta let the negativity out. I see you every day going up and down those stairs, weight of the world on your shoulders. Go on – give it a try?'

Feeling stupid, Cat let out only a squeak. Leila bellowed this time in encouragement, raising both arms and clambering up on a plastic patio chair. Still Cat couldn't do it. Self-consciousness brought flames to her cheeks, made her avert her gaze to the floor.

'Maybe yelling actual words will help?' Leila said. 'I'll start, then you.'

Cat shrugged and watched Leila as she faced the night, still standing on the chair. She did the 'king of the world' pose from *Titanic*.

'Fuck you!' Leila hollered into the night, 'Fuck you, world! I am ENOUGH!'

She turned on her heel, face flushed and happy. Embarrassment coursed through Cat's whole body. What the hell was she doing, hanging out with this crazy person? Everyone thought they knew Cat, thought they could fix her. Whether it was Lawrence lecturing her, Erin tearing a strip off her or this mad hippy yelling into the night, everyone reckoned they had a solution for her. They could all go to hell.

'You try now?' Leila said.

But Cat said nothing. She fell to her knees as if falling prostrate at Leila's feet. The older woman laughed as she looked down on her new friend, puzzled. She was still laughing when Cat clamped both hands around her bony ankles and pushed hard outwards, sending her wobbling towards the edge of the balcony and the black depths below.

Leila wasn't laughing when she went over the balustrade.

SEVENTEEN

CAT

Cat stayed crouched down as time slowed to a standstill. She had no idea how long passed, but she was shocked into complete stillness by her own actions.

What had she done?

How could she have done that?

Why had she done it?

Fear made her woozy as she eventually tried to stagger away from the balustrade and back into the flat. A few steps had seemed like miles.

As Cat finally made it through the threshold and closed the balcony door behind her, she froze again. A million thoughts whirled through her brain as the surge of adrenaline threatened to make her accelerated heartbeat boom straight out of her chest.

She had killed someone, and it had been *easy*. She had never been an impulsive person. This marked the only time she had given into her true desires – and a woman had ended up dead.

The next thought came unbidden: if Cat wasn't careful, she'd be in jail for the rest of her life. She would be as good as dead, too.

What she did next was paramount.

Lawrence was a true crime nut. Their bookcase was bursting with such tomes, most of them featuring lurid black-and-white mug shots on the front: Ian Brady and Myra Hindley, Rose West, Harold Shipman, Jeffrey Dahmer, Ted Bundy and many more. Cat had heard Lawrence pontificate endlessly over why certain individuals were caught straight away when others enjoyed much longer, bloodier careers, flying under police radars sometimes for decades. As Cat cast her mind back, she focused on his many theories.

Killers who aren't connected to their victims are more likely to get away with murder.

Cat had not planned on committing murder that night, so she'd not thought about this. Her actions had come to her in the moment, so she hadn't had time to consider the ramifications of murdering her own neighbour in detail. She was bound to be caught. And rightly so.

That said, being someone's neighbour was not a huge connection. People's neighbours died every day. Cat tried to disperse the fog in her brain and really concentrate. There was no reason for her to be under more suspicion than anyone else who lived there as far as she could see. She had no motive. Even she couldn't really understand why she'd done what she did.

But these killers leave nothing to chance.

Cat's mind turned back to the balcony door. She had closed it behind her, automatically. That was a mistake. The balcony door had a lock like the one on the front door, meaning it was possible to get locked out there. That might be enough for an overly curious police officer to theorise someone could have pushed Leila and then left the apartment, closing the door behind them.

She stepped forward and opened the balcony door again, so it was ajar. The night air rushed in again and Cat listened for sirens. None yet. That made sense: Leila would have fallen onto the dark car park below, away from the road. People in the downstairs flats may not have heard her screams above their TV sets or have seen her body flash past their windows if their curtains were closed. This meant drunk people on the way back from the pub would probably be the ones to discover her. Cat likely had a little while before the alarm was raised.

Such natural-born killers don't go overboard. A clean room is more suspicious.

This memory caused a realisation to come to Cat: *finger-prints. Damn it!*

She had been all over Leila's front room, plus the police would find hers on the front door and the balcony door, too. But perhaps Cat was overthinking again. She had no crim-inal record, so her prints were not on any database. As far as she knew, the police could not demand her prints without an arrest.

Would the room even be swept for fingerprints if they thought Leila's death was suicide or an accident? She had no idea. Even if they did sweep, perhaps Cat had this upside down. Instead of attempting to scrub her presence away and leaving surfaces blank and suspicious, maybe her existing connection to Leila would come in handy. After all, they *were* neighbours. There was no reason they couldn't be friends, or at least friendly. Perhaps Cat had been there for a cup of tea or similar after helping Leila upstairs with her shopping? Why not? There was no way for the police to find out whether this was true, which meant they could not prove it was a lie, either.

Not daring to go into other rooms and contaminate them unnecessarily, Cat had a quick look around the apartment to check she was not leaving anything incriminating behind. As she moved back towards the front door, something else occurred to her.

She could write about this!

This was a real opportunity. Cat had been floundering since Michael's death and her resulting viral article. She'd failed spectacularly to get Erin's attentions with her pitches that afternoon, but not even Erin could argue how newsworthy Leila's death was. Even better, when Leila's body was found, Cat could be first on the scene to report on the death because she lived in the building. She would get the scoop before everyone else and no one could argue she 'shouldn't' have been there. Hell, they shouldn't be suspicious in the slightest.

She was a genius.

Mind made up, Cat turned back towards Leila's belongings. On the worktops in the kitchen area near the landline, there was a pile of mail, mostly bills. Cat didn't pick up or take the post but photographed it with her phone to remind herself later.

Leila's full name – Leila Hardy – was on a payslip clearly marked 'Carmine Media'. This prompted the memory that Leila had worked at Queens Mead Tower too, though their paths had never crossed there. This memory provided a germ of an idea.

What if Cat connected Michael and Leila's deaths in her report?

Perhaps that would be enough to make another article go viral. People died every day, so a mere death report would not cut it by itself. But if she linked the deaths, that could feed into a new narrative: *The Curse of Queens Mead Tower.*

Pleased with herself, Cat quickly typed this idea into her own phone, rather than use a pen from the counter. She also added a reminder to call Hugh for a quote for her article and to double-check she could run with the 'curse' angle. She didn't believe he would object; Hugh was an attention whore who believed there was no such thing as bad publicity.

On the mantelpiece, Cat spied a selfie of Leila, smiling winsomely at the camera. It was not in a frame like her other photographs and had clearly been cut out of another picture. It was held in place by one of those pinch clip holders. She snatched up the small picture in her hand, unable to defy the voice of her subconscious that told her it was a bad idea. She knew she was taking a souvenir – Lawrence had told her about this fascination of killers, too – but Cat told herself no one would miss it. It was such a tiny thing that the only person who'd remember it was there was Leila herself and she was gone now.

Unable to justify staying in Leila's apartment any longer, Cat let herself out and made sure the door clicked shut behind her. She raced across the landing to her own door, praying she'd beaten Lawrence home. As the door swung inwards and the stale cooking smells billowed out of their dark flat, she relaxed. Cat turned all the lights and the television on. She made herself comfortable with a glass of wine, her laptop on the coffee table in front of her and open on her latest piece of writing.

Barely five minutes into her vigil Lawrence arrived in just his shirt sleeves and jeans, clearly drunk and teeth chattering from the late February cold. She made no comment or asked where he'd been. He seemed preoccupied.

'Something's going on out there.' He rubbed his hands and put them next to the fan heater, which Cat had on full blast.

Cat raised her wine glass to her lips. 'Oh?'

'Yeah, rozzers all over the car park. There's cop tape, had to come round the front. No one would say why.'

A delicious frisson of anticipation and trepidation made its way up Cat's spine. This was it: Leila's body had been found. She was also aware from Lawrence's books that police were trained to watch out for people asking too many questions at crime scenes. But Cat was a reporter, first on the scene. The ultimate 'get out of jail free' card. Literally.

Lawrence pulled the cellophane off a carton of cigarettes. Cat wondered where he'd got the money to buy them when she hadn't given him any cash but decided to deal with that later. She acted shocked and sat forward, grabbing her reporter's notebook that was embossed with her initials. It had been a present from her parents when she'd got into university.

'Where are you going?' Lawrence called after her, unlit cigarette dangling from his mouth as he attempted in vain to light it.

'My job,' Cat declared, letting their front door close after her.

EIGHTEEN

WOMAN, 39, FALLS TO HER DEATH FROM BLOCK OF FLATS IN BRISTOL

A WOMAN PLUNGED TO HER DEATH FROM A FOURTH-floor balcony at a block of flats in the city. The circumstances are being described as 'not suspicious'.

Cat Crawford reports.

FATAL PLUNGE

A BRISTOL WOMAN LOST HER LIFE YESTERDAY AFTER plunging to her death from her own balcony.

The body of 39-year-old Leila Hardy was found by police late last night after reports of screams in the early evening. Her next of kin have been informed.

Emergency workers tried to save Leila, but she died at the

scene after falling from the top floor of the building. Police were initially called by a neighbour who reported hearing 'yells and screams' from her apartment.

When police arrived, they discovered Leila's body in the car park that backs onto the building. A police spokesman said: 'On arrival our officers discovered a woman had fallen from a flat.

'Officers attempted first aid and ambulance crews attended but sadly the woman died at the scene.'

GONE TOO SOON

LEILA HARDY WAS AN ALUMNI OF BRISTOL GRAMMAR and a businesswoman, as well as a model in her youth. But behind her jolly façade and her beautiful face it seems there could have been a heart that was breaking.

Following the collapse of her third wellness business in as many years, Leila was forced to live pay cheque to pay cheque as a lowly cleaner. Sources close to her say she'd also broken up with her long-term boyfriend in the run-up to her tragic death.

'She was quite noisy anyway, drumming and doing chants,' says a downstairs neighbour who asked not to be identified. 'I thought it was more of that. I feel terrible now.'

Another neighbour added: 'Leila was a cheerful person. She had a smile for everyone and was always willing to have a chat in the stairwell. Just goes to show you never can tell.'

CARMINE CONNECTIONS

LEILA HARDY WAS EMPLOYED BY CARMINE MEDIA, one of the UK's top media conglomerates working out of the Queens Mead Tower in Bristol city centre. This is the second death of a Carmine worker in as many months (Subeditor note: ADD LINK to Cat's article about Michael's death), but CEO Hugh Carmine insists it's mere coincidence.

'Leila was a valued member of the Carmine family, but her tragic death took place at her own home, not in Queens Mead Tower,' Carmine says. 'Obviously our thoughts are with her family and friends at this devastating time. We will be working hard to introduce new measures to protect all our workers who may have mental health issues to try and ensure this does not happen again.'

These assertions from Mr Carmine were not good enough for Twitter, however.

#CurseofQueensMead has been trending on Twitter for the past twelve hours, with no sign of slowing down. Relatives and ex-employees of Carmine Media have been sharing their views of working for the company, some of them not complimentary. (Subeditor: add Screenshots!):

@Bang2write: URRRGH, my son used to work for this company. He was bullied so badly, he ended up on antidepressants. Not by colleagues either, but bosses! Capitalist vultures KILL!

@KateyLou_9765: Leila was a well-known druggie in this

building. Reckon the poor cow probably got high and then fell off her own balcony. DON'T DO DRUGS KIDS!

@LardyMardy76: Yes, but WHY was she on drugs – SELF MEDICATING! When companies don't have any regard for their employees, death swiftly follows.

Not all of the Twitterati were certain of the cause for complaint, however:

@BlahblahYeah: You can't blame employers for what happens at an employee's home. Typical lefties – you never want to take responsibility!!!

@SashaStrawb: who says she killed herself because of work??? She was just a cleaner. FAR more likely ex made her do it. Men are the worst!!

@Loz53: So everyone's an expert on what was going through this woman's mind and why she did it ... ah Twitter, don't ever change.

When asked about Twitter's notion of the 'curse' of the Queens Mead Tower, Mr Carmine insists he is paying attention.

'People are angry and I get it,' Carmine confirms, 'but I can reassure everyone that practices at the company are under review and we will do all we can to ensure a tragedy like this does not occur again.'

NINETEEN

CAT

At Queens Mead Tower the next day, Cat's day started wonderfully. All the other Carmine drones gathered around her to congratulate her on her 'scoop', making her feel like a rock star. Any misgivings at what she'd done to Leila vanished. Cat had been first on the scene, answering the police's questions. She reported the event to the best of her ability to her superiors. She and everyone else watched a second article go viral as virtue signallers sought to prove how progressive they were, sharing it on social media with their usual predictable comments and hashtags. Cat was on her way up the ladder, she felt certain of it.

Sure enough, it wasn't long before Cat was called away from the crowd and into John's office. For once, she was not worried about being fired: she knew she'd earned some face time with both him and Hugh. (In actual fact, Hugh was on *literal* FaceTime, held up on John's iPad, but it was something.)

The playboy congratulated Cat on a second viral piece and asked her what she'd like to write next. Cat's mind went blank, but she played for time by saying she'd submit some pitches before the end of the week. Both John and Hugh seemed satisfied with that.

After returning from John's office, Cat discovered the bubble had burst. Everyone was back at their desks, staring at screens. Cat was forgotten already. She soothed herself a little by checking the numbers on her viral piece, but the comments, shares, likes and retweets were slowing down.

Cat moved back to her draft copy folder and brainstormed some ideas on how to keep the 'Curse of Queens Mead' narrative alive. Feeding the machine consistently would take some doing. If she wasn't careful, she'd fade back into obscurity.

The internet was one thirsty bitch.

A couple of hours later, Cat saw Erin wander through the cubicle farm from John's office. A smirk curved Cat's lip: just twenty-four short hours ago, Erin had metaphorically ripped up Cat's submission, telling her trolling for clicks was not what Carmine Media did.

She'd just proved how wrong Erin was.

The 'Curse of Queens Mead' had provided a stack of organic traffic for the *Bristol Journal*'s website, exactly what it needed ahead of the relaunch. Both Hugh and John had praised Cat's forward thinking.

Erin was jealous of Cat, that much was obvious. All her talk of them being the same when they'd gone to brunch . . .

that might have been true, but it was obvious now that Erin still saw Cat as a threat. A usurper. She was trying to keep her down, unsuccessful.

Cat needed to make sure she stayed one step ahead of Erin.

The lure of cyber-stalking was a siren call that took Cat back to her computer. First Cat went to Erin's social media and reread all her updates. Then her mouse gravitated to the Higher Ups' shared calendar. She wasn't supposed to know the password, but like everything at Carmine Media, security was sloppy. Cat downloaded the calendar to her own, flagging all Erin's meetings and calls for her own reference.

God, technology was wonderful.

Curious about David, Cat gravitated to Facebook and found him easily. She clicked on his profile picture. She scrolled through his profile and then clicked on the link to his graphic design website at the top of the page.

Cat noted he was talented and boasted several high-profile clients, including a child's cereal company and some washed-up Olympian who'd launched a fitness empire. The site also hosted a professional, well-lit shot of David on his 'About' page. At forty-five, he was a good-looking man's man: chiselled cheekbones and stubble, masculine in a non-try-hard way. She noted David was about as far from Lawrence as a guy could get. Cat's boyfriend looked like an almost-thirty-year-old Eton schoolboy who'd been dipped in oil and then rolled across a dirty carpet.

Unsure what to do next, Cat closed down the tabs on her browser and sat back in her chair. Inspiration would come to her for her next steps, she was sure of it.

After the high of pushing Leila from the balcony the night before, Cat's stomach and bowels had felt as if they'd liquefied. Unable to sleep, she'd written her copy on her phone on the toilet at the flat. Gasping and woozy, she swallowed the persistent, acidic nausea surging up her throat, keeping her bare feet on the cold tiles to quell the sense of falling.

That was all gone now. Whilst it was regrettable that Leila had to die, it wasn't like she'd been making a huge contribution to society. Not like Cat. The gods or fate or whatever were smiling on her. Judith's proud face surfaced in Cat's brain, reminding her, 'She who dares wins.' An opportunity would present itself, soon.

Good things come to those who wait . . . and watch . . . and plan.
Cat felt invincible.

TWENTY

ERIN

I awake in plenty of time for once and walk into the office feeling refreshed and well rested, but it doesn't last long. I'm hit with a million notices via John before I even reach my desk; he fires off all the things he needs from me for the *Bristol Journal* relaunch while we're both standing in the corridor. I smile and nod and promise I will look into them all, trying desperately to retain the details. John gives me the double thumbs up and scurries off, leaving me feeling like he's smacked me over the back of the head with a ping-pong bat.

Next I note there's a cluster of people around Cat's desk in the cubicle farm. All have big smiles on their faces. Cat is seated on her wheely chair looking bashful. She doesn't see me, she's too busy lapping up the attention. I grab some dirty cups and wash them up in the cubicle farm kitchen, looking out through the internal window.

'What's going on over there?'

Dustin, the office Romeo, stands next to me. He's the harmless kind of sleaze: he likes to make silly double entendres and swagger around the office before returning to domestic bliss with his high school sweetheart and their baby. He squeezes the last dregs of his teabag into his mug.

'Something happened at Cat's apartment block last night, so she reported on it.' Dustin takes a sip of his tea. 'First on the scene, apparently.'

'Oh? Good for her.'

I take my coffee back to my office, making a mental note to congratulate Cat on whatever her scoop is later. In a bid to quell my anxiety over my massive To Do list, I decide to do a little feng shui. I move my desk, water my plants, rearrange my desk and papers, then refill my drawer with all the lovely stationery I bought at the weekend. Yawning, I boot my ancient computer up. While I am waiting, I google Cat's article on my phone.

Seconds later I pick up my landline and speed dial Hugh, who sounds as aloof and bored as ever.

'Yeah.'

I count to five and inject cheeriness into my voice, even though I am grinding my teeth so hard my jaw hurts. I stall for time as my brain spasms, trying to work out what I need to say. He sounds distracted, anyway. I can guess why: I can hear not one, but two women's baby-doll voices in the background of Hugh's call. Ever the committed bachelor, Hugh always has wannabe models and actresses on tap to service his every need. Though he's getting older, their ages have remained the same: approximately eighteen to twenty-two. *Ugh*.

'Hi, Hugh. It's Erin.'

'Yeah, I know. What can I do for you?'

I pinch the bridge of my nose between my fingers, trying to ward off the pressure and headache building there.

'Cat Crawford,' I end up saying.

'Ah, yes. Star in the making, that one.'

A sting of unexpected jealousy spears me in the chest. I tamp it down, rebuking myself. It doesn't matter or make any difference to me if Cat is rising through the ranks. I despise the 'divide and conquer' politics of the modern workplace, especially when it's directed at women. Cat is not my competitor. There's room enough for both of us. Even so, I decide to hedge my bets, though I am not sure why.

'I see Cat was "first on scene" to that death last night.'

'Yeah.'

'Did you or the night editor ask her to report on it for the website?'

'No, she showed some initiative and good for her. If only all the word monkeys were like Cat.'

There's a scrape as Hugh covers the mouthpiece of his phone and mutters something to one of the women in the room with him. This sets off another bout of giggling. I cast an eye at the clock: it's only half nine in the morning. Hugh is either partying very early, or very, very late because he hasn't been to bed yet.

'I see. And have you read it?'

'Yes, I did. It's a good piece.'

'Well, yes, but don't you feel it sets the tower up in a negative light with all this "Curse of Queen's Mead" stuff?' I sigh. 'She's had the subeditor include screenshots from Twitter too!'

'Sure, but it's just the tower.'

'Hugh, you own the tower,' I remind him.

'I'm aware of that. But don't you see? It's genius. Bring up all this hokum shit about curses on the building, muddy the waters. People start to doubt it's the company's fault. It becomes just one of those things.' Hugh yawns. 'I'd say Cat has quite the future at Carmine Media.'

I clench my fists, stopping another cascade of thoughts and emotions before they really begin. I visualise locking them away in a box where they can't affect me.

I've always done the right thing.

I say goodbye to Hugh and put the phone down. I sit back in my chair, my brain swirling. I'm perturbed by the fact that Cat has now been in the vicinity of not one, but two deaths. I'm also deeply troubled by her deflection, entertaining the notion that there's a 'curse' on the building. Did she write that for Hugh's sake, to impress him? It feels opportunistic and seedy at best.

I leave my desk moments later. I give the cubicle farm a wide berth, going the long way to John's office via the service corridor so I can avoid walking past Cat directly. I knock on the door and John barks, 'Come in!'

I am relieved that no one is with him. John sits with his small feet up on the desk like a schoolboy, passing a stress ball from his left to right hand.

'Erin!' John grins on full beam like he's surprised to see me. Maybe he is. 'What can I do you for?'

When we worked together at the original *Bristol Journal*, John was a real grafter. Now he's doing as little as possible, just marking time until he leaves. He's still paid a lot more than me, too. Remembering the inventory of things he tasked me with this morning, I'm peeved to see him sitting on his arse like this. Prickles of resentment make their way down my spine, but I bite my tongue like always.

'It's about Cat Crawford.'

'What about her?'

What about her? – the sixty-four-thousand dollar question. Cat hadn't done anything wrong; she'd just done her job. Journalists are *supposed* to be ready to report on events. Even so, something has my Spidey-senses tingling. I decide to jump right in with both feet.

'Don't you think it's odd, Cat being nearby for two deaths in a row, in such a short time?'

John still passes that ball between his hands. 'What would you do, if someone fell off a balcony in *your* apartment block?'

'I have a basement flat.'

'You know what I mean.'

I let my brain conjure images into being. I see Asif dead on the ground, sprawled and bloody, limbs at weird angles like a marionette with its strings cut. Having got to know Asif in the past few weeks, I would be upset. That is without question. He's young, with his whole life in front of him. A tragedy.

But what if I didn't know him?

I am a journalist by trade. I would hear the sirens and go in search of answers. I would gather information, and not because I am a vulture or opportunist, but because people deserve to know what happened. I would honour Asif's life and report on its sad end so he is not ignored or forgotten. It's what I was trained to do.

'You're right,' I admit, 'I just can't help feeling . . . '

I trail off. John doesn't fill in the gaps for me, like I want him to. I sigh.

'. . . this just all seems a bit *handy*, you know?'

John puts the ball down at last. He leans back in his chair, steepling his fingers as he regards me.

'Do you think Michael attacking Cat was "handy", too?'

There's no accusation or judgement on John's face, but even so, I'm horrified. 'No, of course not!'

John nodded. 'Didn't think you did, for the record. So, what's this really about?'

There he was: the John I respected, instead of the more laid-back man I'd had trouble recognising since we'd joined Carmine Media. Yes, he could be a little 'old school' and rigid in his attitudes from time to time, but aren't we all – especially as we age? John has proved he's still sharp and can get to the heart of the matter. I mull his words over.

'Leila died at home. There was no need to mention she was a cleaner here and link it to Michael's death. Most of the staff won't have met or even seen her. All of it just seems rather sensational – sleazy, even.'

'So?'

'So it's obvious Cat is trying to curry favour with Hugh

by trolling for clicks with all this "Curse of Queens Mead" nonsense online.'

'You're right,' John conceded, 'but we're not in Kansas any more, Dorothy.'

'What's that supposed to mean?'

'I mean we don't work for the *Bristol Journal* we used to, Erin. Hugh Carmine doesn't do anything by halves. All publicity is good publicity for him. Cat knows that; she's been here two years. We've been here two months.'

'It's a little longer than that, actually.'

'It doesn't matter. Look, can I give you some advice?'

I nod and brace myself.

'I'll be gone soon, so none of this matters to me – but you? You have so much more in you, but you're idealistic. You think journalism is about the truth. If it ever was, it's not now. We're in the midst of a culture war and it's nowhere more obvious than online. You need to decide whose side you're on.'

I grit my teeth. 'It shouldn't be about sides.'

'You're right, it shouldn't. But it is what it is.'

Leaving John's office, I puzzle over his words some more. He's not wrong; it's been quite the wake-up call to see Hugh celebrating Cat's article whipping bad feeling up online via the 'Curse of Queens Mead'. It leaves a nasty taste in my mouth.

That said, hadn't I suggested she *take advantage* of the fact that her article about Michael had gone viral? Poor Cat was just taking me at my word.

Chastising myself, I scurry back to my desk. This time I

take the route back through the cubicle farm. Seeing Cat across the office, I wave to her and smile. She smiles back, her innocent moon-round face dispelling any previous doubts I'd had. I'm being ridiculous.

Aren't I?

PART THREE

The only place success comes before work is in the dictionary.

VIDAL SASSOON

TWENTY-ONE

ERIN

The week limps on. Even though I can't shake my (surely unreasonable) feeling of unease around Cat, we have plenty to be getting on with, especially after hours. We end up staying late almost every night party planning, but we don't go out for drinks again. A distance has developed between us that I'm sure Cat senses, though she never mentions it. The extra hours mean I get it in the neck from David, who complains I haven't had the boys for dinner during the week like I usually do. I have already apologised to the boys, but David puts the phone down on me as I try to explain this to him.

With John's retirement party on the horizon, Cat and I have caterers to double-check, not to mention the food and drink preferences of all the attendees. Allergies are a particular concern of mine. I'm still haunted by a young man I snogged in a bar when I was at university who literally collapsed as a result. I'd been stunned as people gathered around him, wondering if it meant I was a brilliant kisser. But I learned later it was because I'd eaten a peanut butter sandwich, and the legacy of nuts on my tongue had put the poor guy into anaphylactic shock.

On Friday, Hugh calls an impromptu meeting. Resentful and annoyed at being pulled away from my *Bristol Journal* relaunch work, I make it to the conference room with a good few minutes to spare. I find Cat already there, preparing the room. I note she's set up all the tech and remembered to bring in a jug of water and glasses. She's even laid pads of paper, pens and put out a plate of biscuits. She's really thought of everything.

I greet her warily, remembering how we'd left it last time when I rejected her pitch: she'd looked like she was going to burst into tears. All that angst appears to be gone. I congratulate her on being first on the scene at the balcony death, thinking she will be leaving moments later. She smiles back, then takes her place at the table, but not before pouring water into cups for everyone.

'You're staying?'

I curse as I hear the surprise in my voice. Cat doesn't appear to notice.

'Yes, Hugh asked me to.'

'You know what this is about?'

She shrugs. 'No idea.'

Despite Hugh telling us to be at the conference room at ten o'clock on the dot, he and John are late. At ten past, Hugh, red faced and tightly wound, arrives with John in tow. He aggressively tries the door handle, which won't budge. He makes a perplexed face and I am about to stand and open it for him – it wouldn't be the first time – when Cat leaps up from her place. She races over and wrenches the door open, a wide smile on her face.

'There you go, sir.'

I wouldn't have been surprised if she'd done a little curtsey as well. Hugh traipses in, looking like an aged boffin with his shaggy, curly hair and his ragged jeans, *Transformers* T-shirt and neon trainer laces trailing after him.

I smile through clenched teeth. 'Thank you for joining us.'

Like I had any choice in the matter. Hugh raises a hand as if to say, *don't mention it*.

'Where are we at with John's party?'

Hugh literally clicks his fingers at me. My smile freezes on my face: this isn't even about my proper work and he treats me like a lackey? I want to slide across the big conference table and stab him in the neck with my pencil.

'Okay, then.'

As I start reading out all the preparations and things still left to do, I notice in the corner of my eye Hugh is on his phone. This is not unexpected; Hugh's rudeness during meetings is legendary. Dogged as ever, I rattle onwards to the end of my notes.

'Sounds fine,' Hugh says at last, still looking at his phone.

I turn back to the table, feeling the sting of under-appreciation.

'So, anyway: I need a little change to the party proceedings,' Hugh announces.

Uh oh.

My stomach sinks as I watch Hugh stand up, pressing a remote. The big screen Cat had rigged up for him blinks to life. On it are pictures of the Queens Mead Tower renovations and visualisations of what the downstairs offices are supposed to look like.

The pictures are not far off; just that morning I'd admired the almost-finished building work on my way up the stairs. The rubble and dust have gone and the bank of lifts have been installed at last. Corridors and offices are being fitted with carpets and shiny chrome-and-glass finishings. I also know the new coffee shop, newsagent's and crèche on the ground floor are being painted as we speak. The tower's going to look gorgeous and be quite the tourist magnet once it's done.

'I've signed leases for all the remaining floors,' Hugh says. 'We can fully expect one hundred per cent occupation within two weeks.'

Cat erupts in a burst of clapping but stops when neither John nor I join her. Embarrassed, she looks at the floor.

'With all this in mind, then, it seems sensible to combine John's retirement party with a Tower refurb celebration,' Hugh continues. 'So I want you to invite not just Carmine Media, but all the new people who work in the tower as well. Okay?'

Fury pools in my chest as his words land. Someone like Hugh has never had to do grunt work to get ahead. He has no clue how much organising John's retirement party has taken when considering just Carmine employees. To invite *every single person* in the tower is a mountain more work. The words explode out of me before I can stop them.

'Are you fucking kidding me?'

Hugh blinks, his face as impassive as ever. In contrast, John's eyes bulge in horror and surprise; he's never heard me lose it in a meeting. As frustrated and resentful as I've got over the years, I've always been able to keep a lid on my feelings before. Now Pandora's Box is flying open.

'What I mean is . . .'

I trail off. I have no idea what I want to say, other than telling Hugh to go fuck himself. I don't want the extra work but, more importantly, I *can't* do it. My schedule is full to bursting as it is. This party has already taken up far too much of the time that I am meant to be spending on the *Bristol Journal*. Adding another few hundred guests will take me over completely. I'm already neglecting my family again for the sake of this shit.

Cat coughs, drawing everyone's attention. Even Hugh glances across at her.

'If I could make a suggestion?'

Hugh is looking back at his phone screen but makes no objection. Cat looks to me, then John for permission. Earnest-faced, John nods: *Go on then.*

'Erin is very busy and, as one of the Higher Ups, I don't think she has the time or inclination for all this extra work, so how about I take over this second leg with the refurb celebration?'

I arrest the breath in my throat as conflicting emotions settle on me like second-hand smoke. Relief grabs me first, gratitude following as Cat offers to take this wretched party planning off my plate for good.

At the same time, the mental equivalent of a fire alarm sounds in my brain: if I don't do it, do I look bad to Hugh? Once John is gone, I have to continue working at Carmine Media. If I tell Hugh I won't or can't do the party, perhaps he will consider me unreliable. That kind of reputation is hard to get rid of.

'It's not that I don't want to do the party, Hugh,' I lie through my poker face (Lady Gaga has nothing on me), 'I just worry I won't be able to do Carmine Media proud like I want to, when I have so much on already.'

There's silence as the men digest this. Hugh rubs his not-quite-there bum-fluff beard. He thinks it makes him look intellectual.

'Okay, Cat can take over,' Hugh says. 'But if you can offer secondary support, Erin?'

I breathe a sigh of relief. 'You got it.'

The meeting draws to a natural close. As John fusses around Hugh, I gather my things together and walk back to my office. The door is ajar. I open it, expecting to find someone in there: no one.

I take a quick look around to see if anyone has left any memos on my desk. Nothing, though the third drawer down where I keep my personal knick-knacks and my reporter's notebook is half-open. I try and recall if I'd opened it that morning.

I must have. I slam it shut.

As I sit down at my desk, I process the meeting. Already my

relief about having the party planning taken away is gone. I wonder if I have made a mistake. I saw the triumph in Cat's eyes when Hugh passed the baton to her. It had erupted across the table at me.

A dark suspicion has started to flower in my gut. I already know Cat is an opportunist. Could she be working an angle, here? And if she is, could it end up making *me* look bad somehow?

I don't like thinking like this. I took Cat under my wing. I didn't have to do that; no one did it for me. When I joined journalism in the late nineties, I dreamed of being mentored by the inspiring, trailblazing women who'd come before me. I had a rude awakening: these women saw me as a competitor. They'd climbed the ladder and pulled it up after them, leaving me dangling and alone. I swore I would not do the same to the next generation.

There's a timid knock on my office door.

'Come in.'

Cat appears on the threshold of my office, her face creased with worry. She sits down in the chair opposite my desk, leaning forwards, her gaze sincere.

'I just came to check we're okay?'

I proffer a (fake) smile. 'Why wouldn't we be?'

'I was just trying to help ... take on the burden of the party, that's all.' Cat's eyes are shiny and earnest. 'I didn't want there to be any crossed wires.'

'What crossed wires would those be?'

'That I'm trying to freeze you out in any way.'

I'm touched by her concern. In this moment I let go of any

suspicion I had about her motives. I am one of the Higher Ups. Regardless of how useful she makes herself to Hugh, Cat can't leapfrog over me. I have nearly twenty years' worth of experience on her. I am reacting to the workplace's 'divide and conquer' bullshit again.

'Are you kidding? You've done me a favour. Now I can get on with my real work. I should be kissing your feet.'

'Oh, it's the least I can do.' Cat waves a hand at me.

'When I become editor, things are going to change.'

Becoming editor is what I've dreamed of since Hugh bought the newspaper. But no matter how hard I work or how much shit I put up with, I've seen mediocre man after mediocre man promoted ahead of me over the years. As fond as I am of him, even John has been able to coast and get away with it while I am still grafting away in the trenches. I think I've hidden my resentment and frustration pretty well, considering.

'Well, I hope you remember me when you're at the top!'

Cat titters, but something about her brittle manner gives me pause. I've always believed gut instinct is the key feature not only of good journalists, but all savvy human beings, too. I might not be able to put my finger on what exactly perturbs me about Cat, but it would be a mistake to ignore it.

'Thanks, Cat. That will be all.'

After Cat leaves, my attention is drawn back to my third desk drawer. I'd noticed it was open when I came in this morning. I'm normally so careful. I open it again and cast a critical eye over it. My reporter's notebook is usually on the top so I can access it quickly, but now a bag of toffees, my pencil box and key card sit on the black cover. Again, this doesn't feel like something I would do.

I push the items to one side and take my reporter's notebook out. I flick through the crisp pages, regarding my looped handwriting; I've had it so long, it's journalistic gold. All the notes to self, quotes, reminders, contact numbers, email addresses. If I were a young, up-and-coming – and not to mention *opportunistic* – reporter, wouldn't I want to get my hands on this?

The notebook doesn't seem to have been interfered with in any way, yet a strong conviction comes to me: Cat has read it.

But like a good journalist, first I have to prove it.

TWENTY-TWO

CAT

Cat blinked and time seemed to surge forward like an express train. She was told to report to Hugh and to facilitate whatever he needed to ensure the Queens Mead Tower official opening was a roaring success. She hadn't received a pay rise despite the massive increase in work, but Cat didn't mind. Her promotion came with a (somewhat woolly) new title: *Editorial Assistant*. It didn't make a whole lot of sense given party-planning was hardly 'editorial', but Cat didn't care. Whose assistant she was *exactly* and how long for was not fully explained either, though Hugh sent through a succession of Google invites to various meetings with him that week. After work, she bought a new Thermos to celebrate.

Thanks to picking up the slack for Erin, Cat's boring, soul-sucking entry level job of rewriting press releases and NIBs was taken away from her; she was even relieved of having to empty everyone's rubbish. The tower refit nevertheless meant there was no office for Cat yet.

She didn't even mind still having to sit with schmucks like Helena, listening to her self-diagnosed illness complaints. This week, Doctor Google had Helena thinking she had lupus. Or maybe diabetes. Cat was of the opinion Helena's real problem was she was thick as pig shit and had too much time on her hands. Cat made a note to self in the back of her reporter's notebook to fire her as soon as she made it to that rung of the ladder. At the rate she was climbing, that would be sooner rather than later. In your (orange) face, Helena!

Good things come to those who wait.

With John's retirement-come-Queen's-Mead-Tower-refurb celebration slated for the end of March, Cat had her work cut out getting everything ready. Hugh had written up a punishing schedule of things that needed doing, meaning Cat was working into the early hours almost every night. Lawrence did not like this one bit, though not because he was lonely. Cat's industriousness reminded him she'd gone up in the world whilst he was still in the same place, a little too much for an ego as large as Lawrence's to handle.

Most nights he made himself scarce, leaving the flat empty and cold when Cat came in late. There was no dinner waiting for her in the microwave, or even a note. Cat made herself another note to self in her reporter's notebook: *Dump Lawrence.* She wasn't ready to take that step yet, but she knew she would do it. Her burgeoning confidence made it an inevitability. She'd already wasted far too much time on that loser.

It was not all positive. Cat noted Erin seemed more and more distant as the days rocketed past. She went on to her social media and discovered that Erin had locked them all down when she'd been lax about online security before. She attempted to friend Erin on Facebook, but her request went unanswered. When she queried it with Erin later, she had an explanation.

'Sorry, my Facebook is just for family.' Erin smiled. 'You know, so relatives can see pictures of the boys. That type of thing.'

This seemed both probable and reasonable. Nothing appeared suspect about Erin's demeanour, either, but it nevertheless set wheels whirring in Cat's analytical mind. That evening she attempted to go into Erin's office, but found the door locked. This was unusual; Erin had never seemed to care about keeping people out before. It was not a problem. Cat simply fetched the skeleton key that hung up in the cubicle farm kitchenette.

Letting herself in, Cat made straight for the third drawer on Erin's desk. She knew what she would find in there: Erin's own reporter's notebook. Any worries Erin might have locked her desk drawer as well vanished when she pulled it. It opened right away. Cat was perturbed to find the notebook was gone; Erin must have taken it home with her. *Damn*.

It didn't matter. She'd already taken pictures on her camera phone of the pages that contained particularly juicy information and contacts. Sitting in Erin's chair, Cat spun it round so she could look out across the Bristol cityscape at night as she thought over her next moves.

Erin had been instrumental in Cat's moving up the ladder at Carmine, so it troubled Cat to lose the connection to her. Even though she now disliked and distrusted Erin for rejecting her pitch, Cat did not want to lose the momentum she'd gained at Carmine when Hugh's big tower refurb party was over.

So . . . what next?

Like most mothers, Erin had made it clear her two sons were everything to her, but she kept her feelings about David much more guarded. Hopeful there might be a way of getting back 'in' with Erin via David, somehow, Cat spent every moment she could researching him. She followed his movements online. She discovered he was inactive on Twitter and Facebook but used Pinterest daily for design ideas. He also updated his Instagram every morning at around eight o'clock, checking back in to answer comments around eleven.

Cat subscribed to his newsletter and received his updates once a week. David presented his business in a delightful, conversational tone that showcased his talent and presented him as a normal, reliable 'guy next door'. He also spoke fondly of his sons, his passion for eighties monster movies and walks in the country at weekends. He never mentioned Erin, Cat noticed.

Working all hours, it was tougher to follow David in real life during the week. Cat already knew from a passing comment that Erin took the boys out at weekends. This opened up an opportunity, so Cat made plans to frequent David's neighbourhood that Saturday.

David's home was in Clifton, one of the most picturesque

and sought-after areas in the whole of Bristol, which made it heinously expensive. As Cat made her way down the wide streets in the shadow of the suspension bridge, she marvelled at how the other half lived. It was a far cry from her own apartment building, which was surrounded by huge red Biffa bins and boxes. Until she'd wandered into Clifton, she'd considered her flat block to be pleasant and a cut above Nelson Mandela House.

Here, she realised how naïve and out of touch she was. Cat stared into the windows of boho boutiques at clothes she could never afford, before stopping for a takeaway coffee from a café that had a huge mural of music hall entertainer Josephine Baker on the back wall. Cat was willing to bet the café's proprietor – who was neither black nor French – had no idea who Baker was. He was a short, middle-aged, greasy-looking man with a ponytail and a widow's peak. He took one look at Cat and sneered as though he had shit on his top lip. Cat made her order and paid the exorbitant amount for it, walking out with the cup in her hands like a trophy.

Cat consulted the map app on her phone and wandered towards David's home. It was the smallest and most decrepit house on the street. That figured. Cat already knew Erin had not come from money, which meant David probably didn't either.

She discovered a bench near an old red phone box about three doors up from the address. She had on a disguise, of sorts: her coat zipped up to the chin against the cold, a beanie hat pulled low and a pair of Lawrence's old glasses. She felt confident Erin would pass by, oblivious, but if on the off chance she didn't, there was no reason Cat was not supposed to be there. It was a public place and Erin had no reason to suspect Cat of anything.

At half ten, Erin's little black car came zooming down the wide street too fast. Cat watched as she stopped in the middle of the road without parking. Erin must have rung ahead, because less than a minute later, a tall gangly boy with straggly long hair and a small, thin lad with a shaved head appeared from David's. They clattered down the big stone steps, each carrying rucksacks with them. David appeared after them, holding his shoes in one hand and waving to the car with the other.

He wanted them to wait for him.

Did this mean David was going with them today? That would suggest he and Erin *were* getting back together ... wouldn't it? Cat searched her memory banks for any more proof of this. Erin was the anal type to send Google invites to family outings and barbecues, but she'd not put any such appointments on her calendar.

David hopped down the steps after the boys, pulling his shoes on. He was just in his shirt sleeves; he hugged himself against the cold. If he was going out with them, he would be wearing his coat. He ducked down and muttered something through the window to Erin. Then he laughed and banged one fist on top of the car good-naturedly in that way men do. Erin honked her horn and drove off with their sons. David watched the car go and turned round, skipping back up the steps to his home, letting himself back in.

Cat was intrigued. David and Erin seemed quite tight, but

that didn't necessarily mean they were getting back together. They could just be good parents, committed to co-parenting and showing their sons a united front. As the front door closed behind him, Cat sat forward, crushing her empty take-away coffee cup and leaving it on the bench, an act of juvenile defiance against the otherwise pristine street.

Though she'd made no plan to, Cat found herself knocking on David's door. Her heart hammered in her chest; what the hell was she doing? David would surely know she was up to something. Hell, she wasn't even sure what she was doing. She just knew she couldn't ignore the siren call to see inside Erin's old home and look for clues on how to get back 'in' with her.

Cat barely needed to ring the doorbell before David was back at the door. He returned with a smile, clearly expecting Erin or one of his boys to have forgotten something. When he saw it was Cat, his grin diminished to one of casual but wary interest. He probably thought she was a charity collector or one of those survey people. Cat held out both hands to show she carried nothing with her.

'Sorry to bother you!' Cat giggled. She knew red-blooded men like David liked that. 'I'm Judith.'

'Hello, Judith.' David didn't move away from the door. 'Can I help you?'

'You have a lovely home.'

'Thank you.'

They stared at each other for a second more. Cat could feel her impatience prickle between her shoulder blades and fought the urge to turn on her heel and run away. She decided to dive straight in. She was here now – she might as well.

'I was just passing and, erm, I know this is a weird request ... but I used to live in this house when I was a little kid.'

David blinked as he absorbed this. Cat knew she wasn't speaking out of turn. In her cyber-stalking, she'd discovered the Goodmans had bought the house approximately fifteen years ago according to Zoopla. There was no way David could know she had never set foot in his home before.

'I don't suppose I could come in, have a quick look?'

Cat watched David size her up, then check up and down the street. It was deserted. He sighed, in two minds whether to let her in. Cat knew he didn't consider her a threat; she was half his size. David must be thinking it might look suspect, a middle-aged man letting a young woman into his home, unsolicited.

Faced with the possibility of being denied entry, Cat was seized with the desire to make it across the threshold. She pursed her lips and forced a fake quiver into her voice.

'Please? My mother died recently and I ...' She stopped herself as if she'd said too much. 'Sorry, you don't want to hear my sob story. I'll just go.'

Cat turned away but, before she made it to the top step, David's resigned voice fell on her back.

'Go on then. Just five minutes, though. Okay?'

She turned back, all smiles. 'I promise.'

TWENTY-THREE

ERIN

Cat has fallen into my trap.

My suspicion that she'd been reading through my reporter's notebook is proven correct the week after our meeting with Hugh. Each night I rig my third drawer, fastening a hair across the opening with two small invisible pieces of tape. I'd read this trick in an Enid Blyton book when I was a girl: if someone opens the drawer after I leave and lock my office, the hair will snap.

Both to my dismay and delight, I discover a day or so later that my elaborate trap works a treat. I make my way into my office to find everything in its place bar the broken hair taped across the drawer's opening.

Betrayal burns through me as I piece this all together, but I push it down as I always do. I have to keep a clear head. If I start shouting the odds at Cat about violating my privacy,

I need to prove Cat is up to no good somehow. I can't start flinging accusations around, otherwise the only person who'll get bawled out will be me.

I resolve not to let it spoil my weekend. I pick up the boys on Saturday morning and am delighted to see David looking carefree and happy. He comes down to the car and chats with me, reminding me about Joshua's ear medicine with none of his usual implied judgement. He even grins and winks at me like he used to when we were married. I drive off with the boys with buoyant optimism: even if we are not destined to get back together, perhaps David and I can be friends. At last.

That evening I press David's doorbell, still chatting with the boys who smile and laugh with me. It feels so much easier now; I can't believe I ever found Saturdays to be such a trial. My weekend visits had previously always been a triumph of hope over experience: each time filled with disappointment and resentment. Even mild-mannered Joshua felt the pressure for everything to be perfect, and it often made him erratic and irritable. I understood. Whether Dylan was there or not there with us, he always made his presence felt too.

I feel so much closer to my sons now. That's because of David having that word with Dylan after his drunken misadventures at Turbo Island, but it's also down to Asif. Spending time with him has made me realise I'd been trying way too hard with my sons; I'm also grateful for his help keeping them occupied. I decide to buy him a gift as a thank you. A computer game, perhaps.

I am surprised when David does not answer the door straight away. He often catches up with work when the boys are out; his study is the first room off the hallway near the front door. I look at my watch: it's six o'clock. David is always effortlessly punctual, so I know there's no way he's gone out and lost track of time. He won't even leave home if there's the slightest concern he won't arrive back in time to receive the kids, or even just to sign for packages. I found it one of his many irritating foibles when we'd been married, yet I recall such things fondly now.

'You got your key?'

I hold out my hand to Dylan. I know David has had three or four cut for him since I moved out. Dylan just stares at my palm and shrugs. So that's a no, then. Bloody teenagers. I smile, remembering my own mother's exasperation with me losing keys when I was the same age. Some things never change.

I press the doorbell again, then clatter the letterbox. Joshua takes my lead and bends down to shout through it.

'Hello? Dad! Daaaaaad!'

I expect this to be enough to bring David's shadow into the hallway.

It does not.

For the first time, disquiet blooms in my belly. David *had* been unusually chipper that morning. Now I worry David's excessive cheer might have been symptomatic of something else. I have a vague recollection of reading somewhere that depressed and suicidal people sometimes appear happier just before they attempt self-harm.

I shut this avenue of thought down. I am catastrophising again. David has no reason to kill himself. But the father of a

194

friend I grew up with killed himself and, before that, no one in their family had had any inkling whatsoever their patriarch was in such a dark place.

No. Stop it.

'Mum?' Dylan's dark eyes drill into me as he clocks my expression. 'You okay?'

I force breeziness into my voice.

'Course. Did Dad tell you he was going anywhere today?'

Joshua sniffs. 'Supermarket. I asked him to get me bacon crisps.'

'Great idea. I love bacon crisps.'

I press the redial button on my phone. 'David' pops up on the screen but it keeps ringing. He still doesn't come to the door.

'Where's Dad?'

There's a tinge of anxiety in Joshua's voice. Dylan looks to me and must see that same anxiety, because his Big Brother mode flips on.

'Don't worry, I expect he just got held up somewhere. Right, Mum?'

'Right. He'll be back any minute, I'm sure.'

I work through my options. I'm annoyed with myself for not insisting on a key for emergencies. David is so dependable – I'd never had the foresight to imagine I could end up waiting on the doorstep like this. Though I know I am jumping way ahead of myself, there's a part of me that doesn't want to be the one who finds him, either.

What happens in these types of situations? Do I call the police and tell them my worries? I can't imagine they will be interested. David is a grown man without a history of mental illness. It's his democratic right not to answer the door, even to his ex-wife and children. The kids are safe in my care and there's no evidence to say David might have harmed himself. Aren't they bound to say they can't do anything until David's been missing for days, or even weeks, rather than hours?

Just as I am about to start googling for more information on this, I see movement in the corner of my eye. A shadowy form appears through the frosted glass panels of the front door. Suddenly the door is open and David stands there, hair wet and no shirt on, just jeans and bare feet and smelling of lemon shower gel.

'Sorry, sorry!' He laughs. 'I was in the shower. Didn't hear you down here. All right, fellas?'

Gratitude and introspective embarrassment flood through me at the sight of him. How could I have thought it would be anything different? Work stress must be getting to me way more than I thought.

Everything reverts to normality: our sons nod and both give David high fives as they trudge into the house, just like they usually do. They head straight to the kitchen. Through the bay window I can see them go to the fridge and snacks cupboard. I am looking wherever David isn't, for fear my cheeks will flame with embarrassment at his state of undress.

'Sorry for being "late".' I can hear the smirk in his voice as he says this, though it drops away as he follows up with: 'I wouldn't blame you if you had a go, you know. I did last time you were late.'

'It's no problem.'

I strain to keep my voice neutral as my gaze alights on him at last. A committed runner and fitness enthusiast, David doesn't have the classic 'dad bod'. Even if he did, it wouldn't matter to me. Though I have tried hard to keep him out of my head and my heart, reminding myself of all his many shortcomings, I still love him. Maybe I always will.

'Well, I'd better go.'

Except I don't move. Nor does David.

'Want to come in, have a drink?'

A discordant crash of voices in my head both encourages me to take David up on his offer *and* run away. I want to be in my old home, with him, my sons – even if it's only for an hour. But the last time he'd asked it had ended in disappointment for me, as he'd pushed me away again. I also don't want to confuse the boys or, if I'm honest, myself. I don't want to hope for more, especially if David has moved on and there's no way back for us. David sighs as he watches the internal struggle swim across my face.

'Tell you what, never mind.'

'No!' I blurt out, then laugh: 'I mean, go on then. Just a quick one.'

I can hear Netflix on in the front room as I pour two glasses of wine. Dylan drifts back into the kitchen in search of yet more food. His brow furrows as he takes me in, still here, as his father is upstairs putting a shirt on.

'Don't go getting any ideas,' I warn. 'Your dad and I are just having a catch up.'

'Never said anything.'

Dylan opens the fridge and takes out a pint carton of milk.

I know what he's about to do before he does it.

'Don't . . . !'

Too late. Dylan drinks straight out of the carton and puts it back. He grins, wiping a milk moustache from his face.

'Dad lets us.'

'Does he now?'

I watch him and David, now fully dressed, switch places in the doorway, Dylan disappearing back into the living room.

'You let the boys drink out of the milk carton?'

'Do I hell. Lying little scrote.' David takes his wine glass from my outstretched hand, clinking it against mine. 'Cheers.'

I smile. 'What are we celebrating?'

'Dunno. Been doing a lot of thinking lately.' David sinks onto one of the kitchen chairs opposite me. 'Life is short. I've decided not to waste any more of it being mad at you.'

'I'll drink to that.'

We chat like old friends for the next hour. I regale him with tales about Asif. ('Isn't that the mouthy little sod who called me a boomer?' David says.) I also tell him how we'd all gone to the park to play football until we'd been rained off. David thinks the thought of me playing sport is hilarious; I can't blame him. When we were married, I left him in command of any physical activity with the boys, whether it was playing football or building sandcastles.

Though exercise is not something I enjoy like David does, I can't deny it connects me to the boys and it makes me feel closer to them. I realise now I've been trying to find activities and outings on my level for them – museums, coffee shops, National Trust properties, art galleries. Though both boys like such things too, really all they'd wanted was my time and interest. They'd just wanted to feel like I'm listening and invested in them.

'How was your day?'

'Uneventful. Did some work. Went to the supermarket, then for a run. That was why I was in the shower earlier . . .' David stops, interrupting himself. 'Actually one weird thing did happen. Some woman came round.'

An unanticipated pang slices through me at these words. Thoughts clamour through my head about who this woman could be. Is this David's careless way of telling me he's met someone? I try and keep the tremor I feel out of my voice.

'Oh. Someone from the school gates?'

'No,' David says, 'some random girl.'

The relief feels incredible. David's use of the word 'girl' makes thoughts of Cat swim up into my head. She'd been snooping in my desk, could she have been snooping around David? For what purpose? That familiar sense of unease blooms in my belly again.

'Oh?'

'Yes, she reckoned she lived in the house when she was a child, wanted to take a look around.'

I keep my tone neutral. 'I see. Did you let her?'

'Didn't see the harm in it. She didn't stay long.' David finishes his wine. 'I worried she might be casing the joint, so I didn't leave her on her own in case she tried to nick anything.'

'Smart move,' I acknowledge. 'How old was she?'

'Not sure. Twenty-five, maybe?'

Cat is just twenty-eight.

'What did she look like?'

David casts his mind back. 'Mousy hair. Round face. Short. Plain, but not unpleasant-looking.'

Oh, God.

'Did she say what her name was?' I lick my lips, not sure I want to hear the answer.

'Judith.'

Relief floods through me. It's just a weird coincidence. I set up my empty glass on the table as something else occurs to me.

'Mrs Wells lived here before we did. She'd been here for fifty years, remember?'

'Oh, yeah. Perhaps she meant as a granddaughter, coming to visit.'

'No, Mrs Wells didn't have any children. I remember, because I recall thinking it was odd a committed spinster should have such a big house.'

'Maybe that girl *was* trying to case the joint then.'

I laugh. 'Just as well you were on hand, then.'

Our conversation dies away as we stare at each other for a second too long. I want to reach across the table and press my mouth to his. I feel certain he would not stop me; I see his gaze flick to my lips. I pull myself away and rise from my seat, reminding myself that if it's meant to be, David and I will resurrect our relationship. We have plenty of time.

'I have to go.'

'Right, right.'

David busies himself taking our glasses to the sink. I pop through to the living room to say goodbye to the boys.

Dylan mutters a nonchalant 'bye', still staring at his phone, but Joshua throws his skinny arms around my middle. I give him a big squeeze and tell him I will see him next Saturday, as well as a FaceTime story on Tuesday night like I do every week. Joshua nods happily and joins his brother back on the sofa as I leave the room.

'Bye then!' I call to David as I walk past the kitchen, only to find he reappears next to me from the study, making me jump. He dips forward as if to kiss my cheek. I let him, only to be surprised when he gives me a swift peck on the lips. He draws his head back with a grin, as if impressed by his own chutzpah.

To hell with it.

My own good and responsible intentions vanish. I push David back into the study and against the wall, pressing my body against his as we kiss. I feel his hands on my waist move downwards to cup my bottom. It feels like we've never been apart.

'It's always been you,' David mutters as he breaks away.

I kiss him again. This time, he switches with me and pushes me against the study wall, his hand finding its way underneath my blouse. He always liked to be the dominant one when it came to sex. With regret, I disentangle myself from him.

'Better not,' I sigh, 'the boys are literally *right there*. Especially after last time.'

Rueful, David rolls his shoulders and rearranges his crotch. 'Kids ruin your bloody life, I tell you.'

We both laugh at his daft joke. We'd wasted so much time, but we can't afford to get this wrong again. It is not just us who could get hurt. I'd been wrong: we can't just resurrect our relationship on a whim. We have to *rebuild* it.

'This for real?' I demand, wary after his backtracking last time. 'If you tell me it's all a big mistake again . . .'

'I know, I know.' David holds up two hands in surrender. 'I was a dick last time. I freaked out, I'm sorry. But we take it slow, okay?'

'*Very* slow.'

'I wouldn't mind, though, if you did an adults-only FaceTime story with me next week?'

I chuckle. 'Then it's a date.'

I kiss David one last time and rub a thumb across his lips, making sure none of my lipstick remains. He sees me to the door. As I walk down the steps and towards my car, I glance back. He's still framed in the doorway, the light behind him.

He blows me a kiss.

TWENTY-FOUR

CAT

Cat trudged in through the door of her flat and collapsed on the sofa, face first and shoes still on, screaming into a cushion. Lawrence didn't come rushing through from the bedroom, so he had to be out again. Good. Still face down, Cat balled up her fists and beat the sofa cushions, kicking her feet until she'd yelled out all her frustration.

Sated, Cat rolled over and stared at the ceiling. Though she'd been thrilled to get some one-on-one time with Hugh whilst working on the tower refurb party, the playboy was more of a trial to work with than she was expecting. She'd figured he would at least be interested in her ideas or ask her for the sake of politeness. It was part of the social contract. Yet Hugh appeared to have none of the good graces that had been imposed on Cat as a woman by society. If she spoke to people the way Hugh spoke to her, she'd be considered a monster. It had always been this way.

Whilst she waited for Lawrence to put in an appearance, Cat heated up some leftover spaghetti and poured herself a glass of wine. She was frustrated and felt stuck. She had not been visited by the inspiration she'd hoped for when she'd managed to talk her way into David Goodman's home the week before. David had insisted on showing Cat around the old Victorian house himself, which meant limited chances to see anything that could help Cat gain an insight into Erin.

It was understandable behaviour from David. Her parents had never locked the doors or windows, being miles from their nearest neighbour. Even if some people in cities like Bristol were dumb enough to let strangers into their home, very few would leave that stranger alone. She let him guide her around the ground floor, interjecting with stories about her own memories of the house. Living in that make-believe world was so comforting and at odds with her own upbringing, Cat almost believed her own lies.

As the tour went on, Cat felt certain that if she could just break away from David, she might be able to find something that could help her get back in with Erin. That was why when they reached the second floor, Cat apologised and asked if she could use the bathroom. David had seemed reticent but nodded. Most men don't like to deny women use of a toilet, as if they expect them to explode, literally or metaphorically. Cat smiled and locked herself in, David safely on the other side of the door and unable to see what she was up to.

The bathroom was a small, sloped room under the eaves. It was well finished, though obviously on a budget: a plain white suite and tiles in the narrow space. There was an over-full laundry hamper in the corner, dirty pants and socks gathered around its base like rubbish. In the bath was a selection of toys: a couple of boats, a family of ducks, a frog. There was a medicine cabinet over the sink.

Cat opened it, sorting through all the items inside: cotton buds, toothpaste, paracetamol. Nothing of particular interest. There was also nothing to suggest Erin was staying over regularly: no 'female things' like tampons, hairspray, or so much as an extra toothbrush. Sigh.

She flushed the toilet and ran the taps for the sake of appearances. Opening the door, she hoped to skip across the landing to the master bedroom. She was bound to find something good in there.

But on re-emerging, Cat discovered David was still waiting at the top of the stairs, one step down. Disappointment at being thwarted sent a vivid, violent image searing through her brain. In her mind's eye, Cat saw herself race forwards and give him a good, hard push. She blinked and it was gone again.

'Want to see the rest?' David enquired.

Cat had begged off, saying she was feeling a little emotional about ghosts of the past. David had seemed relieved, like he'd regretted letting her in, which annoyed her. He'd seen her out, then slammed the front door behind her, leaving her stymied on the top step.

Giving up on Lawrence, Cat took a shower. Singing her favourite Disney tunes, she considered the party, less than a week away now. As annoying as it was working with Hugh, she felt certain she was still nailing it. She felt sure her colleagues would be impressed with her hard work. That had to mean Hugh would be too . . . didn't it?

She was so preoccupied, she didn't hear the front door of the flat slam shut, nor Lawrence's footsteps on the carpet then the bathroom tiles. The first Cat knew about his presence was when he whipped the shower curtain back, making her scream.

'Oh, look who's bothered to grace me with her presence!'

Lawrence grabbed her and manhandled her wet, naked body out of the bath, ripping the shower curtain from the rail and wrapping it round her like a wet shroud. Though Cat fought back, she couldn't escape his grip.

'Get off me!'

Lawrence cackled with malicious glee, his breath sour with alcohol. They had so rarely seen each other recently that she had momentarily allowed herself to forget his emotional terrorism: pushing Cat around, freaking out and frightening her were the tools of his trade. He loved it.

'Not such a bigshot now, are you?'

'Fuck off!'

Still naked, Cat managed to slither out of the shower curtain and across the bathroom floor. She made it up onto her hands and knees, crawling away from him.

Lawrence wasn't done. He grabbed hold of her waist and pulled her back towards him, making her hands slip so she fell onto her front, banging her head on the base of the toilet. Seeing stars, she had a vague awareness of Lawrence flipping her over onto her back.

'Your tits are one good thing about you, at least.'

He cupped one of them with his hand, tweaking her nipple. Cat froze where she was, not daring to move in case it unleashed something more predatory and animal in Lawrence. Just as he'd never actually beaten her up, Lawrence had never full-on forced himself on her. Like the violence, his sexual advances had always skirted the levels of propriety. He made her feel like shit, but only within the perimeters of giving himself the get-out clause that any perceived threat from him was all in her head.

God, she hated him so much.

Cat braced herself, but he'd gone again. She heard him moving around in the living area: the blare of the television; the opening and closing of a cupboard door; the roar of the kettle as it boiled. He must have got bored with taunting her.

'Want a cup of tea?' he called through.

Head reeling, Cat sat upright in the bathroom and grabbed for a towel. She didn't want any tea, but she didn't want to antagonise him further, either. Lawrence did not take kindly to being turned down when he considered he was being 'nice'. She had to accept his offers or help, or he took it as a rejection and sign of aggression.

'Sure.'

Emerging from the bathroom, Cat took the mug Lawrence offered her.

'Now what do you say?' Lawrence prompted, like she was a child.

'Thank you,' Cat muttered.

She scurried to their bedroom with it, shutting the door after her. Heart and thoughts still racing, she dried herself quickly and pulled on her Minnie Mouse pyjamas. Lawrence's laughter and shouts came from the living area now, along with the television on full blast. Gunfire and voices. He was gaming. That would keep him occupied for a few hours.

She'd left her laptop on the bed. Getting in under the covers, she wiped a few unshed tears from her eyes. Cat powered up the laptop and went straight to Google. Her hands poised over the keys, mid-air; she wasn't sure what she was searching for.

Part of Cat wished Lawrence was dead. No, *all of her* wished Lawrence was dead. She'd dreamed of it plenty of times: stabbing him in his pigeon chest; smashing in his mocking face; even setting him on fire and watching him scream from the midst of conflagration as it melted his flesh and charred his bones.

Could she kill Lawrence? Absolutely. Thanks to Michael and Leila, the evidence was clear: Cat had the stomach for it.

But *should* she kill Lawrence?

On the one hand, if Lawrence died somehow, that was bound to get Cat the attention she craved at work. People would feel sorry for her, plus another viral article was surely a shoo-in . . . but maybe it wouldn't all be the kind of attention she wanted? The police were bound to ask much more difficult questions of her. Most murder victims were killed by lovers or family members, so she would be a suspect from the offset. Cat could find herself in jail for murder or manslaughter.

There were other practical concerns, too. Cat and Lawrence were not married, plus Lawrence had no will. The flat was bought for him by his mother and Cat would find herself out on the street before Lawrence was cold in the ground. She'd accepted his erratic, frightening behaviour as the price of keeping a roof over her head and she wasn't going to risk her home now that she was finally climbing the ladder.

Cat opened all the spreadsheets, lists and memos about Hugh's big party for John and the official opening of the tower. The event was just days away; excitement and anxiety swam in Cat's stomach. Most of her checklists were done and double-checked, but she still worried she'd forgotten something.

Wresting control of the event off Erin had been one of Cat's greatest triumphs; it didn't even matter to her that Erin hadn't wanted the dubious honour of organising it in the first place. Now Cat had been promoted to editorial assistant, she was on the fast track at Carmine Media, she was sure of it.

If only something could happen at the party.

This thought floated into Cat's mind like a soap bubble. If someone was hurt at the party – or even better, died – she could report on it as 'first on the scene' again. It would be difficult to pull off; both Michael and Leila had died out of range of spying eyes. Killing someone and making it look like an accident in the middle of a party with hundreds of potential witnesses would be a challenge.

Cat wasn't afraid of hard work.

She could feel the blaze of fire within her.

She knew exactly what she needed to do.

TWENTY-FIVE

ERIN

I admire myself in the mirror, smoothing the red dress I'd brought out of hiding for the party this evening. It clings to all the right places: my hips and bust. I take a photograph of my cleavage and send it to David. Seconds later he replies with *HAWT xx*. I feel silly but empowered. Camera phones weren't yet a thing when we'd got together as students, so we'd never sexted each other.

Now the refit on the Queens Mead Tower is complete, other floors have been filling up. Directly below Carmine Media is now an architect firm full of white males who all seem to be called William or Daniel. Below them, a literary and talent agency specialising in marginalised creatives. The rest of the floors are taken up, predictably, by call centres and insurance brokers. If I take the stairs, I can hear a constant hubbub of voices and phones ringing all the way to the top storey. Still, it beats the previous never-ending screech of electric drills and builders cursing at one another before that.

I wish I was taking David with me to the party, but someone has to look after the boys. I'd suggested we pay Dylan to look after Joshua, but David reminded me that Dylan cannot be trusted. He'd lock himself in his room playing computer games with his headphones on, then arrive with his hand out for the money regardless. Meanwhile Joshua could have set the kitchen on fire making porridge, left the bath running or escaped the house altogether and made it to Bristol Temple Meads to catch a train. None of these possibilities are an exaggeration. All three of these events have literally happened in the past when we'd tried to use Dylan as a built-in babysitter. (Joshua had been trying to leave Bristol to meet one of his favourite TikTokers unsolicited. Thankfully a guard found him wandering the station after Joshua had shoved a library card into one of the automated ticket machines. He never even reached the platform.)

Part of me still feels like Cat usurped me when taking on the party for Hugh, though I know this isn't exactly true. I'm too busy and senior to be organising events; rather it's the circumstances of Cat's weird behaviour that has me rattled. After I confirmed Cat had been checking out my reporter's notebook, I've tracked her movements via Carmine's security cameras. There isn't any CCTV in the senior offices, corridors or toilets, but I discovered I could watch her in the cubicle farm and kitchens. All the time I was surveilling her I saw her do nothing untoward, but I still couldn't shake the sensation that she was up to something.

Journalist's instinct again.

One night I had lain in wait outside Carmine Media in my car. When I saw Cat emerge at the end of the day, I got out and followed her at a distance. I wasn't sure why or what I was expecting her to do; I must have been watching too many spy movies.

In any case, Cat strode on up the road, headphones on and hands jammed in her pockets, in a world of her own. About two blocks into this charade, I became aware of a young man in his late twenties across the road. Tall and skinny with a receding hairline, he was smoking a cigarette, his gaze fixed on Cat. Alarm prickled through me as he threw his fag away and picked up the pace, running out in front of traffic near a pedestrian crossing.

I felt certain I was about to witness Cat getting mugged. A flurry of contradictory emotions surged through me. As suspicious as I was of Cat's motives at work, I still didn't want her to get attacked and robbed. Before I could reveal myself and warn Cat, though, she turned around and saw the young man approach. She proffered him a wan smile and they hugged. Relief replaced my alarm. He must be the boyfriend. I'd overreacted, 'catastrophising' as usual.

There's a strident knock at the door to my flat. I open it to my 'date': Asif. He wears a white shirt and black trousers, no tie. His hair sticks up like a duck's arse, though I am too uncool and non-trendy to tell whether this is for the sake of fashion or not. He looks like a schoolboy in his uniform, or a waiter just off shift after a busy night.

'You ready, Mrs G?'

I roll my eyes. It's better than 'Karen', at least. I grab my handbag.

'Let's go.'

There's an Uber waiting for us at the top of the basement steps. We clamber in, Asif chatting nineteen to the dozen about meeting celebrities. I stifle a smile. When I'd been organising the party, I spent all my time pressuring people of note from the area to put in an appearance. I'd managed to scrape together Bristol's mayor, a couple of councillors and an ex *Big Brother* contestant. For the sake of keeping the peace, Hugh has been BCCing me into all Cat's organisational emails, so I know the guest list is slightly better now: a couple of comedians from the nineties and early noughties, a local drag queen and lip syncer called Ophelia Balls.

One guest on the list had given me pause, though: a local actor who'd been in *Game of Thrones*. Asif seems especially starstruck by the last one, so I don't mention I've never seen a single episode. I did, however, interview the notoriously reclusive young woman about eighteen months earlier for John before we were bought out by Carmine Media.

I know *exactly* how Cat found her.

We arrive in the offices on the top floor. The main conference room has been given over to the gathering and I'm relieved to discover I've timed it so I can enter just as the party gets going. I hate being first to these things, it's so awkward. As I greet colleagues and new residents of Queens Mead Tower, Cat passes by with a clipboard and a headset, waving to me in a cheery but distracted way. I step out in front of her, blocking the way.

214

'You've done so well.' I fix an almost-manic smile on my face. 'However did you get hold of *her*?'

I nod towards the actor, who is surrounded by starry-eyed fans all asking her questions and for autographs. She's the picture of professionalism as she signs napkins, books and, in one case, the chest of a young guy who works in the copy room. He shows his friends and they all roar their approval.

Cat grins. 'Where there's a will, there's a way.'

'Isn't there just.' I grit my teeth. 'So tell me: you get in touch with anyone else from my contacts list in my reporter's notebook?'

To her credit, Cat doesn't flinch. 'I don't know what you mean, Erin. You'll have to excuse me.'

She scurries off, swallowed into the throng.

'What was that all about?' Asif enquires.

Before I can reply, a young waiter appears with a metal tray, offering glasses of Prosecco, Coke and red wine. Asif looks to me with wide eyes as if asking permission; it's clear he has never been to an executive function before, bless him. I felt similar at the first I ever went to. I wandered around, feeling pride as well as frustration, knowing it would be left to people like my mother to clean up after such office parties. At ours, I watch as Asif selects a Coke and glugs it back with a big grin.

'Erin!' John appears in front of me, bouncing on the balls of his feet as usual. 'Hasn't Cat done well? The chocolate fountain was a masterstroke.'

'Well, that one was my idea—'

I'm cut off as Hugh appears, still looking at his phone in his hand. He hasn't bothered to dress up as far as I can tell. He's wearing a T-shirt with the Nostromo logo from *Alien*, jeans, trainers. He has finished the look with a corduroy jacket over the top, complete with elbow patches. He looks like a teenage boy crossed with a geography teacher.

'Erin.' He's still looking at the screen in his hand. 'There you are. We need a little word.'

My mouth falls open. Hope flutters in my chest again. I'd hoped the launch party would mean John's successor as editor would be named – and that person would be me. Could this be the moment I finally get the keys to the kingdom? I cross my fingers behind my back.

Hugh shoves his phone in his pocket at last. He looks to each of us this time, even Asif, his lips pressed together in what only he can think is a smile. He looks constipated.

'I must say, I wasn't sure we could make a go of the *Bristol Journal*,' Hugh declares, 'but I stand corrected. The site has been going mental hit-wise, thanks in no small part to Cat's "Curse of Queens Mead" articles. Peter is going to have a great time with this asset now it's been relaunched.'

My fake smile freezes on my face. I'm irritated for a moment that Cat's work is upstaging mine again, before a worse issue crashes through my brain.

Peter?

Before I can ask who the hell that is, Hugh turns on his heel and starts chatting to a young woman with the most plunging neckline I've ever seen. I round on John, who shrinks from my gaze, confirming my worst fear. I don't know how, or why, but somehow I have been usurped. Again.

'What the hell is going on, John?'

'Let's just enjoy tonight—'

'John, tell me!'

He sighs. 'Hugh's appointed Peter Mackinty as my replacement for editor of the *Bristol Journal*. We start the transition next week.'

Disappointment spears me straight in the chest; it's hard to take a breath. Damn it, I worked so hard on setting up and relaunching the *Bristol Journal* with Carmine Media. I went all out to try and get Hugh to realise this. I treated it as a kind of audition, a dry run: *look what I can do.* I worked hard to get John on side too so he would go to bat for me. I decided it was inevitable: I've done my time in the trenches, I've climbed the ladder, I've learned everything I could. I felt certain this was my moment. Yet I've been passed over once more.

What the fuck do I have to do to get my due?

Even worse, the replacement editor is none other than Peter Mackinty. My stomach lurches, disappointment morphing into nausea. Peter's around my age; we went to university together. We did the same course; we were even in the same class. Peter was an over-privileged arsehole who'd landed in Bristol because Oxbridge wouldn't take him. This rejection rolled off him like oil off water. He reminded us of his family's wealth and influence every chance he got.

He's not only my nemesis, he's the antithesis of everything I am and hold dear. At university Peter recognised I was his superior and drew a line in the sand between us even then, competing with me for the best grades and the most attention

217

from our lecturers. Every time I beat him, he started a whisper campaign, calling into question my victory.

I got better exam results? I must have cheated.

Written a better essay? I must have plagiarised it.

I delivered a better presentation? I must have slept with my tutor in return for extra help and credit.

Worse, Peter never took a day off from this, he was relentless. He would give me nothing, let me enjoy nothing. The thought of having to go through all that again, only this time with real-world consequences that could affect my entire livelihood, makes me feel sick.

'Excuse me.' I rush off to the toilets.

After retching up a few mouthfuls of Prosecco and little else, I sit down on the closed toilet seat, head in hands. I feel sorry for myself for a good five minutes, letting tears course down my cheeks. My dead mother's face comes to me in the angst. She reminds me I am allowed to feel like this; I've worked hard and been kicked in the face. Again.

On the sixth minute, her compassionate expression disappears and she purses her lips, telling me to pull myself together. I smile as I hear her in my mind telling me I need to beat the fuckwits at their own game. Mum always did have a potty mouth.

I emit a heavy sigh. I could pre-empt the whole mess by handing in my resignation. I should never have come with John to Carmine Media. It's clear Hugh doesn't really value me or my contribution to the company.

Fuck him. I should leave.

What would David say, though? We are in that delicate

stage of getting back together and rebuilding our relationship. Should I really be serving my notice at the same time? It seems like undue financial pressure at the very least.

Worst case scenario, setting up my own business or job-hunting could potentially knock David and me sideways. Given our previous history of handling such things badly, it could kill any chance of us being a family again. I've wanted this for so long. It's been lonely out in the cold. To kiss the chance of re-joining my precious family goodbye just for the sake of giving Peter Mackinty The Finger seems unbearable.

But how else can I handle this?

My cascade of thoughts is interrupted by a knock on the toilet door. I open it to discover Asif there again. He doesn't seem concerned about being in the ladies', though a woman at the sinks gives him evils while she roots through her handbag.

'You okay?'

Asif scoffs a piece of cheese and pineapple off a toothpick. Cat ordered *ye olde style* typical party food from the caterer. Apparently it's retro and cool now, instead of kitsch and slightly pathetic, like when I was a kid back in the eighties.

'I'm fine.'

Asif lets the now-empty toothpick rest in the corner of his mouth, Clint Eastwood-style. 'That was rough, man. For what it's worth, I think you're great.'

'Thanks, Asif.'

I catch sight of my reflection in the big bank of mirrors opposite. I look a right sight: my meticulous make-up has been ruined by my tears, topped off by smeared panda eyes.

'I look like Alice Cooper.'

'Who's she?'

I laugh. 'Never mind.'

Asif stays with me as I repair my make-up; I can't let anyone else see me like this. As I am finishing up, we hear a scream that makes us both jump. It sounds like it's just beyond the toilet doors, right next to us.

'Help!' the voice shrieks. 'Someone, please help!'

Forgetting my handbag, I bolt out of the toilets, Asif scurrying at my heels. A small group has gathered just outside the door, so I elbow my way through it.

There's a service corridor door now standing open. I run through it and find myself standing on a dark landing, no light. There's a metal staircase leading downwards. Cat stares into the darkness, her eyes wide with horror. I look to where she's staring.

A man lies face down, his arms and legs splayed like a marionette, his face mashed into the floor at the very bottom of the staircase. The back of his balding head looks weird, though I can't process why for a moment. Then my brain catches up. I understand what I am looking at, amidst the black-red blood and the brain matter.

His skull has been staved in.

TWENTY-SIX

CAT

The atmosphere at the party shattered like glass. Upstairs, someone pulled the plug and the music stopped immediately. A shocked hubbub of voices took over the top floor. A woman fainted. People took out phones, shouting over one another about what should happen next.

Only Cat remained where she was, at the door of the service corridor, seemingly transfixed by the corpse below. She was aware of others muttering about her: what to do for the best, whether they should try and coax her away. It was exactly what she wanted them to think. She'd pulled a blinder.

'Oh God, Cat. You okay?'

She was only vaguely aware of someone taking her hand, squeezing it. A waft of expensive perfume, rather than her voice, told Cat it was Erin. She forced herself to look up; it took effort to hold up her own head. The adrenaline was still coursing through her, making her shake and feel slightly disconnected from everything. Like with Leila on the balcony, it was triumph, not shock. She focused on Erin, blinking against her heavy lids.

'Erin, what's happenin—?'

She let herself dip sideways for effect. As Cat predicted, Erin rushed forwards to grab her by both elbows to steady her. Another pair of hands cushioned Cat from behind, grabbing for her waist. She didn't like not seeing who it was, but she knew she had to act oblivious. She was pulled back into the main corridor of Queens Mead Tower.

'Let's get her back in the kitchen.'

Erin's voice was commanding as she walked ahead. Cat's feet barely touched the carpet as a man held her up, letting her rest against his side like a tired child. She allowed herself a peek: Dustin. *Yuk*.

When planning, Cat had half-hoped she might be able to dispatch the sleaze tonight, though she'd recognised he was high risk. Dustin was super-sociable, able to mingle; he was memorable too. If he'd disappeared from the game only to wind up dead, too many other people would have been able to pinpoint his last movements. That would have made Cat's chances of discovery much higher.

Erin was another risk. The older woman was observant as hell. Work allowing that evening, she'd kept as close as she could to Erin and that boy Asif she'd brought with her. Cat had never seen him before, nor had Erin mentioned him to her. A new boyfriend? She attempted to engage him in conversation.

'You new?' Cat had given Asif a toothy grin over the buffet table. 'Haven't seen you in the cubicle farm.'

Asif barely gave her a second glance as he piled his plate high with free food. Cat wouldn't be surprised if he shoved it in his pockets as well. Talk about uncouth.

'Nah. Just doing a mate a favour.'

Cat suppressed a smile. Asif couldn't be Erin's friend. That just didn't track. Erin was a grown woman who had over two decades on this lanky streak of piss. Erin must want something from him. That was the only explanation.

She picked up a bottle of Prosecco and attempted to pour him a glass, but he put his hand over his plastic flute.

'No thanks, don't drink.'

'Religious thing, is it?'

'None of your business.'

Cat froze where she was, unable to compute. This made her offer the bottle again.

'Go on . . . just a little one?'

'I told you, no.' Asif's expression was impassive, but his voice was hard. 'You don't like to hear the word "no", do you?'

'No one does, surely?'

Cat attempted to disarm him with another flirtatious smile, but Asif still regarded her, stony-faced. She shifted on the balls of her feet, uncomfortable under his scrutiny. It felt like he could see right into her very soul. At the very least, she could sense Asif did not like her. She had no idea why.

Most people found Cat to be harmless. Amiability was her superpower. Pain and anger clawed for dominance inside her throat: *he wasn't being fair!* Before she could say anything else, Asif turned away and wandered off, plate of food in hand.

Back in the kitchenette, a cup of black coffee was thrust into Cat's hands. Faces loomed in at her, all pictures of concern. Cat reminded herself they were all going through the motions; they didn't really care about her at all. No one did. She was alone in the world. The only person she could rely on was herself.

'I put some brandy in it,' Dustin confessed.

'Good thinking.'

Erin leaned down by Cat's chair, brushing her hair back from her pale face and tucking it behind her ear. Though Cat loathed anyone touching her unsolicited, she let it go. She didn't want to give them any reason to think she might be faking it. She knew from Michael's death that she had to allow them to fuss round her, however annoying she found it.

'Cat?' Erin sighed, resting one hand on Cat's knee. 'At least you didn't have to find this one by yourself. What are we going to do with you, hey?'

The cubicle farm kitchen door exploded inwards. Asif appeared, eyes wild but hands still in his pockets.

'The police are here, they're asking to see her.'

Those words made Cat's stomach lurch, but she forced herself not to react. As she hoped, Erin shut that avenue down quickly.

'Not until she has been seen by a paramedic.'

'Reckon they must be on first-name basis by now,' Dustin muttered. 'What's this – like, the third death she's turned up in the middle of?'

'Found,' Erin corrected, 'the third death she's *found*.'

'Same difference.'

They were taking note. After Michael and Leila, it had been a wise choice to go with discovery via party crowd. Cat had worried that if she'd come across a third death while alone, tongues would have really begun to wag. Her caution had been justified. People were not quite the trusting fools they once were. Online culture wars, fake news and general paranoia meant people were starting to question and disbelieve things as standard. *Fool me once, shame on you. Fool me twice, shame on me.*

'Cat, what happened?' Erin crouched down next to her.

The sixty-four-million-dollar question.

Cat had worked her guts out on the party, marking off on her clipboard and murmuring into her headset while Erin swanked about in that hideous tomato-red dress talking with her friends and colleagues. Cat had watched over Erin, hoping for a lull where the older woman would go off somewhere. It wasn't imperative that Erin be missing from the main floor, but it would certainly help. She didn't want her noticing when she'd slipped away.

Cat didn't have to wait long; just until John dropped the bombshell about Peter Mackinty taking over the *Bristol Journal*. Erin had the look of every female trying not to cry. There was only one place women went when tears struck them in public.

The toilets.

Knowing she had but minutes, Cat cast an eye over the men in the available vicinity. Most were in cliques and posses; mixed company laughing.

Only one stood alone nearby: a tall, balding man with glasses and a hooked nose. He was about fifteen years older than Cat. She'd cherry-picked the man in front of her earlier when she'd confirmed the guest list. She already knew he had no plus one.

She'd watched him for a week before the party. He didn't work at Carmine Media but downstairs at the architecture firm. Even better, during all her surreptitious surveillance, she'd discovered he had a drink problem.

Cat had followed and watched him sink beer after beer in bars after work. She'd also seen him add slugs of whisky from a secret flask in his breast pocket to lunchtime drinks, even morning coffees downstairs in the Carmine café. In short, there was not a moment this particular guy was not absolutely pickled.

He was perfect.

As she cast an eye in his direction now, she could see him swaying. Since it was a party, he'd not seen the need to hide his habit as usual. He selected yet another glass of red as a waiter strayed too close. Cat grimaced as she watched him knock it back in one. She would need to make a move, soon.

When Cat was a teenager, she had one 'friend' of sorts, Kelly. They'd grown up together from nursery, right through primary and most of secondary. Then there had been that 'unfortunate' episode with Miles Blake in the sixth form.

Cat had been aware right from the off that Kelly thought herself more attractive than Cat: prettier, thinner, more interesting and superior in every way. It had been satisfying to bring her down a peg or two when Miles had asked her to the end of year beach party instead.

One thing Kelly had taught Cat over the years was that men were simple creatures. Some claimed to enjoy the chase, but most were happier if women were straight with them about what they wanted. Add alcohol and men could be the most pliable creatures on earth.

With all this in mind, Cat marched over to the architect in the corner, who watched her stalk towards him like he couldn't quite believe she'd noticed him. Little did he know he'd been on her radar for a good while.

'Hi, I'm Cat.'

'Oh . . . hi.' He blinked against heavy lids and gave her a sloppy grin. 'So, what's a nice girl like you doing talking to an old bastard like me?'

Nice girl. Cat fought the urge to roll her eyes.

'You're not old.'

She let her eyes roam over his body. For an old guy, he was okay. He had the start of a paunch, but he wasn't obese, nor was he overly hairy. He met Cat's standards, at least for what she was about to do. He didn't seem surprised or weirded out by her forthright manner, either. This was a guy who'd been round the block a few times.

'I'm Will.' He hid a belch behind his hand.

It seemed Will was so drunk that Cat would have to take the lead. That was all right. When she was in a mood like this, she felt like anything was possible. She smiled, fluttering her false lashes at him.

'Wanna go somewhere?'

'To do what?'

He liked playing innocent? Fine.

Cat leaned forward and muttered something in his ear. Then she turned on her high heels and traipsed from the room like she imagined a catwalk model would.

Checking no one was walking up and down the main corridor, she opened the door to the service corridor. She slipped into the dark landing, leaving it ajar. The door only opened outwards, if she wanted to get back into the party – and she did – then it needed not to click on the latch. She moved a fire extinguisher over to prop it open.

Seconds later, Will joined her. She'd hoped he would just want to go for it; she didn't want to have to warm him up with chit-chat first. He didn't disappoint her. He pulled her towards him and clamped his mouth on hers.

Cat forced herself not to shudder as his booze-soaked tongue forced itself between her teeth. He had to have been drinking absolutely everything on offer at the party, as well as that secret stash of whisky he carried around. He came up for air and mumbled into her neck. 'You sure?'

She nodded, moaning as he slipped his hand up her dress, between her legs. Even drunk as hell, he was good. Much better than Lawrence. Her intentions for the night faltered as she considered momentarily just fucking Will right there. It could be her reward for all her hard work at the party, not to mention revenge on Lawrence. At best, he'd made her feel unattractive for years; like he was doing her a favour by deigning to be with her. It would serve him right.

Then the shutters of Cat's mind came down. She had a job to do. She had set it all up; she needed to make her next move.

Tonight.

'Wait, wait!' She pushed him away, giggling girlishly. 'We need to get further from the party, I don't want to get caught by my boss.'

Will fixed an unfocused stare on her, grinning in a way he clearly considered charming. He looked like a shark.

'Whatever you say, sweetheart,' he slurred.

Cat gestured down the stairs with a wink and he slowly turned towards them. As he descended, his tread was heavy and unsteady. She followed him closely, looking for her opportunity. She wasn't going to mess this up.

As Will went to take a step, he turned back to catch her eye and smile. She met his gaze with steely determination and curled her foot around his ankle.

As if in slow motion she saw Will lose balance. His weight shifted forward and he grunted in panic, but in his drunken state he couldn't catch himself.

Arms windmilling, he plunged down the stairs.

She closed her eyes but she couldn't drown out the crack of bone on stair. The whole thing lasted no more than ten seconds. When she opened her eyes again, she saw him at the bottom of the steps, broken like a doll. It was horrific.

Everything had gone exactly to plan.

Cat slipped back into the party, the door shut with a

final-sounding *click* behind her as the fire exit bar snapped into place. Music was still playing in the main room. There was no way anyone could have heard them out there, and she'd purposefully picked a service corridor that was not serviced by CCTV.

She'd thought of everything.

She left it another five minutes, spoke to guests and laughed at unfunny jokes. She needed to appear unruffled, the consummate host. Then, once she had steeled herself for the performance of a lifetime, she moved to the door and pushed its big bar down, so she could slip back into the stairwell, making sure it was propped open again. Using her phone torch, she shone it around the enclosed space.

The pool of blood had grown.

He did not move; nor could she discern his chest rising and falling. She could see blackish blood oozing, and smeared on the wall. The steel steps had bitten into the back of his skull like metal teeth.

Not a good way to go.

Cat felt lightheaded, almost on the point of orgasm. She was Sharon Stone in *Basic Instinct*. She inhaled, deep into her lungs to calm herself. She couldn't go back to the party acting like a porn star. Also, she couldn't be one hundred per cent sure he was dead. She had seen too many movies like this: the heroine takes out the monster, only to venture close and have it grab her ankle.

He still didn't move.

Cat was aware Hollywood underplayed head injuries: the human skull is closer to an egg than a rock. The notion you could hit someone hard with a metal object from a height on the back of the head and they not only survive, but walk around minutes later, was ridiculous. Even if Will was still alive somehow, he would surely be in a coma. That was all she needed.

A tragic accident, fuelled by too much alcohol and carelessness. *Oops.*

She stood on the threshold of the service corridor like she'd 'just' opened the door. She hollered up the corridor towards the conference room.

'Help . . . someone, please help!'

Of course, she couldn't tell Erin the true story. In the cubicle farm kitchen, cold coffee grasped in her hands, Cat met Erin's eye.

'I-I'm not sure,' she whispered. 'I was checking we had enough flutes. I was walking past the door and heard a crash. He must have got locked out there somehow and got disorientated in the dark . . . oh God.'

She let her face crumple, hiding it so they couldn't see she had no real tears for Will. She could feel the weight of concern from the others enveloping her; it was going so well. Erin sighed, rubbing Cat's back and making soothing noises.

'It'll be okay,' Erin said, 'it'll all be okay.'

Cat clamped a hand over her mouth as if horrified, but really it was to keep her treacherous facial muscles from smiling.

After being checked out by paramedics and talking to the police about Will's death, Cat was permitted to leave the party. Hugh stepped in, gallantly saying he would pay for her taxi home. Sensing an opportunity as he waited with her for the Uber, Cat pumped him for quotes, though Hugh didn't appear to notice. He was too busy staring at her cleavage. Cat had let another button fall open.

Whatever did the job.

She arrived back at her flat. Still wired with nervous energy and sexual frustration, Cat hurried up the stairs of her block and let herself in to the flat. She went through to the bedroom and woke Lawrence up, who objected for all of three seconds as she clambered on top of him. As a participating lover he was not up to much – literally – but as a phallus, Lawrence's beat rubber, glass or plastic.

It was one of his only true uses.

Lawrence went back to sleep almost immediately, which was handy because Cat was in no mood for talking. In one of Lawrence's shirts, she padded through to the living room and opened her laptop.

Trawling through social media, she found #CurseofQueensMead on Twitter, just as she'd predicted. Perfect. The words, like before, poured out of her. Cat knew it was a good piece before she even proofread it. She called Hugh, who answered on the second ring. He wasn't annoyed at her calling in the middle of the night. In fact, he appeared impressed with her work ethic.

Good. He should be.

She read out the article, including all the quotes she'd gathered from him just hours earlier. He gave his approval, which was all she needed to send the piece to the night sub.

Then, feeling crashing fatigue in her bones, Cat fell onto the bed next to Lawrence.

Content, she descended into sleep the moment her head hit the pillow.

TWENTY-SEVEN

ERIN

I'm disquieted to find Cat's reportage of the architect's death in my inbox when I come in that morning. She'd sent it early, even though last night I'd instructed her to go home and rest. My exact words had been that I would see to it and not to worry about the report. She had taken my burden from Hugh on the party-planning; I felt I owed her, even though she'd felt like my usurper. It's weird how the brain flips back and forth as it processes events and emotions.

Instead, it appears she's stayed up all night combing through Twitter and even interviewing Hugh. It creeps me out: another man dies, and Cat not only finds him but *yet again* has enough presence of mind to file copy?

I regard the printout in my hand, tapping my red pen against my teeth. I strike through all the bits in the article where Cat has centred herself, replacing her musings with 'witnesses' and 'partygoers' instead. I don't like using red; it reminds me of school and teachers' endless passive-aggressive corrections. I have a pencil case with every colour of the rainbow to suit my mood, but I slept at David's last night and forgot my workbag.

We don't want to get the kids' hopes up (especially after the last time), so we're still carrying on like we're having an affair. I've been sneaking in after dark when Dylan and Joshua are in their bedrooms. I leave at dawn via the bathroom window, clambering into the large tree at the back of the house.

This is not strictly necessary; I could leave via the front door like a normal person, but it adds to the thrill. I love leaving David in his dressing gown and scaling the house like a gender-swapped Milk Tray man. Last night wasn't such a joyous occasion, though; I just needed a hug after another death at the Queens Mead Tower.

My corrections done, I settle back in my chair. Something feels off, but I can't work out where the stench is wafting from. Yes, Cat has been snooping around my stuff. No, I don't trust her as far as I can throw her. But Will's death was an accident. How could Cat kill someone right in the middle of a party? That's ridiculous. It has to be a horrible coincidence that she's been in the vicinity of three deaths in such a short space of time.

Through the internal window I can see the cubicle farm, deserted again. Hugh has told only the Higher Ups and senior staff to come in while police comb through the scene. I jump as my phone rings again. My nerves are shot.

'Erin, Peter's here.'

It's John, his own voice filled with false jollity; takes one to know one.

'Oh f—'

He cuts me off, just in time. 'You're on speaker phone!'

Thanks, John.

'Hello, Erin, long time no see.'

It's like stepping back in time twenty years. Peter's plummy accent does to me what it did all those years ago: I want to rip off my own ears and let them fly around the room like grotesque fleshy moths rather than listen to him and his mediocre ideas.

'Can you be a doll and join us in my office?'

John's use of 'doll' rankles, but at least his pleading tone lets me realise he hates Peter as much as I do. Moments later I am ensconced with both men, fake smile painted on as they discuss Peter's transition at Carmine. At least John gets to escape in a few weeks.

When John excuses himself to go to the lavatory, Peter sets his sights on me, full of supposed compassion. I smile back, wondering what angle he's going for this time.

'I was so sorry about you and David. I always thought you were one of those for ever couples.'

Oh, here we go.

A smirk tugs at the corner of my mouth as I consider the fact Peter is closer to the truth than he realises. Me and David *are* a for ever couple; that's why we've found our way back to each other. Peter doesn't need to know that, though.

I meet his eye. 'It's just one of those things.'

'Indeed. Well, I'm part of the divorced club, just so you know.'

Just so you know. There seems an added subtext to his comment; I want him to spell it out.

'No, I'm not sure what you mean?'

'I mean, I think it's rough you didn't get first dibs on this job.' Peter sits back in his chair, rubbing his chin with his left hand as he lets his gaze roam over me. 'Perhaps we could get a drink sometime, discuss the possibility of a job share?'

I have to stop myself from laughing right in his face. He's so transparent. How stupid does he think I am? Even if I wasn't back with David, I'd never fall for a play as blatant as this. As Peter licks his lips, I can fill in the gaps easily.

If I'm nice to you, you can be nice to me.

I feel naked under his scrutiny; I want to reach across the desk and slap his lecherous face. I'd considered the possibility Peter might have been a bastard to me back in university because he found me attractive but I'd discarded it. Those kind of playground antics had seemed beneath someone as bald-faced and ambitious as Peter.

It doesn't fit now, either. He might be prepared to sleep his way into my good books, but it wouldn't be for my sake, but for his own. Sex and power are inextricably linked for a man like him. The only person he cares about is number one.

'I don't think so,' I say, careful to keep my tone neutral.

Peter's lip curls into a sneer. 'That's a shame. I thought we could be friends this time.'

'Did you?'

I smile, keeping it open-ended. I know I need to stand up for myself and show him I won't be beguiled or intimidated, but I don't want to give him enough rope to hang me with either. By my sides, I ball my fists, pressing my fingernails into the palms of my hands. I concentrate on the sting of pinched flesh rather than him.

He slaps the desk, as if to signify the opportunity closed. We both turn our heads as John re-enters the room. He looks to each of us in turn, caught on the hop.

'What did I miss?' John says.

I proffer a grin. 'Nothing. Absolutely nothing.'

'Bye, Erin,' Peter calls after me as I leave. 'I can't wait to work with you, by the way!'

I bet you can't.

TWENTY-EIGHT

MAN DIES AFTER STAIRS ACCIDENT AT OFFICE PARTY

A MAN'S BODY WAS DISCOVERED IN THE MIDST OF A party to celebrate the refurbishment of the 'cursed' Queens Mead Tower

Cat Crawford reports.

Architect William Bridger, 41, has died in an accident at an office party. He was discovered dead at approximately 9.30 last night in a service corridor in the Queens Mead Tower. Police and ambulance crews were called to the scene, but they arrived far too late to save him.

Witnesses claim Mr Bridger must have accidentally got locked out of the main building, then fallen down the steep metal stairs when he became disorientated in the dark.

Partygoers confirm he was on his own at the party, which was to celebrate the official opening of the Queens Mead Tower. Mr

Bridger was an employee of WLM Designs, one of Bristol's most prominent architecture firms.

A police spokesperson said, 'It is our belief this was a tragic accident and details are being passed on to Bristol's coroner for the inquest.'

THE CURSE OF QUEENS MEAD TOWER?

THIS IS NOT THE FIRST DEATH AT THE QUEENS MEAD Tower this year, which is home to media conglomerate Carmine Media. One of its employees Michael Froud died when he fell to his death down an elevator shaft almost three months ago. Not long after, Carmine cleaner Leila Hardy died by suicide at her home.

In both cases, Carmine Media was singled out for criticism by Froud and Hardy's relatives and friends, as well as social media. Following Mr Bridger's death, #CurseofQueensMead is trending on Twitter once more. Screenshots:

@LilMackie45: Seriously, do we not have health and safety standards any more 'cus we left the EU???

@druzif [REPLY to @LilMackie45]: Bristol voted REMAIN, dude.

@ LardyMardy76: Something stinks here . . . and not just the body down the stairs!

240

Not all of the Twitterati were certain of the cause for complaint, however.

> @Blaq6Smak: Here's a thought, it's radical so strap yourselves in! Why not let the police do their jobs?? Or is that too hard a concept for you all …

> @saucelov5: People fall down the stairs and die all the time. Sad, but hardly show-stopping.

> @cinephile89: You can't blame Carmine Media for this one. The poor guy was probably drunk.

When I ask Mr Hugh Carmine about the supposed 'curse' of the Queens Mead Tower, he declines to comment.

'We've been co-operating fully with the police and coroner,' Carmine confirms. 'I can promise all concerned parties we will not be leaving any stone unturned.'

TWENTY-NINE

CAT

Cat woke around two o'clock the next day after the party. Lawrence was gone, the space next to her occupied by Chairman Meow, who regarded her with his typical contempt. She shooed the feline away and grabbed her mobile off the nightstand, eager to read her next viral article.

Cat rubbed the sleep out of her eyes as she struggled to comprehend what she was seeing on her phone screen. She scrolled back to the beginning, to double-check.

Someone had changed her copy!

There it was in black and white: the entire beginning was different. Cat's reference to finding Will herself was gone and had been replaced with inexact words like 'witnesses' and 'partygoers'. Cat had centred herself in the piece because she felt she deserved the credit of being first on the scene, but someone thought she could erase Cat from existence, as if she didn't matter. And there was only one person who would do something like this to her.

How dare Erin neuter her copy?

The more Cat thought about it, the more obvious it became to her. Erin hadn't just been distancing herself from Cat these last few weeks; she'd been looking for a way of sending Cat tumbling back down the ladder she'd been painstakingly making her way up.

Chairman Meow hissed and jumped up from his new spot on the floor as Cat let loose a scream of frustration. She leaned into her anger, drumming her feet on the end of the bed, kicking out with force. Only the crack of wood stopped her, breaking her out of her furious reverie.

She peered at the end of the bed and discovered she'd separated the post from the board. Oh well, it was a piece of shit anyway. Though they had a new mattress, Lawrence had found the bedframe literally next to the bins downstairs. He'd brought it up piece by piece, grinning with his ingenuity at harvesting and repurposing rubbish. Cat had let him because it was simpler. It was his only contribution to the flat apart from the apartment itself, thanks to his mother's money, as well as some curtains from his aunt and a bunch of porno magazines he didn't know Cat had found stashed behind the hot-water tank.

Rage abated, Cat got up and traipsed through to the kitchen to make herself a hot drink. The dark thoughts swirling through her head seemed to match the black coffee as she stirred it. She was so sick of being re-routed. She needed to make *Erin* realise her place. For all her talk of growing up working class, Erin had forgotten where she'd come from.

Well, screw her.

Where was Erin, now? Cat's eye was drawn to the clock. Erin was probably at Carmine Media with at least four or five of the other Higher Ups, or perhaps she'd left early as it was Friday. Maybe she was picking up her kids from school, or about to join them and David at that shitty house in the swanky postcode near the suspension bridge. There was no way she'd get face time with Erin today to sort this out. She would have to wait until after the weekend.

Which gave Cat plenty of time to come up with the perfect way to get revenge.

Cat knew there was no love lost between Erin and that jumpy little weasel Peter Mackinty. She'd even doodled little stick men she'd labelled 'Peter' in the margins of her reporter's notebook. There were targets and cartoon knives, guns and axes around them.

Cat grinned as an idea pinged in her brain. If life were a cartoon, she felt sure a badly drawn lightbulb would be hovering over her head, blinking on and off for good measure.

Looking Mackinty up online, she combed through forums and chat rooms. He was namechecked in several as a particularly bad boss. The general consensus was Peter was bombastic and obnoxious, but Cat knew how to dig deeper. Men were permitted to be difficult, it made them 'leaders'. She needed something more concrete.

Next, Cat followed various handle links back to their sources: websites, Facebook profiles, Twitter accounts. She was always staggered by how lax people were with their own social media. Locking the aggrieved people down was so easy; she made Zoom appointments with half a dozen of them that afternoon and over the weekend. The work of a good investigative journalist.

Some were only too happy to dish the dirt; others were more alarmed about going on record. When Cat reassured them it was just for her own reference and she was not publishing an article about him, more details were forthcoming.

It appeared Erin was bang on the money in her assessment of Peter Mackinty. Cat's contacts regaled her with unflattering stories. It seemed Peter was unaware of his multiple legs-up in life, yet he wielded them like a club on anyone who ever called him into question. That was more like it.

A few handles with feminine avatars or names let slip details that could only be described as sexual harassment in the post-#MeToo era, though none of them would confirm they had followed this up with a complaint to official channels. A couple of men were quite shiny-eyed about him, declaring Mackinty a 'brilliant bastard'. Though no one had the guts to come out and say it, Cat read between the lines: Peter was above nothing to curry favour with people whose influence he required. Dirty deeds or sexual favours, he was one hundred per cent committed to getting ahead.

Cat would have been impressed had Mackinty not been in her way. That was not a problem; she could get him to march to the beat of her own drum soon enough.

The young Asian man who'd attended the party with Erin last night returned to her mind. Just a few years younger than her, the sting of his rejection still rankled. Worse than that, Cat had felt completely exposed. It was as if he'd cast a look at her and seen every dark impulse flowing underneath her skin.

Asif, his name had been. She wasn't sure how he'd done it, or why her ambition had been so repulsive to him. A tiny voice at the back of her head – her conscience, perhaps – reminded her that her ambition had got two people killed, Leila and Will. Three if she included Michael. (She didn't. He'd started that.)

Cat closed this avenue of thought down; it was not productive. The thought of his face and judging brown eyes sent another paroxysm of fury through Cat. Had Erin lied and told Asif Cat was sniffing around her job, or trying to usurp her in some way? Cat was willing to bet real money Erin had. After all, Asif didn't work at Carmine Media; he didn't know how the pecking order worked there.

But what if it was true?

Cat had made serious in-roads at Carmine Media in recent weeks. She'd also been there for two years, biding her time. Erin was the outsider who'd already found herself passed over, just like she always had throughout her second-rate career. Despite Erin trying to bond with her back at brunch, they were not the same. The likes of Erin were also-rans, never destined to make the top spot. Cat was destined for greatness. She could leave Erin behind, kicking dust in her face as she went.

Cat knew just how to do it.

THIRTY

ERIN

I touch the horn lightly twice, hoping it's enough to prompt Asif through the door of his place and down the steps to my car. I've been giving him lifts to university the nights I am not with David since Asif confided to me that he's been struggling with getting himself organised. Keen to help him out, I suggested he treat university like a job, going in for nine and coming home at five. That way, between lectures he can do his coursework and planning, keeping evenings and weekends for himself. I had to do university this way so I could work a part-time job. Asif doesn't appear to have to do that, but everyone benefits from a little structure and routine.

This doesn't stop Mondays being the absolute worst, of course. I still hate them myself, twenty-five years into my working life. When Asif doesn't appear, I sigh and mash my palm on the steering wheel button. This makes a homeless guy presiding over his bag of cans by the bins jump; he turns and gives me The Finger.

I hold up a hand to signal 'sorry'. This isn't good enough for the homeless guy who replaces The Finger with an even more obscene gesture. If it had been four months earlier, I would have been mortified. Today, I simply laugh and shrug.

Asif appears, rucksack on. He trudges down his house steps. His eyes are half-closed and his hands clamped round a coffee travel mug that reads *Not Today, Satan* in glittery purple letters. It's probably been inherited from his mum. I feel an unexpected tug of affection for this woman I have never met who's probably wondering what her son is up to right now. I've no doubt that he won't be phoning home nearly enough as far as she is concerned. I'm glad I can keep an eye on him for her.

'All right.' He slides in next to me, moving in slo-mo.

I grin and gun the engine. 'Hello. Rough night?'

'Poker. I won fifty quid, though. All good.'

'You're rich. Nice one.'

My little car peels off from the kerb and we leave our road. The bins and boarded-up windows fall behind us as we pass off-licences, pubs and colourful, graffitied buildings. As we pass Turbo Island again, I send up another silent thanks to whatever deity it was that made sure Dylan had his mate looking after him when he was so drunk. It could have been so much worse.

'How are you feeling, after Thursday night?'

Asif's big brown eyes blink at me. He's not sure what I am referencing.

'After that guy . . . you know, *dying*. At the party?'

'Oh.' Asif's attention wanders from me, back to the car window. 'Fine. Obviously it's horrible, but didn't really see anything to be honest. Too many people in the way.'

I nod. I wish I hadn't seen anything, either, but I'd been right at the front next to Cat. I couldn't have missed the sight of the corpse if I'd tried. Though I hadn't known the man in the stairwell, flashbacks of that appalling injury to the back of his head somehow keep carving their way through my mind's eye. I won't even be thinking about what happened. I'll be with David and the boys, or at work, or reading a book in the bath and *BAM!* There it is again, in terrible technicolour.

I know this is a symptom of post-traumatic stress. David has been urging me to go to the doctor, but what can they do, really? I saw what I saw. I don't want to take pills. The images are bound to fade, with time. I just have to get through the next few months and keep my mind off it as much as possible.

My own issues do make me wonder how Cat is coping, though. I'm assuming she never saw Leila's body, but the architect is the second dead person she's seen in less than four months. I know the sight of Michael's broken limbs at the bottom of the elevator shaft hole really shook her up.

I'd sympathised at the time but hadn't really understood what Cat was feeling. I do now. Part of me feels a little sorry I've been keeping her at arm's length. Could I have been too suspicious, too harsh on her? Maybe she just got carried away.

I draw up outside the university. I grin and tell Asif to have a lovely day, like I'm his mum. He practically falls out the car and drags himself towards the big double doors. When he turns back to check whether I am still there, I catch his eye and give him a cheery wave. He rolls his eyes and shakes his head, then he wrenches open the doors and disappears into reception.

The morning at Carmine Media disappears in a blur of prep for a big meeting that afternoon. Peter Mackinty is already lording it up, sending memos with various demands: he wants to know all my ideas for the *Bristol Journal* asset in twenty minutes' time. He wants his office painted too; can I call decorators for quotes? He also says he wants a tray of six glazed doughnuts delivered to his desk, toot sweet.

Fucker.

I take the lift and fetch the doughnuts from the new chain coffee shop on the ground floor. I then take it back up all seven storeys and drag myself through the cubicle farm. The vast majority of staff are back after the accident last week, though I see Cat's desk and chair are still vacant. That's something: she *should* stay home this time, collect her thoughts. Maybe she's prioritising her own mental health instead of constantly striving to be productive in the midst of tragedy.

I traipse down the corridor to Peter's office, which is at the back of the building near the storerooms. I knock on the door.

'Come in!'

My heart sinks as soon as I make it across the threshold and see the tables and chairs. John's always kept it informal, no table, just chairs in a U shape. Peter's gone for an old-school set up, creating a long, long table with him at the head framed by the window. The rest of us will be forced to squint at his silhouette while he presides over us like a king in a banquet hall.

Typical.

'Erin, there you are.'

Peter makes it sound like I've kept everyone waiting, even though I've arrived at the exact time he stated. Irritation rankles, but I bury it as I take in the other people in the office with Peter. John's seated next to Peter, looking very uncomfortable. I catch his eye and signify I think the same with a single raised eyebrow. His creased, boyish face does not collapse into his customary grin.

Uh oh.

I bluff it out, placing the box on the table for Peter.

'For you,' I say through clenched teeth.

That's when I notice her: Cat. She's seated off to the side by Peter's massive yucca plant, like she's an observer. She leans forward in her chair, eyes steely with grim satisfaction. A flutter of apprehension replaces the irritation knitting its way through my muscles. Supposed 'editorial assistant' or not, I don't understand why Cat's present in a meeting with three legitimate Higher Ups like us.

What the hell is she doing here?

'Right, let's get started, shall we?'

The anxiety in John's voice is obvious; it transfers to me across the desk. Ignoring him, Peter peers at the box of doughnuts.

'Where'd you get these?'

I fight the urge to roll my eyes. 'The coffee shop on the ground floor.'

Peter tuts and slaps his meaty palms together.

'I thought so. I can't eat them.'

'What?'

My brain rebels. *What the hell is his problem?*

'There was a reason I told you to go to Joe's Doughnuts,' he says, though he doesn't offer what that reason is. 'Get rid of these, will you?'

Peter pushes them across the desk. Seething, I take a step forward to retrieve the box but Cat is there ahead of me. She springs out of her seat like a jack-in-the-box, grabbing the box to her chest and scurrying back to her chair.

'*Okay*,' I say, my tone chosen to signal I haven't the foggiest what's going on, plus I don't particularly care. 'You wanted to see me, Peter?'

'That's right.' Peter has a printout in one of his meaty hands. 'Cat's report on the architect's death Thursday night. She tells me you rewrote the beginning?'

'That's correct.'

'Want to talk me through your reasoning for that?'

My brain spasms at the question. I can't fathom why he would be asking me this. I stare at him and that dreadful affected pose of his: he sits right back from the table, right foot on left knee, hands clasped on his crotch.

'Because I have final say on edits?' I say at last.

My gaze seeks out John for sympathy but I discover he is staring out of the window and across Bristol, his thoughts elsewhere. Perhaps in his mind he is already with Bobbi, his wife of thirty-five years, their adult children and grandchildren. Not for the first time, I feel a pang of abandonment.

'Yes, you do. But I would have thought you'd have a little more understanding of the – shall we say – *nuances* of this case, regarding Cat's copy?'

There's no anger or gloating in Peter's voice. He seems level, reasonable. Men like him always set traps to inspire reactions like anger, betrayal, fury, tears – then step back and play the hard-done-by victim when it all blows up. He'd done it to me at university. I've seen him do it to others as easily as someone might flick a bit of lint off their jacket.

It couldn't possibly be me . . . look how highly strung she *is!*

'And w-w-what "nuances" am I supposed to have missed?'

I curse on the inside as my voice cracks. I can feel mortification creep up the back of my neck as the rest of the table crane their necks to look at me. Hot tears sting the back of my eyeballs. Dammit, what the hell could the problem even be? I'd somehow delivered my head on a platter to Peter just by doing my job.

Peter sighs and leans forward on the table. 'Cat's article about Michael's attack on her and subsequent death at the tower delivered the *Bristol Journal* a total of . . . how many unique hits in the end, John?'

John consults a bit of paper in his hand. 'Over two million.'

'And how many shares?'

'Two hundred and twenty-seven thousand.'

'Retweets and regrams?'

John sighs. He at least has the grace to sound grudging about feeding me to the wolves.

'One hundred and fourteen thousand and thirty-two thousand respectively.'

Peter looked to me, that steely glint in his eye. 'Yet today, we have under five hundred thousand hits, shares, retweets and regrams combined. Why do you think that is, Erin?'

I'm not having this. I won't be blamed for Cat's shitty 'Curse of Queens Mead' clickbait online bullshit running out of steam.

'Because people have moved on!' I hiss. 'They see another death at the tower, it's old news.'

'Nonsense!' Peter slams one of his fists down on the oak of his table, making the rest of us all flinch. 'People should be *more* interested, not *less* interested in a second death literally inside the tower. The readers connected with Cat. You took that element out and the results speak for themselves.'

My mind whirls. 'B-but Leila's death ... ? She just did a straight report on that. I was following what we'd done there.'

'Cat might have been the first *journalist* on the scene, but she wasn't the one to discover the body.' Peter shook his head at me, crumpling the printout in his fist. 'However, she did discover that architect's body. Here was a prime opportunity to milk the internet for clicks like we did for Michael. And you blew it!'

My cheeks flame. *Stick a fork in me, I'm done.*

'I see.'

I cannot conjure any more words into being. I just stand there.

John coughs to break the tension. I feel the weight of everyone's eyes lift off me as their attention moves to him, instead. I feel woozy, like I might faint dead on the ground. He chooses his words.

'I think Erin got the message, Peter.'

Peter almost lets me skulk off, waiting until I try and move towards the door before telling me he 'needs another word'. Heart sinking all over again, I stay. John slopes off, squeezing my arm in solidarity as he passes. Eyes stinging with furious tears, I watch Cat creep by, wide-eyed and giving me a wide berth.

Why the hell couldn't she have raised this with me? Why did she go over my head?

The other two gone, I stand, awkward. Peter lounges back on the table, arms folded. He smiles at me like a caring and compassionate grandparent. Though he can't have more than a couple of years on me or David, he looks a good decade older.

'What am I going to do with you, hey?'

I purse my lips. 'I don't know what you mean.'

'You've not been on your "A" game lately. Anything I can do to help?'

The audacity of his patronising tone hits me in the solar plexus. My rage goes from 0 to 60. As my nostrils flare, I surreptitiously pinch myself at the top of my leg to distract myself. I can't go nuclear, not right here and right now, when we're alone.

It's what Peter wants.

'Everything's fine.'

I drip honey into my voice, in case he might detect the poison: *Die, fucker!*

Peter smiles. 'Oh. Well, that is a relief. Make sure you brush up on viral marketing tactics with Marge, will you? I want to see you've booked an appointment with her on the shared office calendar before the end of today.'

I fight the urge to groan. Marge is one of the head nerds at Carmine Media. She lives online, so there's nothing she can't do when it comes to viral marketing strategies for the assets. But because she lives online, relating to other people in meat space is not her forte. I grit my teeth, my smile more of a snarl.

'Consider it done.'

Peter claps again, his signal that he's done talking and is bored with me. I don't wish him goodbye but turn on my heel and stalk out, keen to be away from him. All the while, my treacherous brain runs a litany in my head: *how the hell are you going to stand working with him without killing him?*

Peter's office door clunks shut behind me like earth on a coffin lid.

THIRTY-ONE

CAT

It couldn't have gone better with Erin. She'd waltzed into Peter's office looking so sure of herself, but she'd been caught on the back foot. She'd been humiliated, good and proper, and Cat loved it.

Erin had underestimated Cat. The older woman had thought she was just a lackey, a nobody, a drone. That would teach her! Cat floated through the rest of Monday, delighting in her own cleverness in going straight to Peter, Erin's sworn enemy.

On Tuesday, Cat awoke with an increased sense of optimism. She fended off Lawrence's lecherous advances and got in the shower, washing quickly to avoid Lawrence wrestling her out of the stall again in revenge. She needn't have worried; he'd rolled over and gone straight back to sleep.

Towelling herself dry, Cat reflected on her massive win

over Erin. She'd played Peter and John like a banjo over her neutered copy. As soon as Cat had seen that likes, comments, shares and regrams were significantly lower with Will's death than Michael's, she'd realised she could take Erin down.

It had worked.

Now Erin was done. This meant she was never going to accept Cat back into her 'inner circle'. That was okay; Cat was sure the older woman had zero to offer her now.

Erin was on her way out.

Cat wanted to accelerate that process, get rid of Erin once and for all. John was basically retired now, no threat whatsoever. She needed to make sure she could ingratiate herself with Hugh and Peter more somehow.

But how?

Cat left the flat without saying goodbye to Lawrence. She arrived at Carmine Media and stalked through the cubicle farm towards her own desk. Helena popped up like a meerkat from behind one of the screens as Cat passed, calling to her across the newsroom.

'Morning, Cat! Peter wants to see you.'

Cat whirled round; Helena's orange-and-rouge-face was hard to miss. As much as she wanted to bawl Helena out, she counselled herself she could afford to be charitable to the bottom-feeders like her in the cubicle farm. Cat was flying high with the big boys now, while poor Helena and her ilk were destined to do the grunt jobs for ever.

'Cheers,' Cat said.

Her cheery disposition matched the smile on her face as she breezed down the corridor towards Peter's office. She felt certain this meeting would confirm it all: she'd proved herself with the party, still bringing yet more hundreds of thousands of clicks to Carmine Media, even allowing for Erin's blatant sabotage. Peter and Hugh would reward her with her own office and view at last, Cat was certain of it.

'Ah, Cat.' Peter's own grin reminded her of a wolf's. 'Do sit down.'

There was something brittle about Peter's demeanour. Cat's optimism took a hit but she did as she was told, her eyes roaming around the office. Peter's surroundings were typically macho and needlessly grandiose. His various business awards were lined up on a shelf behind him, as well as pictures of him shaking hands with celebrities.

Last time she'd been in the room, Peter had been tearing a strip off Erin. Like all good journalists, Cat trusted her gut. Something about Peter screamed a message to her across the desk.

It was her turn for bad news.

'You did a great job with the party.' Peter stretched out a hand and looked at his manicure as he addressed her. 'But since it's over, it's felt your talents would be better spent back in the cubicle farm working with the word monkeys full time now.'

There it was.

A ball of pain lodged in Cat's throat, making it difficult to speak.

'What does Hugh say about this?'

'It was a directive from Hugh.'

She doubted that very much. Hugh had worked one-on-one

with Cat for the second leg of the party. He had also always been very accommodating of Cat, giving quotes for her articles and even waiting with her at the taxi rank after Will's death. She'd felt sure that if she could spend more time with Hugh, he would be the key to accelerating her career. She couldn't see any reason why that assumption was wrong. Peter must be jealous, just like Erin.

'Could I speak with Hugh about this?'

Peter's mask slipped and a bark of laughter erupted from his mouth.

'You'd do well to remember who you answer to, Catrin.'

The use of her full name felt like salt on the wound. Of course Cat's hard-won editorial assistant title was being stripped from her. Why would Peter care about her now he was editor and John's-retirement-party-come-tower-refurb party was over? She raised her head in defiance.

'That's what I mean. I answer to Hugh, not you. I was – am! – his editorial assistant.'

'You're focused too much on "assistant". Hugh's party is done. The key word in your little "promotion"' – Peter provided air quotes – 'is *editorial*. Need I remind you that I am in charge of the writing roles here? I don't have any room for you in the staff reporter positions right now. *Capeesh?*'

His words felt like a stab in Cat's chest. Even though it hadn't come with any extra money, her assistant position had given Cat the validation she craved. She'd hoped to retain it, to help Peter and Hugh on a more permanent basis. She didn't really care how; she just wanted them to think she was indispensable.

Instead, it had been confirmed: she was disposable. She'd been thrown away, boomeranging back to press releases and NIBs and all the other boring shit. She was back where she started.

'Is this because Erin neutered my copy?'

Peter blinked, like he'd forgotten all about that. He probably had; he was that self-absorbed. He smirked at her, oily and insincere.

'Not at all. Besides, if the mood takes you, then you can always write those great articles of yours from the cubicle farm, no?'

So that was Peter's game. He wanted whatever he could get from her, but also to make sure Cat knew her place and didn't get ideas above her station. Just like Erin.

Cat did not make a scene. That would not get her anywhere. She shrugged, making out everything was fine and shook hands with him. Then she went to the cubicle farm and told the office manager she had a migraine. She went straight home, fighting tears all the way.

At the flat, Lawrence was asleep on the sofa with Chairman Meow draped across his chest like a fluffy black and white feather boa. Creeping past them, Cat made her way to the bedroom and opened her reporter's notebook and laptop.

There must be something she could do to recover her position, if not literally then metaphorically? Now that she'd burned her bridges with Erin, she needed Hugh back on side.

Peter was in her way.

She revisited her notes about Peter, combing through them. It was clear he was not well liked by anyone she'd quizzed a few days earlier. He'd still received the kind of grudging, automatic respect-stroke-fear powerful men always do. No one had been willing to stick their heads above the parapet, even the women who'd made veiled accusations of sexual harassment by him.

When she appeared from the bedroom around teatime, she discovered the sofa was vacant of both the cat and Lawrence. He'd left no note again. She made herself a Pot Noodle and retired to bed, feeling desolate and worthless. She slept badly, waking every hour or so, the space next to her unoccupied.

Drifting off around two, Cat awoke at six to find Lawrence asleep, fully clothed with his shoes on at the foot of the bed. When she attempted to make it into the bathroom without waking him, his arm snaked out and grabbed her.

'And where do you think you're going?'

Lawrence's voice was unyielding, like a parent's catching an errant teenager sneaking out the bedroom window.

'Work. Where else?'

He tutted and let go of her.

Cat thought over what she'd learned about Peter as she walked to work, hoping for inspiration to strike. Like so many before him, Peter's bad behaviour was an 'open secret'. He had humiliated female writers in meetings; brushed up against them in lifts, stairwells and corridors; made comments on their clothes, hair and work ethics. He'd shouted down black and Asian women who'd raised concerns about systemic racism; he'd laughed at LGBTQ women raising their own workplace concerns. He'd penalised mothers who needed to pick up their kids early and fired multiple (unpaid) female interns for various imagined transgressions.

The men were not safe, either. Cat had heard tales of Peter taking male writers to strip clubs and threatening to fire those who'd objected, especially gay and bisexual men. He'd mimicked their voices, cussed out their mistakes and sent whispers around offices about their competency. It was no surprise the few who'd attempted to take him on in the past had seen their careers ruined.

Peter Mackinty was, in short, a grade A, old boys' network-protected, over-privileged gammon who thought nothing could touch him because literally nothing had in his forty-eight years.

He deserved to die.

This thought bubbled up and popped inside Cat's brain, bringing an end to the roiling anxiety inside her stomach. It was so obvious: with Peter dead and out of her way, Cat would have the opportunity to get back in with Hugh again. She could remind him of how she'd stepped into the breach with the tower refurb party; that she'd brought hundreds of thousands of new visitors to the *Bristol Journal*. That she was wasted as a mere word monkey. She could be editorial assist-ant again but, this time, as Hugh's number one. She would make sure it was written into the contract, instead of taking it on trust like last time.

She was a genius!

Throughout the day at work, in between rewriting press releases and fielding calls, Cat jotted down a list of possible accidents that could befall Peter. It had to be at Queens Mead

Tower, to make sure Cat could frame it as one of her 'Curse of Queens Mead' articles.

It would be harder now than ever; Cat would have to be even more cunning. She knew people were talking about her string of 'bad luck'. A fourth death was sure to raise alarms. Engineering another accident inside the tower would be a challenge.

At work, Cat looked at her watch: it was just after half eight in the morning. Peter would not be at his desk yet. He'd arrive last, around ten in the morning, barking instructions and demands as soon as he set foot in the place.

She'd scoped out his routine in detail as soon as he'd joined Carmine Media. A fan of *The West Wing*, Peter always demanded everyone 'walk and talk' with him, like he was president of the United States. Then he would buzz up his yoga instructor, an earnest young man who looked like he was there under sufferance and hated every minute.

Forty-five minutes later, Peter would be stretched and meditated but no less Zen. He'd take a tour of the cubicle farm, stopping by computers and reading screens over people's shoulders. If lucky, the word monkey in question was left alone as he passed by; if not, the unfortunate scribe would have to justify every single word choice. Nine times out of ten, Peter would bawl them out and tell them to start again. Then he'd return to his office for Zoom calls.

Peter always took a long lunch because he rarely left Carmine before nine or ten at night. This meant that most days he wasn't seen after lunch again until approximately four o'clock in the afternoon, just as everyone else was winding down. Cat had heard him say he liked being one of the few in the building in the evening as he could 'hear himself think'.

As Cat went to fetch herself a coffee, her gaze strayed to her colleagues' desks as she passed. Framed family pictures; the kids' drawings; postcards displayed. No one ever wrote to Cat or sent cards. Cat rarely regretted going through life more or less alone, but she did when it came to post. She wasn't sure why she wanted to receive a 'miss you' or 'wish you were here' from a pen pal. That would mean maintaining a friendship, which seemed far too much like hard work. Perhaps because sending such stuff through the post would mean someone remembered her? That was what Cat craved: recognition.

She just didn't want to be forgotten.

Cat had been left alone once, but never again. Wasn't that at the heart of her current mission? The problem was viral articles died quickly. Joe Public had a short memory.

Judith Crawford used to say newspapers were 'tomorrow's chip paper'. Cat was too young to remember this. She was born into a world on the cusp of the internet, or 'the information superhighway', as it had been known in the early nineties. By the time she was at primary school, every classroom had a computer. When she made it to secondary school, social media was on every mobile handset.

Cat had watched other girls at school get trolled and cyberbullied, but no one had ever turned their attention to her. They'd barely noticed her at all. Cat had been a ghost in her own life, watching others, never truly part of it. Even those she had thought of as friends were just associates really. No one called her during half term breaks or the summer holidays. She was left alone, always.

Not any more.

Cat had managed to harness the power of internet popularity. Her articles were shared and read by thousands, but it was short lived before they vanished into the digital ether; she had to catch the wave when she could. No one must stand in the way of that. Cat understood the news cycle would continue unabated. Cat's efforts would disappear, as if she'd done nothing at all.

It would never be enough.

As this thought flowered in her brain, Cat grinned. That was where she'd been going wrong! She'd been concentrating on the accidents and being 'first on the scene', when what she needed was to focus on *herself*. Peter had more or less confirmed this when he'd talked of 'nuances' to Erin yesterday, as well as their readers 'connecting' with Cat.

She needed something terrible to happen to *her*.

Whatever it was, the terrible event needed to be big enough for Cat to dine out on for years. She would be brave, but she was not above inviting pity too. She would do all the chat shows. To have any longevity, she needed to divide opinion, which meant courting others' disgust or even disbelief. She had to inspire people to rush to condemn and defend her on social media. People would make videos on YouTube, TikTok and Snapchat, sharing their hot takes. Cat would write a memoir. She'd make bank and Millie Bobby Brown could play her in the inevitable movie that would come next.

The more she thought about it, the more of a slam dunk it seemed.

Cat could find herself 'in trouble' with Peter Mackinty and kill him in 'self defence'.

She would be the whistle-blower for the misogyny in this industry. She would become the figurehead for frontline inequality. Not one but *two* men assaulting her within a single company? No self-respecting feminist could ignore what Cat had been through. She'd discovered that with Michael, hadn't she? In contrast, Peter's ill-behaviour was legendary; no one could say she was exaggerating. She would bring the whole company to its knees.

Cat turned the page in her notebook and started to scrawl in it, listing everything she needed to make it work, as well as everything that could potentially go wrong. *Forewarned is forearmed*, another of Judith Crawford's sayings. Satisfied, Cat sat back and regarded her handiwork, sure she'd thought of everything this time.

All she needed was an opening.

THIRTY-TWO

ERIN

I reach for my mug of tea to discover yet another has gone cold on me. I can't seem to concentrate. There are reports that need writing; piles of copy that need editing; a million appointments and calls that need to be made. I can't focus on any of it.

Fresh from my humiliation with Peter, the stress of the past few weeks (not to mention seeing the architect's body in the stairwell) rushed back in at me like a tidal wave. I woke the next day crying and shaking, much to David's horror. As he fussed around me, bringing me drinks and stroking the hair back from my tear-stained face, I realised I'd never let him see me as anything but the strong woman I'd projected out into the world; not even when my mother died. I'd swallowed it down and got on with it.

At David's insistence, I took the rest of the week off

268

as holiday. I pleaded a family emergency with Peter, who accepted my word with no apparent pushback. It meant I missed John's official leaving drinks that following Friday, but I knew he understood. I let myself flop on the sofa for three days as my brain recalibrated.

Asif was perturbed when he saw I wasn't in my basement flat; he turned up at David's, carrying a bouquet of petrol-station carnations and wearing a worried expression. I reassured him that David was taking good care of me at our old home, bringing me tea and Maltesers whilst I watched old box sets of *Friends*, the only thing I could focus on. Even the boys seemed to know I needed to be handled with kid gloves. They tiptoed around me, speaking in exaggerated whispers. Not once did I hear them screaming at their Xboxes.

After the weekend, I snap out of my malaise. By Monday morning, I'm ready for work again. David is not happy, even attempting to stand in the way of the front door.

'I don't think you should go.'

He folds his arms, resolute. Part of me feels grateful for the choice being taken away from me. I *should* stay here. Life is too short for this crap. Then my inner feminist reminds me I have worked too hard to let men make my decisions for me. I can't let the likes of Peter and Cat destroy everything.

'I have to.'

'You don't.' David's voice is soft, his face earnest. 'I spoke to Peter.'

'You did WHAT?'

He continues, like I haven't just shouted at him. 'Honestly, Erin, he was really sympathetic. He agreed with me, says you

269

can take this week off too. He said you push yourself way too hard.'

I bet he did.

David doesn't quite know Peter like I do. Me being off with stress is a gift to men like him. During my absence Peter will have been swanning around the office, supposedly empathising with people over my 'terrible time' and secretly dripping poison in the ear of anyone who will listen, undermining me. If I am not around, my abilities will be called into question, my previous track record stripped away by his manipulative concern-trolling.

I can't let it happen. I just can't.

So I am back at my desk, wading through my To Do list. I am taking too long; I have to read every sentence twice to comprehend it. Clearly a part of my brain is faulty, its wiring short-circuiting after seeing Will's body. I know the only answer is rest. I need more time with my loved ones, more chocolate and more Netflix.

In my office, I watch Cat in the cubicle farm through the internal window. She swipes through an iPad. Her folders, pens and notebook are sprawled out on the desk in front of her. I look at the clock on my phone and see it's coming up for nine o'clock in the evening. I see a bunch of text notifications from David, asking pointedly when I will be back this evening.

In truth, I would love nothing more than to go home right now. There's a part of me that wants to leave Carmine Media tonight and never return. I could email Peter my resignation, go back to David and ask him to consider changing our family's work–life balance for good. Giving up my flat is a natural step; we'd be saving hundreds of pounds in rent per month for starters. Financially it would still be a struggle if we're both freelance, but there is good equity in our home. We could sell the house in Clifton and downsize. It would mean some considerable changes to family life, but we could do it . . .

Couldn't we?

A renewed surge of energy makes its way through my body as I think about clearing all my admin tasks this evening. Then I can pull myself together tomorrow and really achieve something, instead of going around in perpetual circles. If I can find someone else to do some of the basic admin, I can get it done in half the time.

'Just another hour,' I mutter.

My mind made up, I stalk over to my office door. I open it, calling out to Cat in the cubicle farm. She's the only one still there.

'Cat, can you give me a hand?'

The younger woman looks up, no trace of embarrassment or trepidation on her face. Little madam. The last time we'd been together had been in Peter's office, when he'd castigated me for rewriting Cat's copy about the architect's death. She really does have ovaries of steel.

'Sure.'

She starts to gather up her belongings to move into my office. I catch her as she attempts a surreptitious glance at her watch.

'You have to get back?'

'Just my boyfriend.' She smiles. 'But he's a big boy, he can amuse himself.'

I've never met him, but I've seen him in the street with her, plus there's a photo of him on her desk. Even behind glass, he's one of those public schoolboys who thinks he's 'street'. He's not even attractive, but tall and thin, with a mad mop of Boris Johnson-style hair and a bum fluff beard. If men were gifts, he is not even the consolation prize.

Love or hate her, I still can't imagine what a young go-getter like Cat sees in him. She might not be conventionally attractive, but it's obvious that if she made a little bit more of herself, she could turn heads. Not for their sake, either, but her own. I am pretty sure I saw today's outfit on the rack three decades ago at stores that closed their doors before she was even born. Cat has that steely determination to make things happen; it's weird she still dresses like a twelve-year-old from 1992.

As Cat sits down with me, her gaze falls on my cold tea.

'Let me freshen that up for you.'

Before I can object and tell her I don't want any more tea, she's gone. I return to staring at my work.

When Cat hasn't returned after five minutes, I start to feel impatient. At least, I think it's been five minutes; in truth, time has been a little sketchy for me of late. Sometimes I blink and sixty minutes have passed; other times I feel certain I must have been staring at something for an hour, only to discover it's seconds. I know, I know: I shouldn't be back at work, I should go home and stay there . . . but I just can't.

I can't let Peter take everything away from me. I've worked too hard.

That's when the screaming starts.

Screams do something to you. They are visceral, pulling you to your feet even as a simultaneous dread sinks through your bones. Though I don't want to, I find myself racing to the door and up the corridor, towards the source.

Feeling the crash of blood in my ears, I leave one of my high heels behind me on the carpet, but I don't stop. I kick the other one off and keep running in my stockinged feet down the same corridor I'd run along during the tower relaunch party. Memories sear through my mind like reflections in a hall of mirrors: of the dead man in the stairwell; of Cat's white face and bloodless lips.

Still I run.

I find myself outside Peter's palatial office, the door ajar. I push the door inwards and creep across the threshold. The blinds are closed. Moving from the well-lit hallway into the dark room causes me to pause as my eyesight readjusts.

The faint blue light from a monitor on the wall enables me to see a little better. I start to pick out details in the gloom, smelling the dank air in there. I can taste the acrid stench of sweat and urine and something else, though my brain is not ready to catch up yet.

I find myself standing next to a young woman in tatty blue jeans. It takes me a moment to place her, even though I've seen her only a few minutes earlier.

It's Cat.

I grab her by the shoulder, but she doesn't turn towards

me. She is staring at something next to the far wall, near the television. I can see that same thing in my peripheral vision, but I don't want to look at it. I can't turn my neck to see. It's too much. What the hell is it about this girl? Dark shadows follow her wherever she goes.

'Cat?' I whisper.

I want her to answer. I don't want her to answer. She doesn't tear her eyes away from what she's looking at.

My stomach falls as she raises a hand and points. I brace myself and turn towards the horror, knowing what I will see before I even lay eyes on it.

Peter, dead in his chair.

PART FOUR

I have love in me the likes of which you can
scarcely imagine and rage the likes of which
you would not believe. If I cannot satisfy the
one, I will indulge the other.

MARY SHELLEY

THIRTY-THREE

CAT

Peter was dead. But it wasn't by Cat's hand.

She'd arrived in his office, intent on setting him up in her trap. She knew he wouldn't be able to resist an opportunity to abuse his authority with a young woman, working so late into the evening. Peter was a predator who'd so far got off scot-free. Some might characterise her less as a murderer than an avenging angel. Men like the Peter Mackintys of this world were asking for it.

Unfuckingbelievable!

The police officer assigned to them was a young man, with just a few years on Cat, clearly nervous. This meant he double-checked every tiny detail, much to her chagrin. Cat had been distracted by the irony of being 'first on the scene' for real this time, so had to stop herself from laughing.

'He's dead,' Cat told the young police officer, 'that's all there is to it.'

She had arrived in Peter's office, the sharp letter opener in her pocket. She'd been undecided about whether to provoke his ire or stage it afterwards. She'd come to the conclusion on the way up the corridor that a few knocked-over chairs and a bloody nose for her should do the trick. She'd been almost chipper when she'd knocked on Peter's door and crossed the threshold into his flashy hell-pit of an office.

That's when she saw him.

Peter sat upright at his desk, staring into the distance. His face was contorted, his cheeks flushed red; it reached all the way to his neck. One hand lay palm up in his lap, the other reaching forwards, towards the phone only just out of his reach. At his feet: a glazed doughnut.

Typical!

Cat supposed he must have had a heart attack. He was old and fat and it seemed the most likely scenario. She cast her mind back to when she'd last seen Peter. She'd seen him berate two writers in the cubicle farm that morning, then he'd demanded his usual box of doughnuts around midday, but she'd lost track of his routine after that. From the grey tinge on his lips, Cat guessed he'd been dead and cold an hour at least, maybe more.

David arrived shortly after the police, this time to pick up Erin. He'd stalked into Carmine Media, eyes roaming everywhere. Cat froze where she was, annoyed she hadn't been able to excuse herself before he got there.

His brow furrowed as he took in Cat's face. She knew with an inward groan he was struck by the sight of her, trying to pinpoint where he'd seen her before. Lawrence had been right

278

on the button when she'd said most people don't notice stuff right in front of their faces, but it seemed David was one of the irritating few who did.

Making a decision on the spot, Cat grabbed his hand and shook it.

'You must be David, heard a lot about you,' she said. 'I'm Cat.'

'Have we met?' David replied.

Cat smiled. 'Don't think so. Guess I have one of those faces.'

The tension seemed to dissipate. David smiled back.

Phew.

Erin appeared moments later, tearful. Cat fluttered her eyelashes at the young police officer, who gave her a lift home. She was thankful to discover the flat was empty; Lawrence was nowhere to be seen. He'd left no passive-aggressive notes, nor had he texted.

Good.

Cat grabbed a tub of ice cream from the freezer and sat cross-legged on top of the breakfast bar, spooning it into her mouth.

She was disappointed she'd not been able to enact her plan. She had been excited to make her mark with this death and bring Carmine Media to its knees.

Cat might have launched from obscurity, but there was no reason to stay that way. Her mother had told Cat she could be anything she wanted to be. She had taken Judith Crawford at her word. The internet's relentless memes, infographics, videos, reels and gifs about meritocracy and bootstrap theory had only sharpened this hunger in her; Cat felt it as keenly as the blood that moved in her veins.

She deserved this.

The sugar lifted her spirits. Cat's anger, frustration and pessimism began to recede, allowing her to think more clearly. She understood disappointment was clouding her vision. She'd wanted to be the one to strike Peter down, but the fucker was still dead. That was a win for women everywhere, but especially those at Carmine Media. They'd only had to stand his bullshit for about a month. *Result*.

It was true Cat's plan was as dead as Peter. As fruitful as it could have been, she acknowledged the risk had been huge. It might even work out better this way. Could a second attempted assault have cast her motives in doubt? Maybe.

Yes, it was definitely safer this way. She was unlikely to have got off with a self-defence claim, especially with her family history. There would have been a trial. Whilst Cat was confident she could have been found not guilty of murder, she still might have received a custodial sentence for manslaughter.

Going to jail might have been worth it – especially selling her story as a 'miscarriage of justice' – but short-term Cat would have had to deal with prison life. She was no tough nut. If events got out of control, she might even have died in there.

Peter's unexpected death had shocked even her, but now that Cat had had a few hours to get used to the idea, she realised it changed nothing. Whilst she might miss out on the notoriety of being the journalist attacked not once, but twice at work, Peter was still dead. She could report on it as part of her 'Curse of Queens Mead' series of articles, plus it left the way clear for her to try and get back in with Hugh.

As for Erin, she would hopefully see Peter's death as a sign from the gods and finally leave Carmine Media. She'd outstayed her welcome as it was. *Good riddance!* But even if she didn't, Cat had nothing to fear from Erin any more. Every roadblock Erin had thrown up in her path so far, Cat had knocked aside. The older woman had proved herself a weak adversary. Erin would surely slink away, tail between her legs.

As she should.

Cat licked the spoon and threw it in the sink.

She was back on track.

THIRTY-FOUR

THIRD DEATH INSIDE 'CURSED' QUEENS MEAD TOWER

NEWS EDITOR PETER MACKINTY, 48, FOUND DEAD IN own office

Cat Crawford reports.

A third death has occurred in the Queens Mead Tower, Bristol, leading many who live in the city to speculate again that the recently refitted building is 'cursed'.

News editor Peter Mackinty, 48, was found dead in his own office on Tuesday night. Mackinty's death is thought to be the result of anaphylactic shock.

Anaphylactic shock is a rare but severe allergic reaction that can be deadly if you don't treat it immediately. It's most often caused by an allergy to food, insect bites and stings, or certain medications. Treatment is via an adrenaline shot, but it appears Mr Mackinty was unable to call emergency services in time.

Carmine Media acquired Bristol News Group, publishers of the *Bristol Journal*, six months ago. Mackinty replaced editor John Windsor, 69, who was supposed to retire last month.

'It's hard to believe,' Windsor says, 'I'd spoken to him only the day before, wished him well. Then this happens.'

THE CURSED TOWER

MACKINTY'S DEATH IS THE THIRD INSIDE THE NEWLY refurbished Queens Mead Tower in the past four months. Carmine Media employee Michael Froud died when he plunged five storeys in January. The architect William Bridger died in another freak accident in a service corridor stairwell in April. In March, another Carmine employee Leila Hardy died when she took her life, this time at her own home.

'I'm as shocked as anyone,' says company CEO Hugh Carmine. 'I'm sick at heart to think of three people dying inside the tower in such a short time. However, it's important not to conflate Peter's death with the previous two. There was no accident here, just a sad fact of life: some people are allergic and just shouldn't eat certain things.'

These comments led to a furious backlash on social media, with many users claiming Mr Carmine 'victim blamed' Mr Mackinty.

The death has also led many Bristolians – and those further afield online – to speculate once again that the building is 'cursed'. #CurseofQueensMead has been trending on Twitter since the story broke, as well as #55CentralParkWest, a reference to the haunted New York apartment building where the evil Zuul appeared in the 1984 classic movie *Ghostbusters*. The internet's snark and meme game has been strong too.

@Aristattle66: You don't have to be dead to work here, but it helps.

@Bang2write: Who you gonna call?? Well, not Carmine Media!

@druzif: Honestly, if Queens Mead's gargoyles came alive and killed everyone, literally no one would be surprised at this point.

@99TruthTellers: Did the refit at Queens Mead open a door to another dimension? Because that would explain a lot.

@ParrotSchmarrot: If the offices, stairwells and corridors are that deadly at Queens Mead, I ain't touching the fridge in the break room!

Other internet users preferred less supernatural takes:

@UnicornHair40: This is an OFFICE TOWER, why so many deaths?? Seems suss.

@DevintheCat81: The lack of mental health provision for

employees and shoddy health and safety practices is NOT FUNNY.

@LucyVHayAuthor: Thank goodness we had Brexit, I'd hate for health and safety at work to be a thing ... oh.

THIRTY-FIVE

ERIN

'That's it,' David says after Peter's death. 'You're moving back in here. Permanently.'

I blink at him, unable to compute the sudden turnaround. After Peter's death, I spent another three or four days lying on the sofa again. With David's firm words, I can feel my stupor lift, like I am reconnecting to reality. Hope starts to pierce the numbness I'd attempted to chase away with more chocolate and Netflix.

'But what about the boys and going slow?'

'I think that ship has sailed.' David shakes his head at me, exasperated. 'You've spent most nights here for the past few weeks. They know full well you haven't been sleeping on the sofa. Plus those boys literally came out of your actual body. I'd say "going slow" is at bit pointless at this juncture.'

'I know, I just don't want them to get hurt. What if we screw up again?'

David smiles and pulls me closer to him. 'We won't. Erin, you've taken care of us for years, even when you didn't live here. I want to take care of you now.'

A warm feeling blooms in my chest. This is what I've dreamed of for so long: being back with my precious family. I blew it first time around by being a workaholic, pushing them all away in my bid for greatness. I won't make that mistake again.

'Let's go and get your things while the boys are at school.' David pushes my hair out of my eyes. 'It'll be a nice surprise for them.'

'Good idea. But don't you have a client call at midday?'

David glances at the clock and swears; it's twenty to. I laugh.

'Don't worry, I'll go. I want to say goodbye to the old dump anyway.'

'You sure?'

'Absolutely.'

Leaving David, my limbs and body no longer feel heavy. I send a quick message on my phone to my landlord to give my notice before grabbing some black bin liners and sliding behind the wheel of my car. I surprise myself as I notice I'm whistling.

Taking it as a good sign, I grab my phone again before I start the car engine. I want to check the headlines for Peter's death, something I've put off doing. I'm not looking for the lurid details – I was there, after all – but rather, just one particular byline.

Cat's.

I find it without too much trouble. It's gone viral, its growth fed by social media. She's mined Twitter and even managed to get comments from both John and Hugh.

Hugh must have checked over her copy before it was published; that would have been the deal in return for his quote. I marvel at how brazen he is, courting more scandal in the midst of an existing one. He likes to give the impression of being clueless and aloof, but I realise he would have chosen the words 'sad fact of life' on purpose to enrage the social-justice warriors online. Cat's building a career on her 'Curse of Queens Mead' crap again. She is as shameless as Hugh.

Their tactics have worked: I see countless comments pushing back. As despicable as I found Peter, this all leaves a bad taste in my mouth. It feels exploitative because it is.

It's been a while since I was home at the flat, so the air smells stale when I let myself in. I grab all my clothes, shoes, bed linen and toiletries and shove them in the black bags. I don't have any ornaments of note, just a few pictures and a couple of boxes of books. I manage to clear the whole place in about forty minutes.

Looking at my belongings, I emit a happy sigh. It's not much to make up a life in the last three years, but that doesn't matter. I don't care about what I do or don't own, I have my precious family back. I close the front door for the last time, posting the key through the letterbox.

My things gathered, I emerge at the top of the basement steps just in time to see Asif and his white housemate shoving cardboard into the bins. His eyes brighten to see me.

'Karen!' He winks. 'You back again?'

'No,' I laugh, 'and that's Mrs G to you.'

I tell him I am moving back with David and the boys. I can see sadness in Asif's eyes; he's come to rely on me as much as I've relied on him over the past couple of months. Before I overthink it and chicken out, I grab him and give him a big hug.

'How about dinner, next week?'

Asif disentangles himself and nods in that nonchalant way young lads do, like he's not bothered either way. I can tell he's relieved and pleased.

We stare at each other for a moment, awkward, unsure what to stay. We're bonded by circumstance, whether we like it or not. Asif has helped me work through some realisations about my family and for that I will always be grateful.

As these thoughts glimmer through my mind, something else occurs to me. Before Asif can bid me goodbye and disappear back into his flat, I stop him.

'You met that girl I work with, Cat, at the tower party?'

He nods. 'Yeah. Why?'

'No particular reason,' I muse. 'It's just a case of journo gut.'

Asif looks at me askance, so now I feel compelled to explain. 'You ever feel that someone is dodgy ... *here*?' I rub my stomach. 'You can't explain it, maybe you don't have any evidence. You just *feel* it?'

He nods, accepting my word. 'Yeah, Cat was like that. She's an odd one for sure.'

Finally. Someone who gets it!

I seize on his words, anxious for his thoughts but not

wanting to influence him to tell me what I want to hear. I need details.

'How so?' I prompt.

Asif sniffs. 'Hard to explain. She was a low-key racist for starters, but honestly, that's not unusual. You get used to that, like it's background noise.'

I grimace. 'Anything else?'

'She was really insistent. Too insistent. Like she wanted something from me. It creeped me out. Later, I saw her talking to that architect guy. You know the one who wound up dead?'

This titbit of information sets my brain aflame all over again.

'You tell the police?'

'Yeah, course. But what does that prove? She was the party organiser. She probably spoke to everyone in the tower that night.'

'You didn't see her go anywhere with him?'

'No, I was in the toilets with you.'

Oh, right, of course he was. Damn. Given my concerns about Cat have been continually invalidated since Michael's death, I ask one last question of Asif.

'Do you think I'm being paranoid?'

Asif smiles at me. 'Absolutely not. My mum taught me it pays to be on your guard. It's a dangerous world ... and people like Cat are not to be underestimated.'

His bombshell dropped, Asif goes back inside.

THIRTY-SIX

CAT

The last few days had been brilliant.

Erin hadn't returned to work yet, leaving the way clear for Cat. She didn't want to rush back too quickly and arouse suspicion, so she waited until the third day after Peter's death, then made her appearance to soak up everyone's amazed praise.

They told her she was a warrior, a true professional. She averted her gaze like she was uncomfortable, but secretly she lapped it up. Helena brought her cups of coffee without being asked. People she didn't even know stopped by Cat's cubicle, telling her how brave she was. Cat knew they wanted to hear more details; she couldn't blame them. She would want to hear them, too. Dustin went downstairs and brought her back a muffin, unprompted. She picked it up and inhaled its sweet aroma, before sinking her teeth into the chocolate chips.

It tasted like victory.

The second day Cat was back, she was summoned to John's office. The old timer had been dragged back from retirement, looking strained and very resentful at being there. That figured: John was supposed to be enjoying his leisure time with his wife and grandchildren right now, yet he'd had to boomerang back to clean up Peter's mess, especially since Erin was on compassionate leave.

Anxiety skittered through Cat all over again: she hoped for the best, but her last meeting with a Higher Up (Peter) had been disastrous for her. She could not afford to be complacent. As she shuffled into the room, she noted Hugh was seated beside John, staring at his phone screen as usual. Next to him were a bunch of dour, grey-faced and suited men who all looked identical. Cat was not sure how, but she knew instantly they were lawyers. Was that a good or a bad thing? She wasn't sure.

'Cat, take a seat.'

John indicated the only free seat in the office. Cat's stomach lurched. Was she being let go? What for? She'd brought them millions of hits in the past week – again! – and Hugh had okayed her report and his quotes. Heart skipping in her chest, Cat sat down. Wide-eyed and defiant, she stared back at all the men, like she was a naughty schoolkid in the headteacher's office.

'We're, um, very sorry for the pain and distress caused by Carmine Media's oversights these past few months.' John loosened his tie as he was speaking, then tightened it again, like a noose. 'Obviously we can agree it hasn't been an ideal working environment.'

The other men present all nodded with vigour (barring, of course, Hugh who was still tapping on his phone screen). Cat could feel the earnestness in the room and smelled money. She clamped a hand over her mouth, like she was stifling a sob, before squeezing a few tears out for her captive audience.

'It's been so hard!' she wailed. 'To find Michael was bad enough . . . then the man from downstairs. Now Peter?'

She left it hanging. There were muted croons of sympathy, but Cat was gratified to see the men all looked as if they wished *they* were dead now. It was clear they considered nothing was worse than a crying woman. It gave her power.

'Quite, quite.' John reached across the desk and gave Cat's shoulder an awkward pat. 'This is an unprecedented situation. We would—'

'How much?' Hugh cut in, his tone blunt and his expression impassive. 'Pick a number. We can make all this go away.'

Cat met Hugh's unflinching gaze. She knew she should not accept the first offer, nor should she be too grasping, either. It was a hard balance to strike. She wanted what she was worth, but she didn't want to make them all suspicious. As she grappled with the question, she stalled for time.

'I beg your pardon?' She let a note of outrage creep in. 'You think this is about *money*? You all think I'm that . . . *shallow*?'

It had the desired effect. John appeared on her side of the desk, flustered and apologetic. He crouched down next to her.

'I'm so sorry. I think what Hugh means is that you deserve to be compensated for your distress, plus rewarded for all your hard work during the fallout. Isn't that right, Hugh?'

Hugh's gaze was on his screen again. John shot daggers at him, then returned his eyes to Cat.

'Perhaps it's not just money you want?' John enquired.

There it was.

'There might be something,' Cat said, allowing her voice to waver.

'Name it.' John was as eager for all this to go away as Hugh. 'Pick a department, a job title here at Carmine. We'll make it happen. Right, Hugh?'

The playboy shrugged, still tapping on his phone. Cat met John's eye instead, still playing for time. This was her moment. She didn't want to blow it.

'How about a senior position?' John prompted. 'We have something open in the podcasts department. Culture: sports, movies, that kind of thing.'

That wasn't of interest to Cat. News had always been her passion. Journalists had always fascinated her. After what happened a decade ago, she'd spoken to them on the phone; been ambushed by them in the street; she'd watched them at the inquest and delivered a statement on the steps as they all jostled for position.

Others called them vultures and ghoulish creeps, but Cat had seen only men and women doing their jobs. Their interest in her meant she wasn't forgotten. As soon as the journalists' interests had waned, the world moved on and left Cat behind. She was alone again, only this time for real: she had nobody. She had become a journalist to feel part of the world again, instead of swept aside and disregarded.

An image followed these thoughts: Erin Goodman. She'd

been Cat's idol, a symbol of a woman making it in a man's world. Yet Erin had disappointed Cat. She'd shown her true colours and pushed Cat's face in the dirt. She'd humiliated her and left Cat out in the cold, then wondered why Cat was angry.

Screw her.

'I want Erin's job,' Cat said, mentally crossing her fingers.

John's eyes bulged at this, but no one else's did.

'Hugh, Erin's on compassionate leave. We can't fire her!'

The playboy sniffed like John hadn't even spoken. He met Cat's gaze at last.

'Let's make it happen.'

John disappeared around the other side of the desk. He muttered in the playboy's ear. Cat knew he was pleading for his old friend, but Hugh's face was expressionless. He sighed after a couple of minutes and sat back in his chair, arms folded. His mind was made up.

Forty-five minutes later, Cat had Erin's job title, with her own office and view. She was also promised a small cash settlement, delivered to her account on signature of various legal documents. Unable to let the grass grow under their feet, the lawyers produced the paperwork immediately. Cat signed it all with a flourish and Hugh smiled at her, tapping his screen again. In her pocket, her own mobile buzzed, signalling the payment arriving in her mobile banking app.

They all stood and proffered a hand towards Cat, who then had to shake with each and every one of them.

'It's been a pleasure.' John looked stricken.

'You have a big future here,' Hugh said.

Elation carried Cat home in what felt like the blink of an eye. She stopped and bought herself a Chinese takeaway, her favourite. She never normally bought such frivolous things; a single takeaway was the equivalent of a week's worth of shopping.

The hot bag of cartons banging against her leg, Cat hurried up the stairs. She'd only bought enough for herself. Lawrence had barely been in the flat lately, so there was no guarantee he'd even be home. Even if he was, she didn't want to share: her food, her job news, or the small but significant windfall she'd received. He would piss it up the wall in his latest get-rich-quick scheme, or on drugs and drink.

Tonight was the night.

Her position protected at long last, Cat decided she would break up with Lawrence that very night. She'd eat her Chinese and look at the nicer flats she could afford now. Then she would google some locksmiths and get the locks changed. She'd gather up all his belongings in black bin liners and leave it out in the hallway for him. It wouldn't stick because his mother owned the place, but it would give Cat the breathing space she needed to get rid of him and find a lovely new place, all by herself.

She would be queen of her own castle.

Lawrence wouldn't like any of it, but he should count himself lucky. Since experience had taught Cat she could get away with it, she could have killed him. But she'd loved Lawrence once. Had he always been an arsehole? Probably. She hadn't known any better and her standards had been too low. All that said, she owed him one thing: Lawrence had been the one constant in Cat's life these past ten years.

She would reward him by letting him live.

Letting herself in, Cat was disappointed to hear music in the flat; it sounded tinny, like it was coming from a phone. There went her leisurely evening of eating by herself and scrolling, planning her new life.

As she cast an eye around the apartment, fury surged through her: the place was a tip. The sofa had fallen over on its back like a beetle, legs in the air. All the books had been pulled from the shelves; the cupboard doors above the counters were open; cans had gone the same way as the books, discarded on the sides and floor. The television was missing altogether. The place had been ransacked, but Cat knew they hadn't been burgled.

She knew exactly who'd done this.

Lawrence was not in the living-kitchen area, so she left the takeaway bag on the counter. If she confronted him now, perhaps he'd get angry and sweep out like he'd done so many times before. Crossing her fingers, Cat approached the bedroom door, pushing it inwards.

Lawrence was seated, cross-legged, on the unmade bed, which acted as an island amidst another ocean of mess. The wardrobe doors stood open; the chest was just a wooden skeleton, its drawers upside down, their contents spilled. The duvet and sheets were in tangles on the floor; Cat's small collection of make-up, soft toys and body spray were scattered everywhere as though they'd been fired out of a confetti gun. He'd even pulled the curtain pole down. It lay on the carpet, the drapes still attached.

As he felt Cat's presence in the doorway, Lawrence looked

up from whatever he was staring at in his lap. He raised an eyebrow at her.

'My beloved,' he said.

'What the hell have you been doing?'

Cat already knew. He'd been looking for cash. He'd done this before, which was why she never kept anything but coppers in the flat. She thought of the phone in the back pocket of her jeans; of the settlement she'd received on her banking app less than an hour earlier. Gratitude flooded through Cat as she remembered all the times he'd tried to wheedle her into opening a joint account. She'd always refused.

Thank God.

Her thankfulness was short-lived. Lawrence picked up what he'd been looking at and showed it to her. Pink and spiralbound, the notebook was one of many; every good journalist loved stationery. It was one of Cat's favourites: the cover read *she believed she could*, so she did. She had a matching pen somewhere. Nervous, she licked her lips as Lawrence made a big show of flicking through the pages.

'Interesting reading,' he said, with oily sincerity. 'Lots of notes here about types of death. Electrocution, drowning, falling, stabbing, carbon monoxide poisoning . . .' Lawrence tore his eyes from the page as he said the words, trying to gauge her reaction. He smiled.

'I'm a journalist, idiot. Just research.'

Cat could feel herself uncoil. Lawrence might have his suspicions, but he didn't have anything concrete. She'd been too careful.

'You didn't flinch. Very good.'

She curled her top lip in a sneer. 'Should I have flinched?'

'Considering what you've been up to, yes.'

'And what is that?'

Cat rolled her eyes at him. Lawrence tutted, like he was disappointed in her. He turned the notebook over, so something fell out. She watched in horror as he retrieved it from the bare mattress and showed it to her.

It's just a small photograph, a selfie, but it meant so much more.

It's the one she'd taken as a souvenir from Leila's flat.

THIRTY-SEVEN

ERIN

'I'm really sorry,' John says at the end of the phone. 'Obviously I tried to save your job, but Hugh was adamant.'

'What are my options?'

I try to focus as he takes me through them. Even though I realised a career in the media can be precarious, I can't believe how readily I've been thrown away by Carmine Media. John tells me compassionate leave is at the company's discretion, and Hugh has decided I've had enough chances. I'm one of the last in, plus I've already blotted my copybook with the debacle over neutering Cat's copy, so that's another strike against me.

There's also been an incident report filed about my attitude, John says. I struggle to reconcile this, until I remember swearing at Hugh in that meeting about turning John's retirement party into an event to celebrate the refurbishment of the whole tower as well.

As I hang up, a curious mix of horror, relief and suspicion crashes through me.

It couldn't have *all* been Cat . . . could it?

I boomerang back to the sofa and Netflix, antsy and unsure what to do. I stare at the television screen, not seeing the images. David and the boys give me a wide berth, sure I'm suffering from stress and trauma. I don't disabuse them of this notion. David tries to talk to me about my job loss but I just tell him it's for the best.

Later, when David says we should all go out for pizza to celebrate me coming home, the boys cheer and I paint on a smile for their sake. As they chat about football and movies as they tuck into their calzones, I push food around my plate.

I can't concentrate; my mind is going over the facts, piecing together evidence of the deaths at Queens Mead Tower and the inferences I've made about Cat's character. A young man in a black waistcoat appears next to our table and offers to box it up for me to take home to eat later. I agree, but only to get rid of him, not because there's any chance of my eating tonight.

Asif's convictions about Cat and then her pushing me out of Carmine Media have opened a door and sent me spiralling. I feel as though my brain is caught in some kind of vortex, going round and round. All I can see in my mind's eye are the multiple victims caught up in Cat's 'Curse of Queens Mead' clickbait.

Could she have been behind their deaths, somehow?

I'd always had multiple misgivings about Cat. There is something dark and odd about her, but I'd reframed her disconcerting, exploitative and downright strange ways again and again. I can't shake off the conviction that I should never have tried to kill off what my intuition has been telling me.

There must be some way of finding out if Cat is Behind It All.

I look up from my phone at David, who's seated in the armchair, a book discarded in his lap. He's staring at me, his brow furrowed with concern.

'That girl ... the one who came to the house that time ...' I smile. 'Remember? When I was out with the boys?'

I try and keep my tone light and nonchalant, like it's no big deal. David is not fooled for a microsecond. He takes his glasses off and chews on one of the stems. I carry on anyway.

'What did she look like?'

'I told you.'

'Indulge me.'

'I wasn't wearing my glasses, it was all a bit hazy.' David sighs as he sees my exasperated expression. 'Okay, okay. Short. Thin. Mousy hair. Quite plain ... no, that's not fair. She was all right, just one of those girls you wouldn't really notice if you walked past her in the street.'

'How old?'

'I don't know, twenty-four or five, maybe? You know I'm useless with guessing ages.'

Could this have been Cat after all? Maybe she had come here, not to 'case the joint' as David thought, but because she was scoping out my precious family? But why? My nausea makes way for a hot, fiery anger that blossoms in my chest.

To keep my mind off the burgeoning horror and fury, I tap

Cat Crawford into my phone's Google search bar. Her last five or six bylines pop up; I've visited them countless times already. I will find nothing new here.

This prompts me to remember something else: David had said the girl who'd dropped by at the house had told him her name.

'What did she say her name was, again?'

'Judith,' David says, sounding decisive. 'It stuck in my mind because I thought it was unusual such a young woman would have such an old-fashioned name.'

I want to believe it's all a coincidence. That Cat had nothing to do with any of this. That she really did just find the bodies. That this has all just been 'right place, right time' – if not for the victims, then for her career.

I can't blame her for that. I can't even blame her for usurping me, not really. Women have to look out for number one in the media industry; no one else is going to. I've found that out the hard way.

But why would Cat come to my home?

Perhaps she'd been intent on finding a way to harm David and maybe my precious boys . . . I can't even finish the thought. I am incapable. All I can do is feel the dark fury surge through me, making me clench my teeth so hard it hurts. I want to make her pay. I am shocked at the ferocity I feel.

'Erin?'

I don't answer him. I type *Judith* and add *Crawford*, Cat's surname, into the search bar. Another much older article pops up.

My eyes widen as I skim-read the headline and the

summary at the top. Under the banner is a picture of a young teenage girl, perhaps eighteen. I turn the handset around to show David. He peers at it, putting his glasses on. He nods and confirms what I suspect.

'Yes, she's a bit younger there, but that's her.'

Cat stares at the camera straight on, her expression vacant: some might think it's grief or shock.

I know better.

THIRTY-EIGHT

MURDER-SUICIDE OF WEST COUNTRY COUPLE SHOCKS VILLAGE

REPORT BY J. K. AMALOU

Ernest Crawford, 50, bludgeoned Judith Crawford, 41, to death before hanging himself in his own barn. The couple's only child Catrin, 18, is believed to have been away at university, where she started in September.

A farmer who had 'lost everything' bludgeoned his wife to death at their secluded Devon farmhouse before taking his own life, an inquest heard.

Local man Ernest Crawford, who was born and grew up in the area, murdered his wife Judith at their home in North Devon. Judith was from nearby Ilfracombe. They'd been married for twenty-three years, since Judith was just eighteen and Ernest was twenty-seven.

In an email sent two days before his death, Mr Crawford

confirmed he was cancelling the farm's orders for animal feed. When local wholesaler Noel Campbell queried this with him on the telephone, he was forced to leave a voicemail. Mr Crawford never got back to him.

Devon coroner Aaron Huxtable concluded Mr Crawford killed himself and Judith was unlawfully killed.

'SHAME ON ALL OF US'

MR CRAWFORD LEFT NO NOTE, BUT NEIGHBOURS claim the couple's rented farm had been struggling for years. There were also widespread rumours about the Crawford family locally. It was believed that Mrs Crawford was the one 'who wore the trousers', so locals were blindsided by the news Mr Crawford should do such a thing.

'It's just awful,' says a villager, who prefers to remain anonymous, 'to think we all knew things were not quite right in that house and yet none of us did anything. Shame on all of us.'

The inquest was told Mrs Crawford kept a diary. In it she writes of her pride for her only child Catrin, an A grade student who had recently moved away to study journalism at Bristol University. She had been delighted Catrin had 'got out' of the 'dead end' that farming in the UK had become.

Mrs Crawford also wrote of her fears about her husband's state of mind and of his tendency towards violence. They were startingly prophetic words.

'Ernest has always been unpredictable, but one thing I can

guarantee is his rages coinciding with whatever is happening with Catrin. He never wanted her to leave us.

'Now Catrin is gone, I know it's a matter of time before Ernest erupts again – and this time there will be no going back.'

The inquest in Exeter heard Mrs Crawford died from blows to the head. Mr Crawford was found hanged in a barn.

'VICTIM-BLAMING'

ONE OF THE INQUEST'S WITNESSES TOM GILLESPIE told the inquest Mrs Crawford had run into his co-operative shop and post office 'dazed and confused' with no shoes on, two years earlier.

'She was ranting and raving, saying she had to get her girl out, she seemed really dazed and confused,' Mr Gillespie recalls. 'At first I thought there had been an accident, that she meant her daughter had fallen in a bog or similar.'

Mrs Crawford seemed to 'snap back to normal' seconds later and apologised for her strange behaviour. She started conversing with people in the shop and enquiring after their children. Borrowing a pair of Mr Gillespie's wife's wellington boots, she excused herself and walked back home.

'It's so sad,' fellow villager Susan Jackson says. 'It's clear to me now she never wanted anyone to realise what was really going on up there. I just wish I'd realised at the time.'

Ernest's older brother Clive, 57, also testified at the inquest. He claims that whilst Ernest might have struck the killing blows, he was of the opinion Judith Crawford 'drove him to it'.

'I have no wish to speak ill of the dead and there's no doubt my brother is guilty of murder. But people don't know what was really going on here. Judith was a toxic woman who drove him to it. That's why little Catrin had to get away. She was next in the firing line for her mother's poison.'

Other villagers and witnesses rejected Clive Crawford's testimony, calling it 'victim-blaming' and 'disgusting'.

'This is so typical of men, who are always victim-blaming,' says local farrier Florence Bilson, 28, who works at the stables near the Crawfords' cottage. 'A woman is killed by the man she trusted for twenty-three years of her life, yet somehow it's her fault. It's disgusting, but I am not surprised.'

The inquest heard how Mr Crawford relied heavily on Mrs Crawford's accounting skills in their farm shop business. The coroner said it appeared Mr Crawford 'was unable to contemplate life without Catrin'.

The coroner said: 'Ernest Crawford had helped raise a high-achieving child but could not accept her going away to university. Rather than feel pride for his only daughter's achievements, he blamed his wife for "sending her away". His actions are horrifying and despicable.'

THIRTY-NINE

CAT

'Care to explain how you have this?'

Cat's brain spasmed as she took in Leila's selfie, pinched between Lawrence's thumb and forefinger. Too late, she understood Lawrence hadn't been looking for cash.

He'd been looking for evidence to confront her with.

The smirk curving his lips made Cat want to scratch his eyes out. She pushed this urge down, hoping her lust for blood did not show on her face. She met Lawrence's mocking stare.

'No?' Lawrence tutted. 'That is a shame.'

He stood up from the bed, which in turn made Cat take an exaggerated step back, out of the bedroom. She didn't want to risk being too close to him; she had no idea what his plans were. Her eyes roamed around the flat's kitchen-living area. Lawrence had pulled every drawer from the kitchen counter; each surface was strewn with cutlery, corkscrews, old takeaway menus.

Lawrence flashed her a wolfish grin, holding up both hands to show he had nothing in them but the small photograph of Leila.

'Oh, you're worried about what *I* might do? That's rich.'

'I don't know what you mean.'

'Then let me paint a picture for you.' Lawrence seemed matter-of-fact, like he was describing a trip to the shops, or other banal activity. 'You went over to Leila's. Maybe you thought she'd been sniffing around me and were jealous—'

Cat wasn't able to halt the contemptuous snort that exploded out of her.

'Or maybe it was all a spur of the moment thing, who knows. Who cares? What's important is that you're the one who killed her. You pushed her off the balcony.'

'You're ridiculous,' Cat hissed.

'I don't think so. I think I'm right on the button. You've been making notes, scoping out people and places. Coming and going at all hours . . .'

'You haven't even been here!' Cat spluttered.

'I didn't need to be, I had my phone app, remember?' Lawrence's smile grew wider as he saw the horrified look dawn on Cat's face. 'Forgot about that, didn't you?'

'No . . . no. You're bluffing.' Cat recovered her nerve and stood tall. 'I uninstalled it! Just after you admitted following me to the Mexican restaurant that time.'

Lawrence shook his head at her, like she was a child.

'Oh, Catrin. I live here too, so I just reinstalled it. You

might have changed your pin, but I guessed it. I know you better than you know yourself. Picking the date your parents died? Obvious.'

Cat met his stare. 'So you've got a selfie of a dead woman, some notes about causes of death and my movements on an app. Congratulations. It's all circumstantial. It'll never stand up in court.'

To Cat's chagrin, Lawrence didn't have the decency to look beaten. He just kept grinning at her like the damn Cheshire cat.

'You know, even when I found all this, there was still a niggling doubt in my mind. I thought, "Meek and mild Cat, really?" Then confronted with the evidence, I realised it's all been a carefully constructed persona with you. You've let me get away with all sorts all the time we've been together, not because you're weak but because it suits you. You can pretend to yourself and the rest of the world how hard done by you are. Poor little Cat, left alone in the world, so small, so defenceless. Yet you snuck right under everyone's radar, didn't you? I'm impressed, truth be told.'

Despite his laudatory words, Cat could feel Lawrence's threat still emanating from him like a beacon. A bitter smile played on her lips.

'God, I hate you.'

The scream that escaped Cat surprised even her. She launched herself at Lawrence, her hands hooked like claws.

It was ineffective; Lawrence dodged her, meaning she ran straight into the wall, forehead first. Stunned, she dropped to the floor as Lawrence stood over her, laughing.

'Oh, Catrin,' Lawrence wheezed, 'when are you going to learn?'

Humiliated and angry, Cat spotted a corkscrew next to her outstretched hand. In one deft move, she grabbed it and pulled its two metal arms back. Then with a guttural shriek, she swept her arm sideways with it, level with the unsuspecting Lawrence's calf.

Burying it straight in his flesh.

Lawrence screamed in pain and buckled to one knee, but not before he managed to stamp on Cat's wrist. She felt a crunch, bringing with it bright spots in her vision and an urge to throw up.

Even in the midst of white-hot pain, she knew she had to get away. Cat flipped over onto her front and tried to shuffle away on her uninjured elbow. She didn't get far. Roaring, Lawrence grabbed her by the ankles and pulled her back towards him.

'You ... *cunt*!' he spat.

This word renewed Cat's anger. This had been the insult her father had used against her mother. She'd heard Ernest shout it at Judith when he grabbed her by the ponytail and bashed her face against the table. He'd also used it without his voice raised, like what he was saying was reasonable, daily conversation. The C-word was something men used against women to keep them in their place, to make them feel inferior, to remind them they were lesser due to the bodies and system they were born into.

Cat was sick of it.

She kicked out in desperation as he dragged her across the

cheap cord carpet towards him. By luck rather than judgement, she caught Lawrence in the jaw. He grunted and let go, collapsing onto his elbows.

Cat scrambled to her feet, picking up the empty wooden knife block with her good hand as she did so. She did not hesitate; she gave Lawrence no time to speak or plead his case. Cat brought the knife block down, one-handed, on the back of Lawrence's skull.

Again and again and again.

Cat's body gave way long before her brain caught up with the fact that the man at her feet was dead. She collapsed next to the body, staring at it with unseeing eyes.

She blinked and came to. She was not sure how much time had passed, but the bright red blood on her hand seemed to loom out at her, capturing her attention. This re-opened the door to pain in her left wrist, which flooded through her again like electricity. Lurching to her feet, she staggered into the small bathroom that stank of piss and threw up.

Hissing with pain, Cat took a variety of painkillers in the hope it would take the edge off. She created a splint using two wooden spoons she rescued from the floor, stepping over Lawrence's corpse.

Battling the pain, she tried to concentrate on what to do, how to explain Lawrence's death away. No one would believe Cat was not involved this time. She thought for a brief moment about enacting her #MeToo plan for Peter on Lawrence but decided it wouldn't work. Lawrence was a nobody; this was a tale as old as time. She'd be labelled yet another woman who'd turned against her abuser. There was no story in that, no conglomerate to bring down. Just garden-variety misogyny. She'd get twenty-five years' imprisonment with no possibility of interviews, book deals or film adaptations.

This meant Cat needed to get rid of Lawrence's body. But how?

Cat listened out for any noises beyond her flat that could signal people were coming to investigate the ruckus she and Lawrence had created on the top floor. As ever, the silence was deafening. She supposed everyone was still at work. Or maybe they just didn't care. Britain went out of its way not to get involved.

Satisfied no one was coming, Cat kicked out at the sofa so it landed back on its casters. Sinking into its cushions with a sigh, she told herself she would just take a moment.

She could feel her eyelids droop as her body relaxed, released from the angst and violence of minutes earlier. Cat knew she was fighting off unconsciousness: her reeling brain couldn't cope with either the pain or the conundrum of what to do with Lawrence. She grabbed the armrest of the sofa in readiness to pull herself back to her feet.

Too late.

Cat blinked and passed out.

FORTY

ERIN

I pull up the article on my phone about Cat's parents again and stare at it, hypnotised. Indecision incapacitates me. David and the boys are a blur, appearing and disappearing as I stare at the handset. I hear the front door and refrigerator open and slam.

Later on, David materialises in front of me, bringing me yet more cups of tea and entreating me to talk. I open my mouth, but no words of note come.

John's phone call has crystallised one realisation for me: Cat will stop at nothing. She has taken everything from me: my job, my social standing, my peace of mind. I'd disliked Cat piggybacking on the tragedy and chaos that surrounded her, hailing it as the 'Curse of Queens Mead'. I'd had misgivings, but dismissed them as absurd. Now I am certain what I'd suspected has been Cat's game all along.

She's been killing people to gain notoriety for her 'journalism'.

It's a sickening plan, yet there's a kind of brilliant simplicity to it. You can always be ready to report if you know where and when the next crime will be. I've seen the results, too: most of Cat's articles have gone super-viral. She got what she wanted and then some.

When I reviewed and edited her copy about Will's death, I thought Cat had just got carried away, but now I see her reports for what they are: cold, callous clickbait. She was never sorry to find Michael, Leila or Will. These people were a means to her end.

Unlike my generation, Cat grew up with social media; she knows how to engage and reward her audience online. She can pull at readers' heartstrings or make them outraged enough to click and share. Manipulation is as easy to her as winking. She'd been doing the real-life version to me, making me buy whatever she said, excusing her actions and demeanour if they didn't track.

If Cat is a murderer, then no one is safe, but especially my family. She's already come into *my* home, pretending to be someone else. I have no idea what she'd been planning, or why she abandoned her mission. Deep down I feel certain David dodged a bullet that day, perhaps literally.

I pull the mental brakes. I am getting ahead of myself. As confident as I am in this hypothesis, that's all it is for now. I will need something more concrete. I still feel the need to call the police, but what would I say? I have nothing but suspicions to share. Everything provable has already been said. The police have performed investigations and they have nothing to tie Cat to the deaths.

I need to stop her before she strikes again.

This thought fires something up in me. I scroll through my call history and click on Cat's name. As I wait for her to pick up, fear slices through me: what am I doing? What do I say to her? What do I expect *her* to say to me? 'Oh dang, you caught me! Yeah, I killed them all for my career'? The more this thought rattles through my brain, the more ridiculous it sounds. Yet I know it's true. I've been a journalist too long.

She doesn't answer, anyway. I key off and call through to David's study; there's no answer there, either. I open the door, expecting to see him at his desk or consulting his big project whiteboard on the far wall. The room is empty.

Panic strikes me until I notice the clock: it's just after three thirty. David will be picking up Joshua from school. He looks at his phone so rarely, there's no point in sending him a message. The school is just three blocks away, so they should be back any moment. I whip my phone from my pocket and send a message to Dylan.

Come straight home from school. No hanging about with your friends. I mean it. If you see Dad walking back, tell him the same.

Dylan replies straight away as I know he will. Like most of Gen Z, looking at his phone is the first thing he does when he emerges from the classroom at the end of the day.

What have I done? Am I in trouble???

Despite myself, I smile.

Not one bit. I just need to talk to you all

I'm upstairs packing all three of them some clothes when I hear them traipse into the house. David is pouring milk and making snacks for them when I emerge downstairs, carrying their full backpacks. The boys look up from the kitchen table, curious. I smile, trying to keep my voice and demeanour breezy.

'Hi, guys, how were your days?'

'Fine,' Dylan says, wary. 'What are the bags for?'

I sigh. *Busted.*

'I need you all to go and stay with your grandmother. Just for a couple of days.'

'Her house smells funny,' Joshua complains.

David's mother Lilian has a big dog, Simon. I've no idea what breed he is, but he's a giant, which means his ordinary dog smell is multiplied by a hundred. He is almost as tall as Joshua and farts for England. David is not fooled by my bluff for one second, either. He scowls at me and pulls me aside.

'What is this really about?'

'I'm worried.'

'About what?'

'That girl! You know, the one from the paper? What if she comes back here?'

David crosses his arms. 'So what if she does?'

'It's complicated.'

'Erin, what are you not telling me?'

My gaze strays to the boys, who are watching us both from the table like it's Wimbledon. Maybe I shouldn't have involved them, after all. David seems to pick up on this and claps his hands together.

'Right, go to your rooms, please. I need a word with your mother.'

Five minutes later both boys have been removed from the kitchen and bribed with extra crisps. I know they will sit on the stairs and attempt to eavesdrop. When David comes back into the kitchen I make him close the door and keep his voice down.

'Okay, what is really going on?' he says. 'And don't give me any bullshit about this Cat girl.'

My mouth drops open, agape. 'What's that meant to mean?'

'You've been weird for weeks.'

'Because of what's been happening at work!'

'Yes, I know. I'm not disputing that. It's been rough for you. But now you suddenly want us to all go to my mother's, out of nowhere? I don't want to think it, Erin, believe me, but I'd be lying if I said I didn't think you were up to something.'

I don't like where this is going. 'Like what?'

David leans against the counter. He hesitates, like he's not sure he wants to conjure the words into being. Hands on hips, I dare him. He raises his eyes to the ceiling.

'Fine. Like moving back in here, grabbing the house back for yourself. Possession is nine-tenths of the law as they say.'

'You asked me to move back in!'

'I know. But maybe you set it up so I thought it was my idea?'

Betrayal stabs through me. I can't believe what I'm hearing, but just as abruptly the pain passes. Of course he would feel this way. Despite our promises to each other, we haven't done the foundation work properly in rebuilding our relationship. We've skipped from being lovers to becoming a family again in a matter of just weeks.

With Cat looming as a possible threat, I need to keep them safe by moving them out of harm's way. But of course David is going to jump straight to the logical explanation as he sees it: I never wanted him back at all, I just want the house. The trust between us is too weak. I don't have time for this just now, though; I must stick a pin in it. As this thought surfaces, a solution to the current impasse comes to mind.

'Okay, fine!' I hold my hands up in mock surrender. 'You know me too well. But it's not about the house.'

David regards me, ashen. He looks like he's shitting himself at the prospect of my confession. Even though I hate deceiving him, I'm gratified. Since that fateful day three years ago in our en suite bathroom, when he told me he didn't love me any more, I've worried he still doesn't. I've worried he might be back with me just for the boys' sake. The evidence this isn't true is right in front of me.

'What is it?' he croaks.

'I think I might be pregnant.'

'I see.' David purses his lips and flexes his hands by his sides. 'How long have you thought this?'

'Couple of weeks?'

I'm amazed how I can pluck this lie out of the air.

'For God's sake, Erin. We said no secrets!'

I eyeball him. 'You can talk. You've been swanning about here for God knows how long, thinking I've been plotting to nick the house off you.'

'That's not the same and you know it. What was I supposed to think with you acting like this, not telling me anything?' David slams a fist down on the counter. 'Do you want to keep it?'

I force myself to look agonised about this imaginary baby. 'Yes ... no ... maybe. I have no idea!'

'Well, whatever you want to do, it'll be fine. I promise.'

Damn it, this is not working; if anything, it's making him want to stay and talk when I need the opposite. I want him and the boys out of this house, out of harm's way by whatever means necessary. I take a leaf out of Cat's book and stoke David's ire. He has to take himself and the boys away, where that psychopath can't find or get them.

I cross my fingers behind my back.

'You don't know that. Even on my salary, there were limits to what I could provide. Now I'm sacked and possibly pregnant, things are going to be tight and your job is little more than a glorified hobby.'

I wince on the inside at my cruel – and untrue – words. David's face crumples with hurt. Even if I *were* pregnant, I have never believed any such thing about David's graphic design. He's talented and visionary, plus it's always brought money in. Okay, it's not always been enough but his contribution to the household is measured in more than cold, hard cash. It's important. I have never been the type of person who believes men can't be nurturers and care-givers; David's ability to be both far outstrips mine. Dylan and Joshua are the good, secure kids they are thanks in no small part to their father.

'How can you say that?'

I avert my eyes and shrug like a belligerent teenager. I am afraid meeting his gaze will reveal my true intentions. I can't afford to let him realise I don't really mean what I am doing. David tuts and shakes his head, upset.

'I can't even look at you right now,' David declares, moving across the kitchen and picking up the boys' backpacks. 'You got your wish – I will go to Mum's. I need to cool off.'

I watch David summon the boys from the stairs. I send a silent apology to all three of them as they trudge out of the house to the waiting car, confused and upset. At the last moment, Joshua breaks away and runs back, throwing his skinny arms around my middle.

'Will you be here when we get back?'

I crouch down next to him and brush the hair out of his eyes. 'I promise, everything will be fine. You believe Mummy, don't you?'

Joshua stares at me, doubtful. I don't break his gaze. Then he gives me a sombre nod and stalks back to the car, head down. I watch them go, hating that I've sent them under a cloud but relieved they will be out of any potential harm's way.

Now, to find Cat.

FORTY-ONE

CAT

Cat woke gasping, heart hammering, like she was surfacing from icy water. She blinked furiously as light assaulted her eyes, spinning the trashed room out of focus.

She attempted to rise to her feet, but her legs would not support her. She fell to her knees amongst her the detritus. She swore as her bad arm knocked against the coffee table, sending sharp shooting pains up into her elbow and shoulder.

Once the pain had receded a little, her gaze settled on Lawrence's prone body. It hadn't moved, unlike antagonists in old movies who sprang back to life at will. He was face down so she couldn't see his slack expression, though she fancied death wouldn't make a lot of difference to Lawrence's visage.

The clock on the wall said it was past three o'clock in the afternoon. Cat wasn't sure what time it had been when she and Lawrence had had their little showdown, but she was fairly certain it had been late afternoon or early evening. That meant she'd slept the clock round.

Shit!

Cat thought for a microsecond about picking up the phone and calling the police. They could make it all go away, but they'd make Cat go away too. Cat staggered through to the bathroom and took more painkillers, washing them down with a handful of tap water. Regarding her reflection, she could see the resolve in her eyes. She'd come too far to fall at this last hurdle.

Needs must. Lawrence had to disappear.

Cat grabbed a couple of things from her dressing table drawer before leaving the flat and dashing down the stairs of her flat block. She pulled a hoody on as she went, though she did not bother to thread her bad arm through the sleeve, leaving it trailing emptily behind her. Pulling the hood up over her face, she wrinkled her nose in distaste. It was one of Lawrence's, so smelled of cigarette smoke and stale BO. It didn't matter.

She had a job to do.

She appeared in the street outside her flat block. People parted around her, re-joining like ants in a line. Cat saw none of them, nor did they see her. For what she had planned, she had to remain anonymous, unnoticeable; plain black jumper and jeans were perfect. If she was a big bloke and wearing her hood up, people might have been intimidated by her. In contrast, Cat was small and plain with few defining or remarkable features, drifting under people's radar as standard. Add a dark and shapeless hoody and she might as well be invisible.

She had a destination in mind and darted down a side street, onto a beat-up cul-de-sac full of litter and grey houses with broken-down appliances and plastic furniture on the overgrown front lawns. She'd cut through here enough on her way home to know its footfall was low, especially in the middle of the day.

Her roaming eyes picked out no one in the windows or going to work. The kind of people who lived in houses like this were students at best, more likely the unemployed. Her mother had always called places like this 'vinyl settee central'. She'd regaled the young Cat with tales of common people who had those live-laugh-love signs, singing fish on the walls and laminate on the floor. She'd insisted nobody worked for a living in such places, preferring to spit out kids instead for government benefits.

Judith Crawford had never been wealthy in her life, yet she'd climbed high enough to look down on her own roots. It had been one of her motivating factors for driving Cat so hard. It was also the main reason she'd refused to leave Ernest: disgust at the thought of going back to what she'd come from. Judith had made it clear to Cat over the years that she could put up with Ernest's intermittent outbursts of violence if it meant she didn't have to return to her home streets, tail between her legs.

Trying each door handle, Cat moved as quickly as she could from vehicle to vehicle. She didn't expect any of them to open.

When she reached the end of the cul-de-sac with no luck, Cat dipped down out of sight. She had a collection of niche

325

items she'd discovered a use for over the years. She pulled the one she'd taken from her box of tricks out of her hoody pocket: a tennis ball, cut in half. Her father had shown her how to do this. Press the half ball over the locking mechanism on an old car, it will make the button pop up. He'd had to do this more than once on the farm.

Though Cat didn't have a driving licence, Ernest Crawford had taught her to drive when she was eleven. She'd careered around the mud in an old Mini he'd bought for her from the scrapyard. About a year after that, it had conked out miles away in the fields, forcing her to walk six miles home, dragging a branch after her to give her a boost up over gates, fences and stiles.

Judith had been beside herself, imagining Cat had been abducted by the same types who'd snatched Sarah Payne, Genette Tate and April Fabb from fields and country lanes in the middle of nowhere. Ernest had just looked up from his newspaper and laughed as Cat trudged into the farmhouse, muddied and bloodied.

Cat moved towards a boxy-looking brown car the colour of crayons or shit parked at an angle on the street. The back seat and passenger side footwell were full of rubbish; there was moss growing in between the rubber of the windows and the glass.

No one cared about this car. It didn't even look like it had been driven anywhere in a while. She pressed the cut tennis ball over the brown car's side door and, sure enough, it popped open.

Cat opened the door and checked for the keys, just in case:

none. That was no problem, either: Ernest had shown her the basics of hot-wiring a car too. Out on the farm, it could be a matter of life and death. If someone had gone through the hay baler or got a foot taken off by the rotovator, you didn't want to be arsing about looking for keys the victim may or may not have. You needed to get that person into a vehicle and get them to the hospital straight away.

Thanks, Dad. Turns out you were good for something, after all.

Cat pulled a screwdriver from her bag and jammed it in the ignition, fully expecting to have to take the access panels off the steering column as well to get it started. To her delight, the engine turned over. Damn, this car really was ancient. The crappy car seemed a fitting tribute to Lawrence: it looked and felt like shit. It seemed right Lawrence's body should be spirited away in such a lemon.

Conscious of both getting caught by the car's owner and of time ticking away, Cat gunned the engine. She had no idea where she was going to take Lawrence's body once she'd got it out of the flat block, but no matter. She could find a lake and roll the entire car into the water, Lawrence in the boot. They could rust away in the silt and mud together for ever.

Cat took a deep breath, cracking the vertebrae in her neck as she'd seen her father do right before firing the bolt gun into the heads of distraught cows.

It was time.

She slammed her foot on the accelerator.

FORTY-TWO

ERIN

Once David and the boys have left, I grab my keys and go to my car. As I open the door, there's a flash of red checks as someone moves towards me, reaching for the door knocker. My mind turns it into Cat looming in at me, her face set on murder. Already on high alert, I recoil and shriek, jumping backwards into the hall. Unsteady on my feet, I windmill my arms and fall onto my arse. Peals of laughter reach my ears before I even hit the hall tiles.

'You all right, Karen?'

Asif. It's just Asif.

'I'm fine!' I scrabble to my feet and stalk past him, talking as I go. 'What do you want?'

'I came to check on you,' Asif says, amiable as ever.

I open my car door. 'Well, you've done that now.'

'So, what's going on?'

Dammit. Asif has previous for putting himself in the middle of my dramas and I'm not fast enough to stop him from getting in the car before I can lock the door. I stare at him across the gearstick.

'Get out.' I try and keep my tone measured.

'Where are you going?'

'It doesn't matter.'

Asif just grins at me. 'I'll come with you.'

'No, it might not be safe.'

'I'm a big boy.'

I roll my eyes. Asif is more on the button than he realises: he *is* just a boy. Part of me wants to protect him because of this; it's why I've taken him on as my surrogate 'son'.

I'd mistaken his demeanour for youthful arrogance once, but he is one of life's innocents, someone who strives to see the best in people. He is a stark contrast to Cat, whose nature is far darker.

Or me, for that matter.

Not for the first time I see the similarities between me and her: we came from similar lowly beginnings, had to struggle all our lives. Yet somewhere down the line we deviated onto wildly different paths. I understood there were limits to what I could do as an individual; Cat is the opposite. She thinks that because she wants something, she can take it, no matter how high the cost.

Even if she has to kill for it.

Asif raises an eyebrow. 'Maybe I can help?'

I roll my eyes. I know him well enough now to understand he won't back down. What's more, unlike everyone else in my life, he's the only person to have seen right through Cat. And I can't deny I needed his help with Dylan all those months ago, so perhaps he should tag along?

'You're just an observer,' I warn. 'I don't want you getting involved.'

He shrugs. Fine by him.

I turn the key in the ignition, filling in Asif as I go. His eyes grow wide, but I'm gratified when he doesn't argue the toss or look for alternative explanations.

'I knew there was something up with her,' he says, 'but murdering people to get ahead at work? That is something else!'

It's only as I start to follow the back roads I realise I don't know where I'm going. I press a button on my phone, which puts me straight through to John again on speakerphone. I don't bother with niceties.

'John, what's Cat's address?'

'Erin,' he sighs, 'you know I can't give that info out, GDPR and all that crap. Also I don't think you should go over there and have it out with her about your job.'

I almost snort in derision; my old job is the last thing on my mind.

'I swear, it's not about that.'

'I find that very hard to believe.'

'Look, John, I stood by you no matter what over the past two decades,' I remind him. 'Don't I deserve the benefit of the doubt?'

My minor guilt trip plus something in my voice makes him decide to forego legalities and ethics. John gives up Cat's address without further hesitation.

'Are you going to tell me what the hell is going on?' he demands.

'I'll explain later.'

Cutting him off, we find ourselves off another side street, in a small private car park at the back of a middle-of-the-road low-rise flat block. It's seen better days but it's okay. I park, talking to Asif as we get out and walk across the tarmac, our sights on the building.

'So, what's the plan?' Asif enquires.

I'd been waiting for inspiration to strike on the ride over. Getting proof was the name of the game, but I'm still at a loss on how to extract it from Cat. I doubt very much she'll make a frank and full confession, but perhaps she will say something or do something I can go to the police with? I can only hope.

As I'm about to answer Asif, there's a shriek of car brakes and the backfiring of an engine as a vehicle careers through the car park entrance. It all happens so fast I don't even have time to open my mouth and shriek a warning.

A brown car ploughs straight into Asif.

I struggle to process what happens next: my brain is on time delay. Fragments of the scene in front of me sear through my brain, whilst others don't compute at all. I discern his shocked face; the crumpling of his body against the car bonnet; the way he slumps into the road; the red blood on the ground. Staring at him, adrenaline makes my head buzz and my pulse crash in my ears.

'Asif,' I croak, then a screech bursts from my lungs: 'Somebody, help!'

I rush straight over to him. Outside the car park on the pavement, people on their way back from work stop and stare. A white man in a suit and tie appears, a phone already to his ear.

Asif's broken body is horrific; there's blood everywhere and all over me. I can't take in the number of injuries he has. Some jump out at me: I can see both his shin bones are broken where the bumper of the car hit his legs; his bones protrude through his flesh and his jeans. I'm not even sure if Asif is still alive. I press two fingers to his blood-slicked throat, feeling for his heartbeat. I'm relieved when I feel its weak beat beneath my fingertips.

'Hang on, Asif,' I say in my best 'Mum' voice, in case he can hear me, 'you're okay. You stay with me. Don't you go dying on me, you got that?'

I am sure he squeezes my hand, but perhaps it's just wishful thinking. As I hear an engine turn over perilously close, I realise the brown car is still there.

Right next to me and Asif's prone body.

I look up to see it back up, away from the scene. A little voice pipes up in the back of my head: *the car is not going to stop.* Then I hear the white man is calling 999 as he sees the car attempting to leave. He runs straight after it as it reverses away from him, yelling letters and numbers into the phone.

I don't have time for any of that right now.

Someone else grabs my elbow and attempts to lead me away. Their touch reinvigorates me. A tsunami of thoughts and feelings rush in at me. I scream at them to get off me; I need to stay with Asif. It's like his life is a fragile silken thread, leading from him to me. I can't leave him. I am certain that if we are separated, Asif will die.

What feels like seconds later, the paramedics are pushing me aside, even though I haven't heard sirens or seen them arrive. They're barking questions at me, asking for Asif's name and age. I can barely get the words out. I feel like I'm floating above myself, looking down on what's happening.

Someone wraps one of those foil blankets around me. I look up at them yet I can't discern any of their facial features. A sage little voice in the back of my head says, *That will be the shock*. This realisation does nothing to help me process what's going on around me, or who's talking to me.

'Did you see what happened?' a disembodied voice says.

My thoughts snap into focus. I *did* see who had done this to us. I'd seen her shocked face over the top of the car dashboard as she'd careered straight into Asif. I have no idea how she knew we were coming to confront her today, but it was definitely her.

Cat.

FORTY-THREE

CAT

She was out of time.

Cat ran all the way back from dumping the brown car in a vacant lot, her lungs on fire. Sharp ragged breaths caught in her throat, her chest tight and constricting. Her bad arm sent more shooting pains as it banged against her side. Thoughts ricocheted around her mind, as well as vivid imagery.

Asif, crumpling against the car bonnet.

Erin's shocked face, witnessing it all.

Cat's and Erin's gaze locking through the windscreen.

Her first mistake was obvious. Whilst the stealing of the brown car had gone without a hitch, Cat had failed to take due care driving back to the flat. She had been preoccupied. Disposing of Lawrence's body had consumed her.

This meant she'd taken the corner too fast, careering straight into the car park without looking properly. She'd perceived a flash of blue jeans and red chequered shirt and then BAM! She'd ploughed straight into someone.

Not just someone. Someone she knew: Asif.

In front of Erin.

Fuck!

What were the odds of both Erin *and* Asif being in Cat's flat block car park as Cat burst through the barriers in a stolen car? Too late, Cat appreciated it must either be millions to one ... or, more likely, Erin had decided to confront her.

Cat had just given Erin all the ammunition she needed. She had hit Asif, then legged it from the scene. It could even work in Erin's favour and lend credence to her story: it would seem like Cat had tried to murder them to stop them going to the police.

It would no longer be a massive stretch for anyone to believe Erin if she made a case for Cat doing other terrible things, like murdering Michael, Leila, Will or Peter, for the sake of her journalism career. (The fact Cat had only *technically* killed two of those people was by the by; why let the truth get in the way of a good story??)

Her second mistake was also clear now. Cat had thought that if she could steal a car, she could manhandle Lawrence down the stairs unseen and into the boot before continuing her life as normal.

Now Cat could appreciate how naïve this had been. Even if Lawrence hadn't stamped on her wrist just before she killed him and she still had two working arms, she wouldn't have had the strength to drag him down so many flights of stairs. Even if she'd somehow managed to roll him down, inch by agonising inch, it would have taken so long that she'd never have got away with it unseen.

Idiot!

There was only one play left. If she couldn't move Lawrence, then Cat had to be the one to leave. She had no choice.

But first she had to get back to the flat.

Every instinct inside Cat screamed against this. If Erin had had the presence of mind to give her statement to the police outside Cat's block and name her as the driver of the hit and run, the police could be waiting for her there. Cat should stay in the wind.

There was one big problem: whilst Cat needed to disappear, she had no money, no wallet and no passport with her. She didn't even have her phone; it was back at the flat too. Her only real chance of getting away was – ironically – returning for them.

Cat pulled her hood up as she neared her flat block. A much larger crowd had gathered than she anticipated. She'd underestimated the melee road accidents bring with them, but at least it offered some cover. She slipped back in amongst the voyeurs, dodging several who were filming on their mobiles.

Keeping her head down, she tried to blend in just in case Erin was nearby. She didn't worry where that mobile footage was going; if anyone caught her face on their phones or even the actual accident, by the time it was uploaded she would be long gone. She had to believe she was going to be successful in slipping away. Now her precious career was gone and she had to leave the flat, it was all she had left.

There were paramedics and police nearby; men and women in black uniforms were moving people back. Cat stood on tiptoe as she negotiated her way around the throng; she could see Erin in the distance near an ambulance, a foil blanket wrapped around her shoulders. Cat could see Asif on a gurney, being tended to by a woman in a green paramedic's uniform. Wow. She had felt certain she would see a body bag. Yet there Asif was, alive and with an oxygen mask over his face!

That was something, at least. Cat was staggered the student had withstood being hit by a huge chunk of machinery when all it had taken to kill Will was a fall down five or six metal stairs. It was true some people are built of 'sterner stuff', as her father had always put it.

Cat made it through the crowd and slipped down the side alley that took her to the front of the building. She was gratified to see it was free of people; everyone was congregated around the back door. Without further hesitation she pressed the entrance code into the keypad and made it into the bare reception. Grabbing the rail with her good arm, she pulled her exhausted yet adrenaline-filled body up the stairs to the fourth floor.

Conscious that every second wasted could mean the arrival of the police, Cat almost fell through her flat door in her haste to get back in. Ignoring Lawrence's body, she picked her way across the kitchen-living area and went straight to their bedroom. She grabbed her work rucksack: her wallet, phone and iPad were already inside. She shoved in a change of clothes, some underwear and her passport. She could buy toiletries and anything else she needed on the road. All that mattered was getting away.

If only she could slow them down, somehow.

As this thought occurred, Cat's gaze fell on Lawrence's corpse as she emerged from their bedroom. If she could cause a diversion of some kind, that might give her the extra time she needed. *But what?*

Cat raced through to the kitchen area and checked the timer switch on the boiler for the hot water: six o'clock, as always. Swearing, she raised her hurt arm to check her watch: ten to six. Her wrist was still painful, but it no longer incapacitated her; with a bit of luck it was a minor crack or bad bruising, rather than a complex fracture.

She screamed as Chairman Meow surprised her by jumping onto the counter next to her. Sighing with relief, she opened the window for him. She watched him skitter across the rain-soaked roof and jump onto the balcony opposite. If he had any sense, he would not be back this time. The bastard feline was deserting the sinking ship, and she should do the same.

Shutting the kitchen window, Cat switched all the cooker dials to 'on', pulling the blind closed so gas would fill up the small space just in time for the pilot light blinking on in less than ten minutes.

That should do it.

She could still do this. Cat grabbed her bag and opened her flat door.

FORTY-FOUR

ERIN

Asif is loaded into one of the waiting ambulances. Another paramedic fusses around me, taking my blood pressure and shining a light in my eyes. I can't bear the ghoulish crowd watching. I want to round on them and yell at them, ask them if they're enjoying the show.

'So, did you see the driver?'

A young police officer stands near me, her notebook in her hand. She's about Cat's age; she even looks a little like her too. For a moment, my shocked brain warps the picture in front of me and suddenly it *is* Cat interviewing me. I take a step back, like she might fly at me, murder in mind.

'Ma'am? Are you okay?'

I blink and Cat is gone. It's just the young police officer again.

'No, I didn't see the driver,' I find myself saying.

Before I can wonder why I am saying this, the paramedics interrupt. They want me to go to the hospital to get checked out some more, but I refuse. I can't face being around yet more people, prodding and poking me. I look around and the young police officer has replaced her notebook in her pocket and is helping another officer move the crowd back.

I take my chance and slip away.

It's easy to mingle and get lost in the crowd at the back of the building. I make it down a side alley and find myself in front of Cat's block by the roadside. As I gather my thoughts, I try and put myself in Cat's shoes. Where would she have gone, after knocking Asif down? She is alone in the world, barring that useless boyfriend of hers. Would she call him, ask him to bring her money, clothes, passport so she can go on the run?

It's a possibility I can't ignore.

If I am to accost the boyfriend, first I need to get into the building. I press the button on Cat's flat block intercom. When there's no answer, I start pressing other buttons in the hope of irritating another resident into letting me in.

My tactic works, sort of. An old-sounding woman's voice crackles through the tinny metal box, heavy with accent, though I'm unable to guess where she's from.

'Wha' the fuck you doin' eh! No orders, no bible basher!'

As I process these words, I realise the truth in them: what the fuck *am* I doing? I don't know what I am trying to achieve. I should have just told the police what I know – that I *had* seen Cat behind the wheel – and let them handle it. Am I trying to be a hero? I must be out of my mind.

'Please, let me in.' I cross my fingers.

'You forget key? Your problem, missus.'

There is an abrupt pop as the old woman appears to lose interest. When nothing is forthcoming, I press down on her button and leave it there. I know she can't ignore it. Seconds later I am buzzed in, along with some more choice words from her.

I run into the bare hallway. I take the stairs two at a time. As I make it onto the first landing, blue jeans through the stair bars catch my eye, prompting me to look up. I can't believe it as I catch sight of Cat on her way down. How did she get back here, undetected? Her face is creased with pain; she's got a backpack on and is cradling one arm. As if she feels the weight of my stare, she freezes where she is. Her gaze fixes on mine.

'Cat!'

It is a low-rise block; there's no lift and only one set of stairs. If she makes it back up into her apartment, I won't be able to get her back out.

To my confusion she doesn't turn on her heel but rushes down the steps towards me, her good arm out in front of her. I realise she is planning on muscling past me and getting out of the building regardless.

WTAF?

'Cat, stop!' I put my own hands up and stand wide-legged on the stairs so there's no room for her to push past. 'We can talk about this?'

'Get out of my way!' she hollers.

I don't move, sure she will relent at the last minute. She

does not. She crashes into me and we both go flying down the stairs.

She cries out in pain as her bad arm bashes against me. The breath is forced out of me too as I land hard against the concrete; I feel the hard bite of steel stair bars in my lower back. A burst of pain hits me in the elbow where I land on it. I've broken Cat's fall. Dazed, I watch as she scrambles off me and attempts to escape through the front door.

'No, you don't,' I growl, grabbing her ankle.

'Not again!' she squeals, which is weird, then: 'Get off me!', which I do understand.

She kicks out but I duck, so her foot finds only air. Holding her ankle with both hands, I twist, making her fall against the wall.

Standing up, I don't let go of her. It destabilises her.

One-legged, she slides down the wall, still cradling that bad arm of hers and staring at me like she hates me. She probably does. Psychopaths like Cat not only hate being busted, they always blame those doing the busting. They never blame the bad choices and behaviour that lead them into trouble in the first place.

'We need to talk.' I'm breathless, both from exertion and adrenaline, and it's difficult to force the words out. 'There must be some kind of agreement we can come to?'

Just like my refusal to tell the police it was Cat behind the wheel, the words feel odd, even as I say them. What *agreement*? Why would I care? Cat has been behind this insane palaver from the beginning, killing people to get ahead at work. I've just been caught in the crossfire. I am blameless.

'You don't understand!' Cat is almost hysterical. 'There's no time for this!'

'Look, I get it,' I gasp. 'It's shit being a woman in a male-dominated industry. You wanted to be taken seriously, you thought this was a good way to play the system at its own game. But they were *people*, Cat. This is not the way!'

'Will you shut up!' Cat screams. 'None of whatever you think you know matters now. We have to get out of here, right this second. The building is about to—'

An all-encompassing blast rips through my ear drums and my body, throwing me to the floor as showers of masonry and plaster come down. I see my own pain reflected in Cat's expression as she is hurled sideways.

Before the noise can recede there is another, smaller, explosion, followed by screams from the landing above. Disorientated, I'm unsure if whatever exploded was right next to me or somewhere above. My brain's already spongy with shock after Asif; this shuts me down. I can no longer compute and my vision blurs. Blood runs into my eyes from where a piece of debris hit me in the head.

Even so, I know who caused the explosion: Cat.

I try and raise my head, move my limbs, but I can't. I watch, helpless, as her shaky outline forces itself to its feet and stands over me.

'Bye, Erin,' she says.

Everything goes black.

FORTY-FIVE

CAT

Cat limped along the Bristol streets, careful to keep to the back roads, away from prying eyes, human or CCTV. She could barely keep her eyes open; lethargy infected her bones, threatening to drag her under. She knew it was shock, that she could not afford to succumb. If Cat fainted in the street, some good Samaritan was bound to find her and take her to the hospital.

Then it would all be over for real.

She concentrated on the terrible pain in her arm to keep her awake. Had it only been yesterday she'd been in that office with John, Hugh and the lawyers? She'd been given what she deserved at last. Cat had left the room recognised and rewarded for her efforts, ready to begin the next chapter – only for it all to be snatched out of her grasp.

Why did life never go her way? Fuck!

No, no, that wasn't right. She had to count her blessings; that's what her mother Judith Crawford would say. Erin might have nearly got her killed this afternoon, but Cat couldn't have gone back to Carmine Media anyway. Her time there had come to a natural conclusion, thanks to Lawrence's snooping. He'd paid the price for that.

Cat had always known deep down that keeping him around was a mistake. Lawrence had never truly cared about her; she had known that, too. He'd just been there when she needed him, alone for the first time after her parents' deaths. Her gratitude and nostalgia for the past had almost destroyed her. Her mother had said failure was a learning experience. Cat would not make that mistake again.

Thank God for Hugh's money. Ten grand was not much in the scheme of things, but it was a start. Cat had had the presence of mind to grab her passport and notebooks as well as a change of clothes. She could still make it abroad easily in the time it took for the authorities to make the flat block safe *and* discover Lawrence was dead *before* the explosion. It was never meant to be a cover up that would hold long term, just a short-term diversion to let Cat escape.

She needed to make it to Bristol Airport. That was her literal ticket out of here; she didn't care where she went, as long as she couldn't be dragged back. Cat supposed she would need to go further afield than Europe; somewhere like China. That was okay; she had always fancied seeing the Great Wall. Maybe she could pick up some work teaching English.

It would all be okay.

Cat was intrigued that Erin had picked that day of all days

to confront her. It had been clear from Erin's talk of 'playing the system at its own game' that she'd worked out what Cat had been up to. But how?

She could only guess. Perhaps David had finally remembered where he'd seen her before, or maybe Cat had neglected a tiny detail Erin had been picking at in her subconscious which had made the whole thing unravel. Or perhaps it had been the culmination of several things. Whatever.

It didn't matter now.

Erin's earnest pleading returned to Cat again. What was it the older woman had said, holding on to Cat's ankle in her block's concrete hallway?

There must be some kind of agreement we can come to?

The memory fired a realisation in Cat's brain so vivid it took her breath away. She fought the urge to go back. She wanted to confront Erin herself now over a crucial point she had missed in the moments before the explosion. Cat had been concentrating on the *how* of Erin working out her plan.

She should have been concentrating on the *why*.

If Erin knew what Cat had been doing, then why hadn't she told the police? The police could have re-interviewed Cat and subjected her to DNA testing or finger-printing, previously unavailable to them without an arrest. They could have put pressure on her to confess. Plenty of legal cases had been won this last way; perpetrators languished in jail because the tiniest and most random of details had whipped the rug out from under their feet.

Yet Erin had not told the police, she'd come straight to Cat. Why?

As Cat turned down a side street she grasped the answer. Now she had worked it out it seemed so obvious.

Erin Goodman killed Peter Mackinty.

SIX MONTHS
LATER

EPILOGUE

ERIN

'Mummy, look at me!'

Smiling and waving, I watch Joshua line up a ball in the park. Goalie Dylan stands between two jumpers, ever the dutiful big brother. David cheers as Joshua boots the football straight past Dylan, who makes a show of trying to catch it and failing.

Joshua doesn't appear to notice the theatrics and whoops with joy. He runs around in circles, arms in the air like his football heroes. David winks at our eldest son and pats him on the back for being a good sport and letting his little brother score.

'You all right, Karen?'

I turn my head to the other person seated on the park bench with me: Asif. He's been out of his casts for a while now, but he still needs to use crutches. After the hit and run and all the surgery he's had, he gets tired easily.

I'm sitting with him so he doesn't feel left out. Asif's mum had wanted him to go back to Slough with her, especially after the university had told him he could repeat the year once he'd recovered. But he hadn't wanted to go home. I'd told his mum we would look out for him.

'I'm fine.'

For once, I am not lying to myself or others. I'd come round from the explosion in hospital, filled with wonder I was still alive. Asif was conscious and seated next to my bed in a wheelchair, attached to a drip and with both legs in plaster. I'd been delighted and relieved to see him. His presence felt like a good omen.

Asif told me that, somehow, no one had been seriously hurt other than me in the gas explosion. The swearing granny was on the next ward. She'd been as obstreperous with the nurses as she had been with me on the intercom. Asif confirmed she had no knitting with her, just a Jason Statham box set on her iPad. That tracked.

In the days that followed, I spent lots of my time thinking about Cat – mulling over her past, her motivations, her choices. At first I was angry, but over time I realised Cat is not some supervillain, but a mixed-up, opportunistic young woman with a very, very wonky moral compass.

I've tried to be empathetic, to imagine what she must have gone through to end up like this. I also recognise I can't take this too far. Trauma and abuse does not automatically create killers. If they did, there would be a lot more like Cat out there. Most kids who grow up in abusive homes, witnesses to the toxicity of domestic violence, don't just survive adversity, they thrive. Cat is an anomaly.

After I'd stayed in for observation, David and the boys came to get me from the hospital. I admitted to David I'd never thought I was pregnant, that I'd just wanted him and the boys out of harm's way. David had tutted and told me he'd figured as much when he'd heard what had happened at Cat's flat block. All forgiven, he and the boys insisted I do absolutely nothing, Dylan and Joshua taking my food and drink orders on little notebooks like I was a paying guest in a fancy hotel. David cooked me up steaks and elaborate ice cream sundaes.

Two hours after I returned from the hospital, Hugh was calling me on FaceTime, Skype, Facebook Messenger and every other platform he could think of in the hope I would answer. I did not, though I listened to some of his messages.

Hugh told me how he'd made a big mistake in firing me. He told me how invaluable I was and how he was willing to give me a pay rise, a nicer office and control of any asset I wanted at Carmine Media. I laughed as I heard this, thinking just a few weeks earlier I would have needed this validation; his offer would have been my greatest wish. Now it sounded like shackles.

I pressed 'delete' without hesitation.

As my relief and gratitude just at being alive has waned over the past six months, I've found other emotions niggling at me. My new media consultancy business might be doing well, but it's always a slow burner when you first go self-employed.

This is matched by the curious frustration at no longer being the breadwinner. David is now the one with more demands on his time as he earns more than me, so the house-work, taking care of bills and childcare duties are on my shoulders. Whilst I enjoy this change of pace and being with the boys more often, the school run and drudgery of running the house again takes some getting used to.

Without workaholism to distract me, I have more time to think, too.

About what happened with Peter.

Sometimes it all feels unreal, like a dream. Sometimes I fancy it was. I'd been fighting the effects of seeing Will's body in the service corridor stairwell, not to mention being humiliated by Peter shortly afterwards, thanks to Cat. I'd felt I couldn't take the time off I needed, because someone like Peter would use it against me.

That, at least, is true.

I'd wandered down to his office, knocking and pushing the door inwards. His fruitless gasps for breath reached my ears as soon as I crossed the threshold. Before my eyes adjusted to the darkness, my brain skipped ahead. I'd imagined he was having an asthma attack. I rushed towards his desk, intent on making a grab for the phone to call 999.

Then I stopped.

I froze where I was. I want to say it was the horror of seeing him, his face cherry-red with anaphylactic shock, his tongue swollen and misshapen.

That would not be the truth.

Something fell from his hand as I watched. My gaze followed it to the floor: a doughnut, a single bite taken out of it.

I can't eat these, he'd said.

He'd told me before to go to Joe's Doughnuts, but I'd thought it was just that he preferred them. When he'd called on me yet again to do his errands, I couldn't be bothered to leave Queens Mead Tower. I had too much on my To Do list to take an extra fifteen minutes out of my day to get doughnuts for him.

In haste, I collected six from the chain store coffee shop on the ground floor of the tower without a second thought. I put them on a plate and gave them to Peter.

In his office that fateful evening, I wasn't sure if Peter could see me or not. His eyes were bugged out, his gaze on a far-off point in the distance. Drool dropped from his slack mouth, which opened and closed like a dying goldfish's.

I took a deliberate step back from the desk and the phone. I stood and watched as the light vanished from Peter's eyes. Then I turned on my heel and walked out, waiting for someone else to find him – Cat, as it turned out.

I let Peter die.

I watched him asphyxiate. A dark part of me says Peter deserved it. He had been a symbol of every patriarchal ideal that contributes to the ills of society. He'd been the epitome of privilege: a misogynist, homophobe and racist, riding on the backs of those more talented and harder-working than him.

I know this excuse does not cut it.

I could have saved him; there had been plenty of time for that.

When Peter was dead, I left the office as I found it and withdrew to my own. Noticing Cat was the only one still in the cubicle farm after-hours, I called her in, so I would have an alibi when his body was found. It had been Cat who found Peter which had surprised me at the time; but it worked for me so I didn't question it.

Now I realise she'd been scoping Peter's office out for her own reasons; blind luck meant she hadn't seen me come and go earlier. I also understand now we are more alike than I ever thought possible.

Takes one to know one.

'You coming for dinner, Asif?'

David appears in front of the park bench, the football under his arm, sweaty and happy. Dylan and Joshua bound up after their father.

'If that's okay?'

We always do this dance: Asif eats with us most days, but we still ask and he still checks. I put an arm around his shoulders, helping him with his crutches as he stands up.

'Of course. You're our extra son, aren't you?' I smile.

'*Mum!*' Dylan chastises.

I'm being uncool again.

As we leave the park, my mobile buzzes in the back of my jeans pocket. As David and the boys chatter, I pull my phone out and open the notification. I don't recognise the number, but I know instantly who it's from. I've been dreading this, but on opening the notification, my anxiety dissipates.

A weird sense of calm comes over me as I read the message:

I will be seeing you soon, Cat's text reads.

I don't falter. I tap out a reply and send it in seconds.

I'll be ready.

ACKNOWLEDGEMENTS

'I tell women, that whole "you can have it all" – nope, not at the same time; that's a lie. It's not always enough to lean in, because that **** doesn't work all the time.'

In 2018, Michelle Obama took aim at the #GirlBoss and *Lean In* culture and confirmed what every woman on the planet already knew:

We <u>can't</u> have it all.

Hearing a successful woman that I very much admire saying this felt like validation at last. Whether we're rich or poor or somewhere in between: white, black or Asian; heterosexual or LGBTQ+; able-bodied or disabled, this simple truth unites all of us:

The system was not built for us.

This book started the germ of an idea ... one in which a woman can try and play the system at its own game yet discovers even KILLING for our ambitions won't work!

Cat and Erin should have known, shouldn't they? For every

man who is admired for building something, there are countless women dismissed, mocked and condemned as we attempt to do the same.

'Female empowerment' is a red herring. We are already powerful. We are just not recognised as such. That's why it doesn't matter how – or even if! – we choose to play 'the game'.

The game is rigged.

Cat finds this to her cost in *Kill For It* and since she is the antagonist (not to mention a serial killer!), we are glad about that.

Erin finds herself in a similar position. She means well and has worked hard all her life ... yet that 'game' will take her to the brink. Patriarchy will destroy her self-esteem, her sense of self, her family. Worst of all, it will take her conscience.

Thankfully, my journey in writing this book was not as troubling as Cat or Erin's at Carmine Media.

First up, my gratitude as always to my uber-agent Hattie Grünewald and 'collaBRO' JK Amalou. You were both there for me during my biggest wobbles on this project. You rock!

Thanks also to Darcy Nicholson, Callum Kenny, Thalia Proctor and Charley Chapman at Sphere Books. It was great to work with you all.

Many, many thanks for the moral support to my B2W group chat: Debbie Moon, Elinor Perry-Smith, Sophie Gardiner, Liam Kavanagh, Drew Hubbard, Chris Lunt, Zee Zomorrodian, Karen Martins, Kefi Chadwick, Olivia Brennan, Sally Abbott and Hay November. I literally couldn't have done without your musings on getting ahead at work, dealing with problem bosses, parenthood and more!

Many thanks to the rest of the 'Bang2writers' too. All our discussions online and at workshops, talks and panels about female characters, feminism, politics, double standards and societal myths and expectations have helped shape *Kill For It*.

Lastly, many thanks to my long-suffering husband Mr C. Not because he's 'hen-pecked' (he's far from it!) but because he was the body in lots of my re-enactments of the murders. He spent many Saturdays lying on our living room floor while I tried to think of ways I could kill him and make it look like an accident (yet he's not scared of me because I'm a tiny woman?? Gawd what a sexist. KIDDING!).

Finally, thanks for reading! I appreciate you.

Lizzie x

Did you enjoy *Kill For It?* Check out Lizzie's other gripping feminist thriller ...

Let me repeat myself, so we can be very clear.
Women are not the enemy.
We must protect them from themselves.

Imagine a world in which witchcraft is real. In this world, mothers pass on peaceful powers to their daughters, but the men in charge decide that this secret knowledge is dangerous. Not only dangerous, but illegal.

As witches around the world are imprisoned, one young woman discovers a power she did not know she had. This terrifying force puts her at the top of the list in a global witch hunt. But she – and the women around her – won't give in easily. Not while all women are under threat.